Denise Ke

was born in Fairli
the southern half
Wellington in the 1950s, later settling in Naenae. Early ambitions to be an engine driver or archaeologist were replaced by the idea of writing novels, a notion overtaken by the need to earn a living. After graduating from Victoria University she had a variety of jobs and spent some time travelling before working for the public service in a range of policy or human resource management roles. However, she recently returned to fiction and now does the usual juggling act between writing and the demands of the day job.

ORIGINAL

The STOVE RAKE

Denise Keay

Flamingo
HarperCollins*Publishers (New Zealand) Limited*

National Library of New Zealand Cataloguing-in-Publication Data

Keay, Denise.
The stove rake / Denise Keay.
ISBN 1-86950-406-2
1. New Zealand fiction—21st century. I. Title.
NZ823.3—dc 21

Flamingo
An imprint of HarperCollins*Publishers*

First published 2002
HarperCollins*Publishers (New Zealand) Limited*
P.O. Box 1, Auckland

ISBN 1 86950 406 2
Set in Electra
Designed and typeset by Chris O'Brien
Cover photo Mahan & Halford, Timaru
Printed by Griffin Press, South Australia on 80 gsm Econoprint

Acknowledgements

This comes with thanks to Phyllis O'Connor Keay, who dredged her memory for details of life on a South Canterbury farm in the first quarter of the last century; Kay Wall, for her constant support; Libby Tregear, Paul Kingdom, Chris Martin, Gwenyth Wright and Vivienne Hill for their advice and encouragement; and Mike Hill for what can only be described as blind faith.

Chapter 1

The men had gone outside to see the foal and lingered in the yard, talking. They were talking about the devil, of all things, and Mrs Kelly didn't care for it. Hell's a thriving enterprise and Lucifer has his agents: suave Mephistopheles and lazy, loitering Beelzebub, Apollyon the bullyboy and moony Ashtaroth. The men spoke of them as they might a troop of vaudevillians. She shut the kitchen window, briskly enough for her husband to notice, but not with a bang that would startle his friends. Her ear had picked out the name of a poet she knew to be great, and it may have been a literary discussion after all.

Dan should have had an education; that was why he liked Mr Fernon. Mr Fernon had an education, though much good it did him. Now he lounged beneath a southern sky, smiling at damnation. Mr Harraway was enjoying the conversation too. Perhaps he felt he owed it to his father, who was said to be a bishop — Protestant, of course — and not best pleased with his son. But Dan would have started it, as he always did, by declaring that he'd sell his soul to own a Cup winner.

Mrs Kelly sometimes wished her husband's taste in friends a little less catholic, or a little more so, but he said one man was as good as another and it didn't matter which church he went to. He himself no longer went to church at all. He was known for hard work and sober habits, and his steady manner concealed a taste for something quite contrary: the rare, the beautiful, the freakish, anything exceptional of its kind. He bought retired racehorses to pull his gig so that nobody should pass him on the road. Even their cat had six toes on each foot, and with them the capacity to grant a wish every seven years. Or so the children liked to think. Dan had brought him home as a stray, and since no one knew how old he was his talent had never been tested.

A moment ago Lily Macgregor had come in to take some mending. 'The only thing she's ever been known to do for anybody,' Lily's grandmother often said.

Indeed it was a strange way for a youngish woman to want to spend her evenings, intent upon the socks of another woman's family, but as Mrs Kelly had never been a needlewoman and Lily's darns were better than most people's embroideries, she was grateful and thought no more of it.

Lily's grandmother was a Mrs Davidson. It was her considered opinion that Mrs Kelly was an ignorant Irish biddy who, if you suffered a seizure on her kitchen floor, would send for the priest ahead of a doctor. Mrs Kelly regarded Mrs Davidson as an extraordinarily good woman with all the petty preoccupations of her kind. When Lily was a girl scarcely a day had gone by without her displaying some piece of stupidity that Mrs Davidson never failed to communicate, with an odd mix of triumph and contempt, to Mrs Kelly. Lily didn't know how to peg sheets on the line. She stood around staring, then laughed at nothing. She made a real business of setting the table or putting flowers in a vase, and they didn't look any the better for it. 'Hoity-toity! She's been spoiled, that's what it is.'

Lily had been used to trailing about after the maids in her stepfather's hotel, and Mrs Kelly thought it only natural the girl's notions of housewifery should differ from those of her grandmother. However, she could think of no reply that wouldn't be interpreted as either a criticism of Mrs Davidson or an admission of some failing on her own part. So instead she would exclaim in her most Irish of accents, 'Well, Mrs Davidson, you know what they say, don't you?'

To which Mrs Davidson would respond, 'We are never sent a burden we cannot bear,' smile tightly and be content. They were neighbours, and obliged to get on with each other.

Lily leaned against the bench and gazed into the yard while Mrs Kelly brought out the mending basket, its contents furred and flattened by the warm bulk of Oedipus. The men had drifted further off, taking their conversation with them.

Lily asked, 'Who's the fair-haired one?'

'Mr Fernon. Dan reckons he's a remittance man.'

Lily saw remittance men in the hotels. As a rule they had beautiful manners, no money, and were very seldom sober.

Something of this entered Mrs Kelly's mind too. She added, 'It was at the races they met.'

'Is he a gambler, then?'

'I don't know what he is,' said Mrs Kelly. Nor did she care, so long as he behaved himself in her house. In any case, Dan's enthusiasms were often short-lived.

'I don't think I've seen him before.'

'Well, you may not have.'

'How old is he?'

Lily asked that about almost everyone she met, and Mrs Kelly took it to mean she was afraid of growing old. There was something of the faded child in her, and at times she affected a precarious girlishness that was unsettling now and would make a marionette of her in years to come.

'Oh . . . thirtyish?'

'He's not bad-looking.'

Mrs Kelly didn't really agree. She liked men to be dark, and lively with it. 'They're coming to dinner on Saturday night. You can make his acquaintance then.'

'I said he was good-looking, not that I wanted to meet him,' said Lily, turning from the window to inspect the contents of the mending basket.

As a child, Lily had been considered very pretty. Her face was pale and bright, and she'd had hair like a fall of new-minted pennies. The hair was much darker now, but her complexion was still so fine her flesh seemed to shed a light drawn from deep beneath the surface of her skin. This natural radiance caused the most indolent of eyes to veer towards her when she entered a room or passed along the street; perhaps that caused her to overestimate the sum total of her charms.

Mrs Kelly tried again. 'Bob Graham's coming, too.'

'Is he back here now? Then at least I'd have somebody to talk to. Though you'll have too many men.'

There were always too many men. 'But there'll be you and me and young Cathy,' said Mrs Kelly, undeterred. 'She's quite grown up now. She's even offered to make burnt cream for pudding. And Mr Harraway'll bring his wife — they're on their honeymoon.'

'It seems to be a very long honeymoon.'

'Dan thinks Mr Harraway's another whose family prefer him at a distance, and that could be because of her. He's even spoken of settling here. He might be interested in your grandparents' farm.'

'He might, but I don't think they've quite made up their minds to sell.'

'Well, you can talk to his wife and find out what she was before he married her.'

One of Lily's shoulders twitched dismissively. She didn't share the district's current fascination with the mysterious Mrs Harraway. Returning to the window, she placed her hands flat upon the bench and craned in the direction the men had gone.

'What are they doing?' asked Mrs Kelly, startled by her sudden concentration. Lily's chin was almost on the sill, and her bent elbows made the sleeves of her blouse sit out like filmy wings. Her hair, tied back with a Gibson-girl bow scarcely suitable on one of her age, lay in a dull red mass between her shoulder blades.

'Talking,' she said, without lifting her head. She remained motionless for another minute or two, then straightened and drew back, adding, 'Pat's with them now.'

'Then I hope they mind what they say.' Pat was a little pitcher with very big ears. 'Are they coming in?'

'I don't know,' said Lily, who thought that they were. 'I must be off, anyhow.' She gathered up the mending and slipped into the hall.

Dan Kelly was too quick for her. He came in the side door and called to know where she was going with that basket.

'Why, to my grandmother's, of course,' Mrs Kelly heard her answer in a voice of squeaky innocence. Then the front door banged, Lily's steps were brisk on the verandah, and she scampered, positively scampered, down the drive.

Mr Harraway had gone back to town; his wife didn't like to be left alone for long. But Mr Fernon came in, and sat down at the kitchen table while Dan brought out the whisky and Pat his Latin homework. Mr Fernon accepted a drink, propped his head on one hand, and applied himself to Pat's task. Mrs Kelly, reflecting that Lily had called him good-looking, considered him more carefully now.

His looks were of the kind that go unremarked by other men unless they are inclined to malice, but which leave few women unmoved to some degree or other. He was clean-shaven, with dark blue eyes that had bluish shadows beneath them, as though they'd been rubbed with inky fingers. In repose his mouth drooped at the corners, giving him a sad, rather than sullen, expression. He put her in mind of a schoolboy himself, one some women would ply with kind words and cakes while others sniffed, 'He'd make a lovely girl,' or 'That face is wasted on a boy.'

He had the hands of a gentleman, which was only to be expected, but as one pale forefinger tracked along the page in pursuit of a verb — more elusive things in Latin, it seemed, than in English — she wondered if his fingers were very slightly swollen and that was why his skin appeared so smooth. One of her cousins had died of the drink, and she knew the signs.

'That's a plural verb,' he was saying to Pat, 'so it's the nominative plural you should be looking for now. I think that what you had before might have been the ablative.'

Pat pointed to the page and mumbled something.

Mr Fernon asked, 'Is that how you pronounce it?'

'It's how Father O'Reilly does,' said Pat cautiously.

'Then do not let me corrupt you. Can you see anything that looks like the accusative?'

'There'll be no trouble finding a name for the foal,' murmured Dan, but Pat seemed happy enough.

And he can't be out of his twenties, decided Mrs Kelly more hopefully. Her cousin had been given to wine, not whisky, and died a bachelor; if he'd married and settled down things might have gone differently.

Dan also seemed inclined to play matchmaker. He was disappointed to hear that Lily hadn't said for certain she'd be there on Saturday night.

'She's away into town to match some thread, Mr Kelly,' said her grandmother, when he rode over with a reminder. 'She's been sewing till all hours. It's ruining her eyesight.'

'Oh, surely not, Mrs Davidson.'

'She peers. I think she must need spectacles.'

'She has not yet found what she's looking for.'

'And she never will if she keeps on at this rate.'

Lily did not fail him. He went out to fetch a little more coal for the stove and almost fell over her in the back porch where she sat huddled in her evening cloak, changing her boots for indoor shoes. Her face above the dark velvet was as pearly as the sky; by the light of his lamps she'd be luminous.

'Is that blouse new?' asked Cathy Kelly when Lily came into the parlour and every head turned in her direction. 'Did you make it yourself? I wish I could make something like that.'

There is none now left to remember Lily as she looked that night in her triumph of lace and crêpe de Chine, but Michael Kelly was sufficiently dazzled to think kindly of her for eighty more years. Michael was just old enough for such occasions then, and his mother knew he'd open his mouth only to put food in it. Mr Fernon was there of course, accompanied by the amiable Mr Harraway and his wife, a tall, dark, bold-featured woman with a stunning figure sheathed in sea-green silk. She too seemed disinclined to say a word.

Mr Kelly thought she might have been a governess or a music teacher before her marriage. He'd heard her singing one day he was in town and called at the house the Harraways were renting there. She'd stopped as soon as he knocked, but he said her voice was strong and showed signs of training.

His daughter found this impossible to believe. 'Do you make your clothes, Mrs Harraway?' asked Cathy, with another glance in Lily's direction, but Mrs Harraway merely gave her a rather hard little smile and shook her head.

Mr Harraway asked about the local fishing.

'I think she was a mermaid,' whispered Lily, skipping into the hall close behind Mrs Kelly. 'He caught her at the Bay, and now he's brought her inland so she can't escape.'

'She's not been well. The doctor recommended a change of air.'

'I'd say the same in his position. I'm sure there's nothing in the medical books about a change of water.'

Lily's eyes were bright and her cheeks tinged with colour; she was in one of her flighty moods. Mrs Kelly supposed the men would like it.

'You don't need to do anything,' she said. 'I'm all set.' She added slyly, 'Go and talk to Mr Fernon.'

'Dan is.'

'Then step into the dining room and tell me if the table looks all right.'

Mrs Kelly said 'dining room' on an exhalation of pride, and Lily stepped. When Mr Kelly did the introductions and Cathy let everyone know her blouse was new for the occasion, the corners of Mr Fernon's mouth had lifted in something like recognition; his expression was knowing. She had no intention of talking to him yet.

Bob Graham arrived late but splendid in a new suit, and Mr Kelly was mightily relieved to see him. Bob was an educated man, he'd travelled, he could be relied upon to help any conversation along. The Grahams thought they were a cut above the rest of the district, but nobody held that against Bob. It was said that no matter who called at the Grahams', if Bob was there he'd come out to greet them as though he'd been looking forward to their visit for days. Mrs Kelly thought him delightful, and rather wished Lily would too.

'Phemie!' he exclaimed with his sudden, sweet smile when he caught sight of her. 'I didn't know you'd be here. I thought you lived in Christchurch now.'

'I did,' said Lily, 'until about a month ago. We had a very swank establishment there. But my father's moving back to the Bay, and I'm staying with my grandparents for a while. I always do, most summers.'

Her answer seemed to amuse him. 'You haven't changed at all.'

'Nor have you.' She didn't know what time had done to her, but Bob's face had settled. His eyes and eyebrows had lost their faint, impish slant, and his cheeks curved gently inwards now, making him look quieter, somehow, and more thoughtful.

'It must be almost ten years,' he said.

'Easily.'

'Your father was at the Bay then, too.'

'And you were still at school. Or perhaps the university.' He'd gone away to be a lawyer, and married a girl whose name Lily couldn't remember; she'd died not long after, so there wasn't a child.

'Just as well,' Lily's grandmother had said in her significant way.

'Why just as well?'

'A young fellow like that doesn't want to be left on his own with a baby.'

'I don't see why not,' Lily had said. 'Women are left with babies every day of the week, and not only because their husbands have died.' But her grandmother wasn't to be drawn on that topic.

Lily asked Bob how long he'd be home for.

'That depends,' he said.

'On what?'

'On what I decide to do next.'

She didn't know what else to say to him. It seemed silly to offer condolences on the death of a woman she'd never seen, and anyway, he hadn't sat at home and pined. He'd gone off to England. Bob wasn't the sort to sit anywhere for long. He turned his attention to the Harraways, eliciting a flicker of interest from the mermaid, and began to tell them of his newest ambition. He wanted to buy a motorcar. Darracqs were good on the local roads, but he also knew of a chap just back from America who was thinking of selling his brand new Buick because his wife found it bad for her nerves.

Mr Harraway was doubtful about Buicks. He'd heard the company was going under.

'That mightn't be the motorcar's fault,' said Lily.

'No, indeed not,' said Mr Harraway earnestly. All the same, he favoured English cars. 'I had a Wolseley at home for a while. My wife used to drive it everywhere, didn't you?'

A nod this time.

'Then I'll look to you for driving lessons, Mrs Harraway,' said Bob.

'Ruby,' she said in a hoarse whisper, and Mrs Kelly decided to seat them together at dinner. Which meant that Cathy would be next to Mr Fernon, and she wasn't at all sure about that. No, it would do, because he'd have Lily opposite, with Mr Harraway beside her. Lily could talk well enough when she chose, and that was usually to the men. And there weren't too many of them; Dan's bachelor brothers had finished their work early and gone off in pursuit of their own pleasure, so if you didn't count Michael the numbers were just right.

Chapter 2

The Harraways and Mr Fernon were planning to visit the mountain. Mr Harraway told Lily he was looking forward to it *immensely*. He and his wife had caught up with Mr Fernon in Dunedin, and they'd agreed to meet again here. 'But you're staying at the Grand, aren't you, Fern?' he called over his almond and asparagus soup, and Mr Fernon inclined his head.

He looked tidier than he had the other day. Thrown on, Lily's grandmother would have said of his clothes if she'd seen him then, and Lily had thought that he would require very little encouragement to throw them off again. But perhaps she'd misjudged him; tonight he seemed subdued.

Mr Harraway made up for him with gleeful tales of missing trunks and missed trains, night rides over potholed roads, and cheerless lodgings with stewed tea in towns where a real drink was not to be found. At intervals he appealed to Mr Fernon for comment or confirmation. 'You've been there, haven't you, Fern?' and 'Didn't you think so, Fern?' It was almost as if he were trying to coax him into speech, a strange thing for one grown man to be doing for another.

'And are you enjoying yourselves?' asked Lily, to see if she could succeed where Mr Harraway was failing.

'Oh, very much so,' said Mr Harraway with great satisfaction and the mildest of lisps.

Cathy Kelly also wanted to hear more from Mr Fernon, and Mrs Harraway gave her an opening by asking Bob Graham about a burnt-out house half a mile or so from town. Cathy had heard there was a title in Mr Fernon's family, and since all families of note own an ancient seat or two and such great houses have their ghosts, she saw a way of encouraging him to reminiscence. 'That house was haunted,' she announced.

Bob agreed that it was, but then everybody differed as to the nature of the manifestations. Mrs Kelly said the maids were always leaving.

'They left to be married,' said Mr Kelly. He maintained there'd been a poltergeist, a very dull one that had done nothing more than tramp up and down the passageways and rap on a few windows. It frightened nobody.

Cathy said she'd never heard of any poltergeist, and Mr Kelly told her she was too young to remember.

Bob and Lily could remember the house perfectly. They'd gone to children's parties there. 'And we often smelled burning,' said Bob, then grinned. 'Or at least Phemie said she could, so I thought I did too.'

'I could,' said Lily. 'It used to worry me. And this was well before the fire took place.'

Mrs Kelly said a maid had told her that she'd felt one of *them* give her a push as she came down the stairs, causing her to drop a full – and here Mrs Kelly blinked and faltered – a full soup tureen.

Her husband laughed and said he hoped they weren't splashed by its contents, or they'd be sorry to have ever left Ireland.

Cathy, disliking the cryptic turn the conversation had taken, opened her mouth to press for more detail, saw Mr Fernon was smiling too, and stammered that she really didn't know whether she could remember the house or only what she'd heard of it.

'Oh, well,' said Lily, 'that fire was a good twelve years ago.'

'Nearer sixteen,' said Bob. 'You wrote to me at school about it.'

'Oh, sixteen to be sure,' said Mrs Kelly. 'For Michael was the baby then.'

Women who record events by babies are never wrong. Lily conceded graciously, and Mr Harraway began to tell them about a ghost he'd encountered in a country house in England.

That gave Lily the chance to study Mr Fernon again. His air was one of resignation. When she'd seen him in the yard the word 'dissolute' had come to mind, though she wasn't quite sure what it meant; the sound suited him. But that may have been unkind. He made her think now of an animal wearied by illness or injury, not yet ready for death but beginning to distance itself from life. She felt the unease such creatures always caused in her: a feeling akin to distaste, but so faint it was scarcely a feeling at all.

He's bored, she thought. He must know he's Mr Kelly's latest acquisition. I expect he's only here because he's hungry.

Mrs Kelly was a famous cook. She was concerned to see he had enough to eat and that the cat wasn't bothering him. They'd progressed from smoked trout to lamb in a berry sauce, and Oedipus was partial to a bit of lamb.

'Not at all,' said Mr Fernon. 'He's promising me my heart's desire.'

'We're not sure how old he is,' said Cathy eagerly. 'Or if he could do it when he was one and then again at eight, or in the seventh year of his life. When he was, or will be, six.'

'He'll be on the table in a minute,' muttered Mr Kelly, as a hint that Cathy should remove him, but she had ears for Mr Fernon alone.

'Is he so secretive about his age, then? Here, little Swolfoot, you've deceived me. Take that and be gone.'

There was a quality about his speech, a gentle precision that made everything he said sound humorous. Cathy certainly seemed to think so. She beamed.

Actorish, thought Lily with sudden disdain. His hair was too long. His voice, though, wasn't overloud, nor was he at pains to draw attention to himself. She wondered what he'd done to earn his exile. Maybe women didn't interest him at all.

'He's of no use whatsoever,' she said. 'He does nothing for his keep.'

'But he stared at me so, Miss Macgregor,' said Mr Fernon. 'How could I refuse him?' His tone was humble, but his eyes met hers in a manner so intent yet impersonal she had to look away, and wished she'd kept her mouth shut.

The others didn't notice. Their talk had turned to the local farms: who owned what where, and how they'd come by it. Mr Kelly was explaining that most of her grandfather's land was leased to him. The tedium that came when she'd been too much with other people began to settle on her, and she started to work out how soon she could slip away.

'And was your mother their only child?' asked Mrs Harraway. Her voice was deep and hesitant, with an accent approximating, though not perfectly, that of her husband and Mr Fernon.

A parlourmaid, thought Mrs Kelly triumphantly. She knew the airs and graces creatures of that ilk gave themselves.

'They had a son too – my uncle,' began Lily, then saw Bob's eyes were on her. 'My uncle,' she repeated, and finished in a rush, 'but he had an accident.'

'A fatal one,' said Bob soberly and waited, his lips slightly parted in expectation of what she might say next.

'In the ba-arn,' added Lily, making two syllables of the word.

Bob's eyes were dancing. 'It was a dreadful thing.'

'A dreadful thing,' echoed Lily.

Bob seemed about to say something more, then busied himself with his table napkin.

'Oh, I am sorry,' said Mrs Harraway into the little silence that followed. 'I didn't mean . . .'

'No, no, it's quite all right,' said Lily. 'It was years ago.'

'We never knew him,' said Bob.

'I was just a whippersnapper at the time,' said Mr Kelly, and went on to speak of the alterations that had been made to their house since he was a boy. Mr Harraway was fascinated. At one time he'd thought of becoming an architect.

After the *crème brûlée* everyone went back to the parlour. Bob and Mrs Harraway sat on the sofa between the two big windows that overlooked the lawn. Bob was talking about theatres in

London. Their names meant nothing to Lily, but Mrs Harraway was all ears; she'd taken a real shine to him. Her speech was not hesitant now, nor her accent so refined.

Cathy began to tell Mr Fernon about a play she had seen.

'*The Face at the Window*,' said Bob in chilling tones, and Mr Fernon laughed.

'Do you know it?' Cathy asked him.

'No,' he said, 'not yet. But I'm sure I would enjoy the piece, had I the opportunity to do so. What do you think, Miss Macgregor?'

Lily had thought the reflection of the late sun on the kitchen window would have prevented him from seeing her there, but he had and he wanted her to know it. He was amusing himself with her, and he'd make the most of this. 'I didn't see it,' she said.

'It was terrifying,' said Cathy. 'And whenever the face was about to appear there was the eeriest sound. But I won't tell you about it in case you do see it and I spoil it for you.'

'You could never do that,' said Mr Fernon kindly. 'Could she, Miss Macgregor?'

Bob kept glancing in her direction as if he wanted her to join him. Impossible. The tedium that had begun at dinner threatened to overwhelm her, and she was no longer interested in making herself agreeable to anybody.

Through the window she could see the pale backs of sheep, and dark outlines of the trees beyond them. The mountains were violet now, their crevices of snow invisible. The lamps were lit in her grandparents' house. Michael Kelly began to light theirs, and Mrs Kelly summoned Cathy away. Mr Kelly and Mr Harraway were talking about the fishing again.

Mr Fernon joined her at the window. 'Is that where you are spending the summer?'

Lily nodded. His reflection didn't look at hers, but there'd been a subtle change in his manner.

The two half-wild cats that lived under the verandah and did everything together were coming up the drive, carrying a rabbit between them.

'Do you like animals, Miss Macgregor?' This in the indulgent tone of one attempting conversation with an imbecile.

'I dislike people, Mr Fernon.'

'You seem very fond of windows.'

'It's an old habit of mine. I always liked to sit by the door at school, or by a window if that wasn't possible. It was a nervous habit then, I suppose, but it's nothing now. Except I still don't like to stay anywhere I'd rather not be.'

'And how long do you intend to stay here?'

'You're right,' she said to his reflection, 'I should be more sociable.' She moved to the sofa and perched on the arm beside Bob. He started to rise, but Mrs Harraway sprang up.

'Sit here — I want a word with Joss,' she cried, and went to Mr Fernon's side. 'Oh, what've those cats got?'

Bob murmured, 'We disgraced ourselves at dinner.'

'You started it.'

'I didn't.'

'You did. I could tell by the way you were looking at me.'

'I wanted to see if you remembered.'

'I did, but you lost your nerve.'

'We'd have embarrassed Ruby Harraway even more if I hadn't.'

Lily fell silent; Mrs Harraway and Mr Fernon had moved away, but her hearing was acute and she'd learnt long ago to listen to other people's conversations without seeming to do so. Mrs Harraway picked up a book that Mr Fernon had brought for their host. 'What's this about?'

'What are you thinking?' asked Bob. He'd often asked Lily that when they were children, and it had always annoyed her.

Nothing that concerns you, she used to say, but now she said, 'Is that a new seal on your watch chain?'

'No, it was my grandfather's. You've seen it before.'

'Let me see it now.'

He handed her his watch and chain. She tossed the seal gently in her hand, feeling its weight on her palm. The gold around the stone was finely ribbed and whorled, the ornate stem knobbed like a blackberry.

She'd missed Mr Fernon's reply, but Mrs Harraway still held the book. She read out, '*Holy Living and Dying, with Prayers, containing The Whole Duty of* A *Christian*. That doesn't sound much like you, Joss, if I may say so. Or him either, for that matter,' she added, with a toss of her head in Mr Kelly's direction.

'It is his prose we admire, rather than his principles,' said Mr Fernon.

'That's what blokes always say when you catch them reading something a bit peculiar.'

Lily held the seal towards the lamp where Mr Fernon stood. The stone lay in its setting like a pool of dark ale. 'Lucky your grandfather's initials were the same as yours.'

'You used to tell me I couldn't possibly wear it because my initials were BG, not RG.'

'Oh, the print!' exclaimed Mrs Harraway, and came nearer the lamp. 'Poverty, or a Low Fortune. The Charge of Many Children. Violent Necessities. Death of Children or Nearest Relatives and Friends. Untimely Death; Death Unseasonable; Sudden Death, or Violent. Being Childless; Evil or Unfortunate Children. Our Own Death. Cheerful chap, isn't he!'

'He is,' said Mr Fernon mildly.

'For Temperance! He's thought of everything. For Chastity, to be said especially by Unmarried Persons. I hope you know that one by heart. Ah, this is more like it. Ejaculations to be used any Time that Day, after the Solemnity is ended. Well, there you are.'

'You are more than welcome to borrow it if you think it would interest you.'

'Who wrote it, anyway? Oh my God, another bloody bishop. No thanks, I'll stick to Elinor Glyn.'

'Definitely not a schoolteacher,' whispered Lily, tilting the seal to catch the lamplight in the stone. Its back was faceted, and as she turned it this way and that the light carried through to the gold within.

'I never thought she was. That's not enough to unsettle a bishop. Even an English one.'

'I like the way the stone holds the light. It reminds me of the creek.'

'Muddy.'

'No, the way the sunlight catches in the water. The creek's brown, it's never muddy.'

'It is when it's in flood.'

'Don't argue. How old do you think she is?'

'About the same as us. Old enough to have a past.'

Mr Fernon and Mrs Harraway had put the book aside. There was a ripple of laughter, first from her and then from him.

'The stage,' murmured Bob, 'I'm sure of it. Or to be exact, the music hall. Is there a prize for the correct answer?'

'Ask Mr Kelly,' said Lily, with a last look at the seal. 'It's beautiful, it matches your eyes. Is that enough to unsettle a bishop?'

'I've never sought a bishop's opinion of my eyes.'

'The music hall, you idjit.'

'That would depend upon the bishop. And her repertoire.'

'Anyhow, she's very handsome, but pantomime's the best. I'd like to see her as Dick Whittington or Prince Charming.'

'Ooh, so should I,' sighed Bob with exaggerated ardour.

The others were going out to smoke cigars on the verandah. Bob said he might too, but he showed no sign of moving. Lily looked in the direction of her grandparents' house; there was a glimmer of light from their bedroom, and then it was gone. The house would be settling into silence now, ruled by its own spirits, not theirs.

'Are you enjoying yourself?' asked Bob.

'Oh, very much so,' said Lily through her front teeth. 'Immensely.'

'I think you should've gone on the stage.'

'Why?'

'You're such a good mimic. And I never know what you're thinking.'

'If the audience didn't know what an actress was thinking they'd ask for their money back.'

'You know what I mean.'

'I have to speak to Mrs Kelly for a minute,' said Lily, rising. 'She'll be in the scullery.'

Michael Kelly followed her out to the back porch. 'Are you going now?'

The sound of his voice made her jump. 'Yes, I must. My grandmother'll be waiting up for me, and it's getting late.'

'Would you like me to see you home?'

'No, I don't mind walking alone in the dark. In fact I enjoy it.'

He vanished. Lily finished tying her bootlaces and undid her hair. Soon she would be herself again, with Mr Fernon and to-night's half-formed hope behind her. As she went down the steps she heard someone else in the porch, and then a shadow fell on the grass beside hers.

'Are you leaving so soon, Miss Macgregor?'

'Yes, Mr Fernon, I am.'

'I would be honoured if you would permit me to accompany you.'

'That's very kind of you, but it's only fifteen minutes or so across the paddocks. No distance at all.'

'That's why I offered to walk with you.'

'As you wish, Mr Fernon.'

'I wish you would call me Joss. Or even Josselin.'

'Why?'

'Because it's my name.'

'That's not what Mr Harraway calls you.'

'He's not a woman.' He added dolefully, 'We were at school together.'

'Josselin,' said Lily, 'is an unusual name.'

'It was my mother's before she married. You might describe her as unusual.'

He had not liked school; he didn't like his mother. They were alike in that.

Mr Fernon made no further attempt at conversation, and seemed to expect none from her. After a little she said, 'Mrs Harraway was rather shy at dinner,' and wondered if he knew how much of their later talk she'd overheard.

'That's because she takes no pleasure in pretending to be anything other than what she is.'

'A mermaid.'

'Precisely.'

'She doesn't need to with the Kellys. They don't care what people are as long as they're interesting.'

'Really? I would have never guessed that.'

There was the same barely discernible hesitation in his step as there was in his speech. Lily lengthened her stride, but he kept up with her easily.

'You walk quickly, Miss Macgregor. I think you are too used to walking alone.'

'It's what I prefer, Mr Fernon.'

'I would prefer to call you by your Christian name, but I've forgotten it.'

'It's Lily.'

'That's not what Bob Graham called you.'

'He forgot and called me Phemie, which is short for Euphemia and that's even worse. Once I'd finished school I told everyone my name was Lily.'

'Lily is a name for whores and housemaids.'

She laughed. Whatever might be said for his face, his manners were far from beautiful. 'Perhaps that's true. There was a maid called Lily at the first hotel we lived in with my father — my stepfather, that is — and she had a string of followers.'

Anything was possible after all. She marvelled that she could have found him, however briefly, distasteful; that languid air made him irresistible. But she could think of nothing to say that wouldn't sound like an appeal of sorts, and they went on in silence until they reached the gate.

'There,' she said, 'you've had your walk. I told you it would be a short one.'

'But long enough,' he said, and touched her hair. 'I like it better loose. Goodnight, my fair-spoken one.'

'Goodnight, Mr Fernon.'

Chapter 3

Lily knew her grandparents' house well, because she'd been born there. She lived there until she was five, sometimes with her mother but mostly without, for reasons that were never explained to her. Nor did it occur to her to ask. It was not a time when explanations were thought necessary or desirable for children.

She was born in summer, but winter was the season she liked best. Somebody lifted her up to touch the icicles hanging from the roof, and earwigs lay frozen in the dish of milk put out for Soot. One of the kitchen chairs was left against the stove; its back was scorched, and it grew bitter and envious. The other chairs didn't like to be placed near it after that. When the house was too quiet and everything smelt of burning, Lily sat under the table and listened to their whisperings, and got to know them well.

Soot came home with his sides sunken in and one front leg crushed and flyblown. Her grandmother said he'd been caught in a trap, and spread a sack for him in the shed where he crouched, nibbling at the shreds of fur and bone. The shed was through Prince's stall. Whenever Lily took Soot the day's scraps she had to reach up to slap his side and say, 'Gee over, Prince', and he'd step away from her on huge white-feathered feet as lightly as a dancer. Those same feathery hooves could make the ground tremble when her grandfather unhitched the team from the plough and Prince led the way down to the dam. She liked to watch the horses' collars sliding on their necks each time they bent their heads to drink and lifted them again. Then they'd fling back their heads to settle the jingling collars on their shoulders before they walked to the gate and stood waiting to be let in.

One shimmering day Lily and her grandmother returned from taking food out to the men and found her mother in the house. She had come on the Bay train and walked from the railway station, and when her feet began to hurt she'd taken off her boots and stockings and walked barefoot. She thought nothing of that, but Lily's grandmother was not pleased. 'Who saw you?'

'Nobody was coming this way,' she said, yawning sunnily, 'or I'd have got a lift.'

She was a loud, ungainly creature who seemed neither child nor adult, and she ran about poking into everything. When she tried the swing it complained of her weight; she sat twisting the fat gold ring on her finger and wondering if it were safe.

'I'm Mrs Macgregor now,' she said, seeing Lily's eyes on the ring.

Then she made Lily show her her marbles, pestering her for their names. 'Which one's your taw, Phemie?'

'My name's not Phemie,' said Lily, but she picked out the prettiest and silliest for her.

'Oh no,' her mother said, 'that's not a taw. A taw should be old and worn so it doesn't slip in your fingers. This one here was my taw.'

Next she sat on the floor with her skirt bunched up while her hands scooped and scattered knucklebones and she exclaimed at their remembered skill. At teatime those same hands cut up the meat on Lily's plate, and when Lily refused to eat it she jabbed a finger in the gravy and tasted it for salt.

'*She* still loves me!' she cried, as Nancy stood up like a dog to put her forelegs on her shoulders. 'We had such fun when she was little. We used to chase each other along the verandah. Nancy'd chase me one way and I'd chase her the other. And when she had a lamb of her own and it got through the fence, she didn't stand there bleating like any other silly sheep. No, you didn't! She came to the door and bumped it with her head. Dad went out and she led him to the fence, looking back all the time to make sure he was following. She's so clever. Yes, you are! Wouldn't you like a little lamb to play with, Phemie?'

'No.'

Each night she took down her hair and brushed it, counting the strokes. It hung in streams of cream and honey, with here and there a thread of gold. At her neck and behind her ears it was the soft, shining brown of a mouse's back. When Lily lay in the grass to see what Soot saw, the green blades against her eyelids splintered into all the colours of the rainbow, and she thought that if she were to put her face against that hair it might do the same. Then her mother flung back her head, her face red from the brushing, and held her hairbrush over some torn-up pieces of paper. They leapt at the bristles. 'Shall we see if your hair can do that?' she asked, and Lily backed away.

They all went on the train, a day trip to see the sea. Her mother unwrapped the apples she'd dipped in toffee the night before, and sat licking hers with her broad tongue as if it were the most natural thing in the world to do. Lily held her apple so awkwardly it fell off its stick and got covered in sand.

'If you'd been holding it properly that wouldn't have happened,' said her grandmother, pleased to have something to snap about.

'Here, have mine,' called her mother instantly, pressing it down on the stick with her wet red mouth. The thought of eating anything licked by that tongue and pressed by those lips turned Lily's stomach. She shrank against her grandmother for no better reason than it was expected of her, and that was no reason at all.

'Well, there isn't any more of them,' cried her grandmother triumphantly.

Her mother bought a storybook while they were at the Bay, and whenever she read aloud the whole house listened. The broken darning needle had a wonderful opinion of herself: she lay in the gutter and thought she was a sunbeam, but soon everyone was tired of her. The beetle in the stable was affronted to see the emperor's horse shod with gold. A butterfly had trouble choosing a wife; when he was caught and pinned in a glass case he thought it quite as good as marriage. One crackling night the snowman looked into the kitchen and felt a terrible longing deep within him: he wanted to break through the window and lean against the stove, but the yard dog, who knew what love was worth, barked 'Be off, be off'. Lily sat arranging the buttons from her grandmother's button box to fit the pattern in the rug.

'Phemie, are you listening?'

'Yes.'

'Don't you want to see the pictures?'

'No.'

'Would you like to hear another story?'

'Yes.'

'Then why won't you come and sit beside me?' implored her mother, patting the sofa.

'Because I do not like the way you smell,' Lily had replied, and this caused greater consternation than anything she'd said or done so far. When pressed she could name nothing her mother smelt of other than shop soap and rose-water, which was not a matter of grave offence, but she was sent to bed, where Soot came to lie beside her.

His fur smelt of sun, and of the peppery scents other cats left in the places where he walked; his breath of the rabbits he'd caught and killed when he had all his legs. Once, in the pump paddock, she'd watched him take one that was bolder or more stupid than the rest: the dash and tumble in the grass, the way he braced himself as it lay kicking beneath him, the tender precision of his sleek black head as he sought and tightened his grip on its throat.

That such delight was gone from him, that her grandfather had spoken of shooting him if his leg didn't heal, meant nothing to him now. He did not want or offer love. Lily knew better than to touch him, he didn't care for that, but she could draw his thoughts into hers until his vast, unruffled soul lay in and all around her.

The others were arguing. Her mother's voice was high and nervous, her grandmother's low and reproachful; she heard the sombre tones of her grandfather and then his heavy tread as he left the house, for he never stayed indoors for long. The women's voices sharpened, and Lily knew for certain they were quarrelling over her.

'You have set her against me!' cried her mother, as if the person she called Phemie could have had no views of her own.

The next morning they were loaded into the wagon to be taken to the train. Lily turned for a last look at Soot where he sat on the verandah and her mother said, 'Oh no, we can't take him. Soot wouldn't like it in town.'

And then Lily felt strange, because nothing seemed to fit. She was away from herself; she could see herself quite clearly, squashed between her mother and her grandfather, in her faded blue coat and the new boots that shone and sneered at it. Her coat had just lost a button and was dangling its long twisty thread; her mother was smiling and talking, and even though Lily was too far away to hear what was said, that was when she knew she would have to start all over again or she'd always be away as she was now.

Then her mother's flushed and toothy face was close to hers. She was saying, in her stupid way, 'Don't sulk, Phemie. I'll get you another cat, a dear little kitten. Soot's a bad-tempered old thing.'

Which wasn't what it was about at all.

And so Lily went to live with her mother and the pink-faced man who was to be her father, though when he heard her grandfather was Dad he said she could call him Mac like everybody else did. They lived in a succession of hotels, in Naseby, Dunedin and Middlemarch, until her mother went off again, for good this time, and Lily was sent back to the house where she was born. She found things much as they'd been, yet not quite the same. The furniture was less inclined to let her know its secrets; Nancy was gone from the pump paddock, and a different dog walked with its nose at her grandfather's heels. A ginger cat sat blinking in Soot's old place on the verandah.

Her grandmother had soured. Lily remembered her as a heavy, tight-skinned woman, full of the importance of being clean and doing things properly. Now she was quick to anger. A chance remark or careless gesture would cause her eyes to harden and her face turn dark. She'd swipe at Lily with wooden spoons or wet dishcloths, accusing her of ingratitude, silly talk, airs and graces; there was the occasional frenzy with the razor strop.

At first Lily took pleasure in provoking her, as one might test any unpredictable creature for its limits, but these were unequal contests. Beneath her grandmother's rage was steel, the same steel Lily had to find in herself when she cut her finger to the bone with the carving knife, or was sent to shovel the maggoty remains of a rat from the wash house. That steel masked disgust and fear, and met the need for distance; Lily came to understand that her grandmother was ashamed of her, and afraid of what she might grow to be in her turn. So she learnt to do things properly, and kept quiet, in return for being left alone as much as possible.

For a while she'd gone to the local school, trudging to and fro with Jean Graham and her brother Bob. They were very much alike, 'as like as one egg to another,' said her grandmother when she saw them waiting shyly by the gate. Which was unusually clever of her, for they reminded Lily of two nice brown eggs. They had smooth, clean faces with gently rounded cheeks, and the faintest of speckles across their noses. As they walked along they watched her from beneath fine eyebrows with eyes that were both dark and bright. You could see what those eggs might hatch into.

Lily tried to entertain them with imitations of the dominie at Middlemarch who'd caught her and Jamie Macpherson playing truant. Jean pursed her lips and drew her eyebrows together in a cautious expression that ripened into a pout of disapproval when Lily went on to show them how drunkards stalked or staggered out of the hotel at night.

'I've signed the pledge,' said Lily airily, but that didn't seem to please her either.

Bob's was a keener spirit. Often she caught him looking at her with all the eager concentration of a young animal whose very wariness might be an invitation to play.

'I'll help you with your sums, Phemie,' he said after a disastrous day. 'Try this. If it takes one man one whole day to dig a ditch, how long will it take two men?'

'Two days.'

'No, Phemie, it takes half as long, not twice as long. Because there are two of them to share the work, you see.'

Lily knew she was in danger of losing the small piece of ground she'd gained. 'It takes twice as long because they keep stopping for a yarn and a smoke,' she said.

Bob and Jean exchanged looks.

'No, Phemie, listen,' he said. 'It would take one man one whole day to dig the ditch, but now he has a friend to help him. If they don't talk and they don't smoke, how long will it take?'

'Two days, because now he has a friend they decide to dig a longer ditch.'

'I'd give up if I were you, Bobby,' said Jean.

After Jean went to high school Bob had a horse to ride, and as soon as they were out of her grandmother's sight Lily climbed up behind him. He said he and Jean used to have ponies for school, but one day his had bitten hers on the backside and she'd fallen into a patch of mud. Jean wouldn't ride with him again, and having to walk with her had been his punishment for laughing. Bob was indifferent to bumps and bruises; he rippled with delight at the memory.

'I'd have laughed too,' said Lily, but the horse's back was slippery and she was a long way from the ground. She tightened her arms around his middle and put her cheek against his warm back.

He told her she was different from everybody else he knew.

'That's because I'm a townie,' replied Lily grandly. 'I hate the country.'

'So do I,' he assured her, with a sidelong glance to see if she believed him, but by then she knew him better. When he stood barelegged in the creek with his hair rusted by the sun and his lips stained by blackberries, or slid on the ice, or searched the grass for a fluttering dotterel's nest while Lily tiptoed behind him whispering, 'Leave it, Bobby, let her think she's deceiving you, let her keep her secret,' he seemed formed of and for its elements. Without Jean they were always late home.

Then Lily's grandmother decided she was too old to be running round the countryside at all hours of the day and night with Bobby Graham and God only knew who else.

'How old's Bobby?' asked her grandfather.

'Twelve,' said Lily.

'He won't be twelve forever,' said her grandmother. 'I'm not making that mistake twice.'

'The Grahams are to have a tennis court,' said Lily by way of distraction.

'A tennis court! Some folk've got more sheep than sense. What do they want a tennis court for?'

'To play tennis on.'

'Well, you needn't think you're going to. You can stay home and make yourself useful. You can learn to cook.'

'I know how to cook.'

'Omelettes and sauces! That's playing at cooking. Good plain food and plenty of it, that's what the men like.'

In the country, Lily knew, *the men* had a strength and significance they didn't have in town. Once the men come in. When the men have eaten. What the men like. Town, thought Lily, was better.

Bobby went away to high school and grew very grand in his stripy blazer. When he came home for the holidays, Lily played tennis at the Grahams'. Everybody did. She went up to his room and inspected his school prizes, heavy books with gold-stamped covers, while he wrinkled his nose modestly and explained that as he was in the first eleven and the first fifteen, nobody minded those.

He and Jean had friends to stay, smug boys and prissy girls who sat around in circles talking of nothing. The girls were the worst. They had a knack of indicating that a conversation was closed unless they chose to reopen it. 'Well, of course.' 'So it seems.' They all went to dances and the boys hung round Lily then, but she usually danced with Bob because there was no need to say much or appear to be enjoying herself any more than she was.

He asked, 'Have you worked out how long it takes two men to dig that ditch?'

'Well, of course.' Then she forgave him his friends. 'How long is the ditch to be?'

'Long enough to take one man twelve hours to dig. They don't talk, they don't smoke, they don't even stop to boil the billy. They start at six in the morning and they'll get nothing till they're done. When will that be?'

'You're a hard man, Bob Graham, and they hate you for it. As soon as your back's turned they go off to find a better job.'

His eyes were dreamy; he hadn't listened to her answer. He put his hands around her waist and told her that last night on their lawn the pink glow from the sky had turned her curls to crimson, and she was like the girl in her old storybook, 'the one who was the colour of milk and blood.'

'She was light in the dance and lighter in the mind,' said Lily.

'She was a town lady,' said Bob.

'She was a fallen woman. And she was chased along the seashore by the ghost of her bastard crying, "Dig me my grave."'

He blushed unhappily. 'I don't think I can have finished reading it,' he said.

'It was the talk of the Bay. My dear, the picnic was utterly ruined.'

But Bobby didn't laugh. He'd lost his old immunity from hurt. After an evening when Lily danced several times with Bertie Fraser, Jean conveyed that there'd been a falling-out between Bertie and Bob. And as she, Jean, was bound to take Bob's part there was now a coolness between Bertie and herself.

Lily thought they were being silly. She'd never regarded either boy as a possible suitor, and she wasn't about to shun Bertie just to please Jean Graham. Pleasing the Grahams had almost ceased to matter, because her father now had a hotel at the Bay and she was old enough to spend more than the occasional weekend there. He'd written to ask if she might come for the winter.

'Mac's a very kind man,' said her grandmother. 'Most wouldn't bother.'

Lily wasn't so sure. She looked well behind the bar, and barmaids were supposed to be superior to the general run of hotel maids. She remembered them taking their meals with her parents, quite like members of the family. But it meant freedom in a proper town with ships and trains to everywhere and boys who wouldn't hang round long enough for misunderstandings to occur. That little upset with Bob and Bertie hadn't been the first of its kind.

Nor was it to be the last. A midshipman told another of the barmaids he didn't know why Miss Lily hadn't been nicer to him; he'd have sent her all sorts of pretty things from overseas. The artist she invited to tea because he looked so hungry bought her an expensive box of chocolates, then sulked when she wouldn't hold his hand. And not long after, Bob kissed her properly, or perhaps improperly: a sensation so like a mouthful of cold porridge she couldn't keep a straight face, though she accepted that the fault lay with her, not him.

Other girls, other women, managed these things better. They met men, they went about with them, and when asked they married them and seemed happy enough, though it was often hard to see why. Her inability to find a man she might ever wish to marry, and her attraction for those whom she regarded as no more than friends, sprang from inattentiveness on her part — a failure to grasp some basic principle, or a lack of application similar to that which causes promising lads to falter in their chosen careers. She grew wary.

And in the end it was Jean Graham who became Mrs Bertie Fraser. 'His taste's all in his mouth,' sniffed Lily's grandmother, as if Jean weren't at all pretty, but she was right. Soon Jean's preoccupation with what Bertie would and would not eat overrode all. In victory she grew gracious and confiding: Bertie had to have meat at each meal and was made itchy by tomatoes. Lily accepted these peace offerings with every appearance of goodwill, and was glad that the future combination of her maiden state and a move to Christchurch with her father would save her from having to see much of the Frasers, together or apart.

She knew what she wanted now. It was there or it wasn't, that was all. One wild night when she was hurrying to meet her father she'd glimpsed a young man sheltering in a doorway: bright hair, rough clothes, a sullen face, his eyes on her. Lily passed him in seconds and didn't look back. The street was almost empty and there was a sourness in him, but there was something else as well, something that set her heart racing and not from apprehension. She saw it again in a swaggie at the farm, dusty and unshaven as he'd been, but his blue eyes flicked away from her as soon as she'd given him tea for his billy and some cheese and mutton sandwiches. There'd been a commercial traveller who lingered at the bar; she was busy, then he was gone. And none of these were men she could have married

For a while longer she looked, from the best and safest of vantage points, then grew tired of looking. When she was not behind the bar she wore her hair down her back like a schoolgirl and left off her stays. She bought a bicycle. She took drawing lessons, and was seen at public lectures with some very odd friends. She referred, loftily and with increasing frequency, to her 'independence', and wore a large wristwatch and a collar and tie. She even spoke of going to sea as a stewardess.

'Our Lily seems set on having a career,' observed Bertie Fraser. He'd always thought her game as a pebble.

'And what do you think that career could be?' asked Mrs Bertie Fraser.

'Now, Jean,' said her mother. 'Phemie's a nice enough little thing.'

'Wasn't Bob sweet on her once?' asked Bertie.

'A lot of men have been sweet on her. Once,' said Jean.

'Oh *really*, Jean,' said Mrs Graham.

She could afford to be generous now her darling boy was engaged to be married, thought Jean. Bobby was their mother's favourite: Jean knew it, her dull old brother Alec knew it, even clever Connie knew it, though she kept on being clever.

Most summers Lily came back to the farm and made herself useful. If she went to dances it was with the Kelly boys, Dan's two bachelor brothers. Their cheeks were so freshly shaven her own stung in sympathy, their hands against hers looked like slabs of corned beef, but they were as light on their feet as lambs at twilight and they weren't overly susceptible to Protestant girls.

People began to forget what a flighty piece she'd been. A pity, some thought, Mrs Kelly among them, that Lily Macgregor should be left on the shelf and her grandfather's farm be sold. Perhaps she'd set her sights too high. Or not high enough.

'I can't see Joss Fernon as a farmer,' said Dan, who knew which way his wife's thoughts were running when she asked what kind of impression Lily had made on Saturday night. Lily's evasion of what he'd taken lately to calling 'the new and undiscerned chains of marriage' amused him. Anyway, he wanted the Davidsons' land for his brothers, or for Michael, who'd foregone his chance of an education and worked like a hind for him so Pat and Kevin and little Danny could have theirs.

'Nor can I, now I've had a closer look at him,' admitted Mrs Kelly. 'Though he didn't take much wine at dinner, and it came from the Grahams' cellar. Lily told me there'd be nothing finer at the Grand.' Bob had sent it over in a picnic hamper with sets of glasses neatly stowed, as if everywhere the Grahams' wines went their glasses did too. Mrs Kelly thought his tact exquisite. 'I was thinking of Bob Graham,' she said.

'I can't see him settling to anything. I thought he'd be looking to join a law firm, but he said he's staying on here for a month or two. Now there's a waste of an education for you.'

'He's still young. Mrs Graham'll be pleased to have him home for a while, and at this time of year his brother'll be glad of an extra hand who knows what he's doing.'

'He's nearly thirty. Mrs Harraway liked Lily.'

'They scarcely exchanged a word all evening.'

'That's what she told me. "I like Lily," she said, "she's my sort." Mrs Harraway's been lonely, and Nigel Harraway said that seeing she's made some friends here he might stay for the summer.'

'He probably thinks Alec Graham's the local squire.'

'Well, if we don't disillusion him I'm sure the Grahams won't. And next time I go into town I'll take Lily to visit Mrs Harraway. That'll make a change for them both.'

Chapter 4

Lily raised no objection to calling on the Harraways while Mr Kelly went about his business in town. Ruby Harraway was very lively in a red silk wrapper and not much else, even though it was the middle of the afternoon.

'I've done the washing! I don't mind doing washing, in fact I'm quite good at it.' Now she was making a cake. 'Nige went out so I thought I'd surprise him. I'm glad you're here — see what it's done.' She thrust the bowl under Lily's nose. 'I creamed the butter and sugar like you're supposed to and I beat the eggs, but when I put them in it curdled.'

'That doesn't matter,' said Lily. 'Just keep beating.'

'My arm's aching. You do it. I thought the eggs were bad when it did that — I've tried making cakes before. I said to Nige, farms everywhere and we can't even get good eggs. I've been throwing it out. Just as well we're not short of a few bob!'

'When an egg's bad you know as soon as you've cracked it,' said Lily, wondering how much money the Harraways had to lead their venturesome life on.

'Should you be putting the flour in yet? Mrs Kelly said to do it when it was white and fluffy. That still looks yellow and crunchy to me.'

'Mrs Kelly's a famous cook. This'll do, believe me. Have you greased the tin?'

The stove had gone out. Ruby said her husband had been chopping wood that morning, so Lily went out to the yard to see what was there. A collection of corsets, men's underwear, and what the fashion books called *lingerie* was pegged all anyhow on the line. She found coal and kindling in the shed.

'God, I'll never make a farmer's wife. He's mad even to think of it.' But they'd seen the lakes; they had been to the mountain. 'It's lovely, isn't it?'

'I suppose so,' said Lily with a shrug. 'I went once when I was little, that's all.'

'You should've come with us! I wish we'd thought to ask you. I'd have had someone to talk to.'

Lily, busy with the stove, was glad Ruby couldn't see her face. 'It'll take a while to heat.'

'Come and talk to me while I dress, then.'

'Shall I bring your washing in?'

'Oh, there're other things in the trunks.' Ruby led the way into a dim, cluttered room with an unmade bed and threw off her wrapper.

Lily flinched. She'd never seen another woman naked, and the sight was both repellent and reassuring. Ruby's breasts sat like steamed puddings above her gaunt ribcage; her belly was flat and her hips bony, but there was an odd bulkiness about her haunches and thighs. The patch of hair looked very thick and black against her sallow skin. Strange what the men liked. You could hardly suspect Mr Harraway of marrying her because he needed someone to cook and keep house for him.

Ruby heaved open a trunk and rummaged through its contents. Kneeling there in the half-light with her hair falling over her face and shoulders, she looked something other than human. *They will live in one kennel, they will gnaw on one bone,* thought Lily and tried to remember who'd said that. It didn't sound like her grandmother. She sat on the edge of the bed and studied the wrapper where it lay on the floor.

'Pretty, isn't it? I've another just like it somewhere that I've never worn. Peacock blue. You can have it, it'll suit you.'

'That's very kind of you.' Lily glanced up; Ruby had dispensed with the idea of underthings and was shaking out a mass of flame-coloured chiffon.

'Well, blue never does much for me, and I was hoping you'd make me a skirt. Here, have a look at this.' She thrust a silver-framed photograph into Lily's hand. 'That's our wedding photograph. Poor old Nige looks rather glum. Too much champagne the night before.' She stepped into the gown and arranged her breasts inside its bodice. 'What was so funny about your uncle's accident? I saw you and Bob at dinner.'

'It wasn't an accident. He killed himself.'

'That must've given everybody a really good laugh.'

'We never knew him. It was a silly game we used to play, that's all. My mother said something to me once, about her twin brother. I never knew she had a brother, and I asked where he was. "Well," she said, "you're bound to hear sooner or later so I might as well tell you now. Your uncle done a very silly thing, Phemie." I said, "Why, what did he do?" I was hoping he'd held up the mountain coach or run away to sea.'

Ruby was looking thoughtful. 'I'll wear the sash.' She gathered up chiffon by the armful to expose an embroidered silk lining, and handed Lily a boned and fringed length of matching silk. 'Do you mind tying it underneath at the side for me? Nice and tight, now.'

Nice and tight was easy. There seemed a good six inches of nothing between Ruby's hip bones and her ribs. 'Go on,' she said.

'My mother said, "He shot himself, Phemie." And I said, "Where?" Still thinking of the coach, and that he'd shot himself in the leg as he drew his pistol. And she said, "In the ba-arn." Just like that. In the ba-arn. And it was "a dreadful thing, a dreadful thing" and I wasn't to talk about it. So I kept it a secret for years until it burnt a hole in me and I told Bob on the way to school. After that, we used to practise it every morning. I'd say, "My uncle done a very silly thing, Bobby." "Why, what did he do, Phemie?" "He shot himself, Bobby." "Where did he shoot himself, Phemie?" And I'd say, "In the ba-arn." Then we'd be sheep and sing the chorus, "In the ba-arn, in the ba-arn, you can come to ha-arm, in the ba-arn." Then he'd say, "It was a dreadful thing." And I'd say, "A dreadful thing." And he'd say, "And we're not to talk about it."'

'Little horrors,' said Ruby, thrusting pins into her hair.

'Oh, we were. But nobody ever told us anything the least bit scandalous, so we had to make the most of that.'

'Bob's nice, isn't he? Has he bought his motorcar yet?' Ruby turned in a swirl of chiffon and struck a pose in the doorway. Clothed, hers was naturally the shape all women wanted but few could achieve. The gown's opaque lining clung to her body while the sheer overdress flared against the light. Its brilliant colour lent a creamy resonance to her skin and made her mouth and eyes mysterious. 'And now I'm in me teagown, we can 'ave a cuppa tea. Pity the cake's not ready.'

They put the cake in the oven and went to drink tea in the front room. Later Mr Harraway came in. Mr Fernon was with him.

Ruby said, 'I thought you were going on to Christchurch, even if we did stay for a bit.'

'Not yet. I thought I might stay too.' He acknowledged Lily with the slightest of bows. 'For a bit.'

'We'll be your guests at dinner tonight then. Lily'll come.'

'I can't,' said Lily, who didn't have the sort of gown that Ruby could doubtless pull from one of those trunks and wear to dinner at the Grand. 'I've things to do at home. I'll have to go now, because I came into town with Mr Kelly and he'll be ready to leave.'

Ruby was not put off so easily. 'Ask the Kellys to come as well. Joss owes them a dinner. You can do whatever it is you have to do at home, and come back with them.'

'My wife is an extraordinarily generous woman,' said Mr Harraway.

'Strike while the iron's hot,' said Ruby.

'Mrs Kelly needs more warning,' said Lily. 'She can't come away at such short notice, and he won't come without her.'

'Another time, then. Wait a minute and I'll see if I can find that wrapper for you. What I really want is a maid.'

'We can't afford one,' said Mr Harraway, following her, and Lily was left alone with Mr Fernon.

'What pleasant weather we are having, Miss Macgregor,' he said.

'Indeed.'

'I did think it might rain this afternoon.'

'Tomorrow, perhaps.'

'I suppose the farmers will like it.'

'They have to cut the hay.'

Ruby returned waving the wrapper and tossed it at Lily. 'I'm sorry it's so creased. Silk's the devil to iron.'

Lily felt exposed, clutching the gaudy thing in front of Mr Fernon; she trembled. 'I iron silk while it's still damp,' she said, 'though not with too hot an iron. I just wrap it in a towel and then I iron it dry.'

'That's handy to know,' said Mr Harraway to his wife. 'Isn't that handy to know?'

But Lily's composure was irretrievable, and it was only by moving about that she could keep herself from shivering. 'It does feel a little cooler,' she said. 'It might rain after all.' She made for the door. 'Mr Kelly . . .'

'I'm going to the hotel now,' said Mr Fernon kindly. 'I shall walk a little way with you.'

'You have to go out the back way,' announced Ruby, 'so you can see what I've made.' She winked at Lily. 'Will it be ready?'

Cakes were something Lily was at ease with. She took it from the oven, and in the absence of a rack turned it out to cool on a tea towel.

'Oh I say, how absolutely splendid!' cried Mr Harraway.

'Lily helped me,' said Ruby, with the air of one who can take no credit but what is her due.

'Ah,' said Mr Fernon gravely, and turned to contemplate the cake. Then he said, 'That does not make it any less splendid,' and Lily wondered if he found the Harraways as odd as she did. He opened the door and followed her down the steps. The light dazzled her; she felt feverish again. When he offered his arm she edged away, and saw the amusement in his eyes. The over-dry washing still hung across the yard; she flung herself under it, but he caught up with her as she turned onto the narrow side path that led to the street.

'Do not run away, Miss Macgregor. Are you quite well?'

'It's the heat, nothing more. The stove, in that little kitchen . . .'

'Then you ought not rush about so.' He slid one arm around her waist. 'Why, you're all aquiver. Is there anything I can do for you?'

Humiliation made her reckless. She clung to him. He kissed her on the mouth, forcing her head back and her lips apart. Her body slackened of its own accord and she seemed to lose all consciousness of herself and everything about her save the wall at her back and the pressure of his body against hers. The sensation then was of falling into darkness and it frightened her. With an effort, she raised her hands to his shoulders and turned her face away. He did not release her, but stood stroking her breasts with his free hand as absently as if it were Oedipus he had there.

'They'll see from the street,' she said.

'Don't go back with Mr Kelly. Tell him you intend to stay in town tonight.'

She made a slight movement of denial, but asked, 'Where?'

'At the Grand.'

Perhaps she'd misunderstood. 'I can't. I'm not dressed for it.'

She felt his smile. 'In the circles in which I move, it's customary to undress for it. It will be too late for you to go home after dinner, so I'll take a room for you.'

His ignorance restored her. 'The circles in which I move are very small ones. It's not customary for a woman to stay at the Grand in a room a man has taken for her, especially if the night's fine and she's used to walking alone.'

The absurdity of it. A remittance man and Phemie Whoever. It would be all around the district before the cows came in for milking. But there'd been no misunderstanding, and she had the advantage now.

'Then we'll come back here,' he said. 'The house has a second bedroom.'

'The Harraways will know. And Mr Kelly's waiting for me now.'

He moved away from her. 'As you wish, Miss Macgregor. Though I think you should straighten your hat before you join him. Allow me.'

Lily said very quickly, 'I'll come tomorrow evening at the same time as the train, but not for dinner.'

'I languish upon the hour.' He turned in the direction of the Grand.

Mr Kelly was naturally eager to hear how the Harraways were.

'Very well,' said Lily, as he handed her into the gig. 'I helped Ruby make a cake. Mr Harraway said it was absolutely splendid.'

'What's happened to your blouse?'

'My blouse?'

'There's dust on it.' He settled himself beside her. 'Shall I brush it off?' She presented her back, and felt the edge of his hand beat against her shoulder blades. 'It's like chalk. It won't come out.'

'It must be paint dust from the house — I leant against an outside wall. Mr Fernon was there too. He was talking of staying a little longer.'

Mr Kelly made a sound of annoyance. He had forgotten to bring Mr Fernon's book with him and he'd meant to return it that day.

'I shall see Ruby tomorrow evening,' said Lily. 'I'm to make her a skirt. I could leave the book with her, or at the Grand if he's still there.'

'Ah, would you now!' cried Mr Kelly, and she started, but it was only that they'd been proceeding at a sedate trot and somebody had had the effrontery to overtake them. She clutched at her hat and the side of the gig as their horse plunged forward.

Lily walked into town the next evening. The day hadn't been so hot; rain was almost certain. Pale drifts of mist hung low among the trees, and the mountains were grey above them. She told herself Mr Fernon would be gone, or wouldn't be alone; that she should turn back now, because it would be impossible for her to find his room, but still she went on, though every step seemed strange to her.

The train was in, and there was much to-ing and fro-ing between the station and the hotel. Lily entered the lobby, expecting at every moment to be hailed by somebody she knew, but there were enough tourists milling around to screen her from the desk.

Jack Dennehy was staggering towards the stairs with bundles under both arms and a suitcase in each hand. He was a nice boy and a smart one. Mr Kelly and Father O'Reilly agreed he should have had an education, but Mrs Dennehy was a widow, or said she was, and took in washing.

'Oh, Jack!' called Lily, fluttering after him and holding out the book. 'Can you carry something more? There's a Mr Fernon staying here and this belongs to him.'

Jack turned and looked, first at her and then the book. He cocked his head to one side, and for a moment she thought he was inviting her to wedge the book under that arm. Then she saw that he was peering at the lettering on its spine, and held it closer.

'*Holy Living and Dying*,' he read thoughtfully.

'It's a book of prayers and things. It's by a bishop, an English one like Mr Harraway's father.' It was her strength and her shield, but she didn't think it was what one of Father O'Reilly's most cherished pupils would care to have a quick skim through before he gave it to its owner.

Jack smiled. 'If I take it I might drop it. You follow me, Miss Macgregor, and I'll show you which is his room. If the door's locked you can leave it just outside.'

Lily followed him up the stairs and along a passageway, and waited till he'd gone on before tapping at the door. There was a murmur from within. Mr Fernon was lying on the bed, dressed in riding clothes. He must have been out earlier with Mr Harraway.

'You came,' he said. 'I didn't think you would.' There was neither pleasure nor surprise in his voice, but it was the sight of his boots on the clean bedspread that concerned her more.

'I've brought your book.'

He indicated that she should put it on the mantelpiece. There was a neat little cupboard set between the shelves, and Lily opened it to see another book and a sticky-looking medicine bottle, but no liquor. That was something.

The room was at the back of the hotel and overlooked the garden. It was brighter outdoors than in. People were drinking tea under the trees, swapping travellers' tales and exclaiming at the splendour of the scenery and the brilliance of the roses.

He said, 'You may draw the curtains if you wish.'

They were of gold watered silk and filled the room with yellow light. The tourists' voices still carried through the window.

'Turn around,' Mr Fernon said. 'Take off your hat.'

She did as she was told. She too was in an unfamiliar country.

'Untie your hair.' He lay watching her, his hands behind his head. 'Now come here.'

Lily hesitated, but did not take her eyes from his face. This is what you want, she told herself, this is why you came. And why you sewed all night and went to dinner at the Kellys', and were nice to Ruby Harraway. He knows that, you haven't deceived him, why cheat yourself by turning timid now? And it doesn't matter, it means nothing to him. He's done this a hundred times; he'll do it a hundred times more. In a few weeks' time he won't even remember your name.

That last thought gave her courage, and she sat on the edge of the bed to remove her shoes and stockings. He unfastened her blouse and pushed it down over her shoulders. She pulled it free from her belt, then shed both belt and blouse and lay beside him. His expression was as impersonal as it had been at the Kellys' table. When his hand slid down inside her skirt her stomach tensed, and for the first time he smiled.

'You are more than welcome to do the same to me, Miss Macgregor.'

Not for him the eager, guilty clutchings and half-apologetic glances; he knew something different about women. He was used to being sought, he was open to possession. She began to undo his shirt.

He withdrew his hand from her waistband and pulled up her skirt. She felt his hand between her thighs; as he bent to kiss her neck and shoulders he slipped one finger into her body. To seem at ease she brushed her lips against his, then against his throat and saw a streak of raised flesh there. She tested it with her tongue: it was firmer than the skin around it. After a moment he sat up, swung his legs over the side of the bed, and began tugging at the heel of one boot.

'Take everything off,' he said over his shoulder.

'I'll do that for you.' While she knelt to pull off his boots he fondled her hair, and drew her towards him when she stood to finish unbuttoning his shirt. The sight of his fair head at her breast made her feel faint. Once she was naked she finished undressing him, though clumsily. Her fumblings amused him; she could see that in the corners of his mouth and in the way he fell back on the bed and arched his back so she could take down his breeches.

The sight of a naked man was infinitely preferable to that of a woman. His clothes merely served to cover him; they weren't designed to conceal the true nature of the creature underneath. In the light from the curtains his flesh was the colour of ripening wheat, the hair on his body a little darker than the hair on his head. Yet somehow his easy manner made her shy again; she sat on the foot of the bed and lowered her eyes. His feet were like his hands, long and pale. One ankle had a small protuberance of bone below the joint. She placed a fingertip against it and thought again of the pale line on his throat.

The tourists beneath the window had turned querulous, as tourists will. They were complaining of the uncertain weather and the state of the roads.

He drew his leg up and away from her. 'I broke it once, in three places. The ankle had the worst of it.'

'Does it hurt?'

'Not at all. It set a fraction shorter than the other, but it's never painful. You are running away again, Miss Macgregor.'

'I'm not.' And to prove him wrong she stretched out beside him. 'I'm surprised you're still intact, that's all.'

'I might say the same of you.'

'I lack application.'

'I had hopes you would apply yourself to me.' He could move quickly when he chose; he spread her legs and knelt between them. Lily turned her head towards the window and put her fingers to her mouth. A tourist spoke satirically of the socialistic manners of the populace. There were shrieks of recognition.

Mr Fernon stroked her thighs. He said, 'You have the body of an adolescent.'

'Is that what you like?'

'Not particularly.'

She thought of Ruby, that exact arrangement of jutting bone and solid flesh, the swelling breasts with their dark nipples. 'Then what is it you like in a woman?'

He too gazed in the direction of the window, his lower lip caught beneath his teeth, his expression soulful. Then he said, 'A cunt.'

That silenced her. It was a word she knew, she'd even heard it shouted in drunken brawls once or twice, though not in a voice like Mr Fernon's. Lowering his head, he put his mouth there. This was not what she expected, but she'd seen dogs do as much to bitches. The sensation was more wet than anything.

'Do you like that?' she asked.

'Oh, very much so,' he said, and she wondered if the echo of the foolish Mr Harraway was intentional. 'Don't you?'

'I don't know. I shall have to think about it.'

'Do not think too much, Miss Macgregor. I wouldn't care to see you overtax yourself.' He returned to probing her with his fingers, rather less gently than before, and added, 'I should like to put my cock in there,' yet made no move to do so. Instead he lay beside her again.

The words he used. But now that he'd named it, she felt free to examine it: the way it resisted yet seemed to seek her touch;

the taut, slightly shiny skin whose darker colour contrasted with that of his belly, as white as kid leather. The tip made her think of the plump grapes she liked to peel and suck to prolong her pleasure. She flicked it with her tongue to feel its texture and catch the drop of moisture there, and heard him sigh. Something made her savage then; perhaps the harsher mix of odours on his skin and the hint of salt in her mouth, or the way he shifted on the bed and caught at her hair. She thought he meant to pull her away, but his fingers did no more than press against her scalp, relax, and press again. Her head was full of the sounds from her throat and her breath as it strained in her nostrils, but above those she heard another sound, puzzling at first, that came not from her but from him. So she could make him moan and shudder, for all he liked to laugh at her; she could feed on him. Then her throat filled with warm liquid and his cock softened; she let it slip from her mouth and swallowed, wondering if it were possible to choke at this. The room was suddenly quiet.

'But at last,' came an extravagant voice from the garden, neither American nor English — German perhaps. 'New Zealand has done something right.' He was praising the honey, and there followed a brief discussion on the qualities of clover.

Mr Fernon lay on his side, his eyes closed. His lips twisted in a half-smile, and Lily, thinking he was about to make one of his odd remarks, decided that this time she would get in first. 'Are you quite well, Mr Fernon?'

'Never better, Miss Macgregor. Do you make a habit of this?'

She shook her head, watching him through her eyelashes, still half-afraid she'd offended him. Then he sighed and stretched, saying, 'This is the first time since you came in that I haven't had an erection.'

'I noticed.'

'How observant you are.'

'How did you break your leg in three places?'

'I decided to drown myself, so I jumped into my grandfather's moat.'

'Why did you want to drown yourself?'

'I was unhappy in love.'

'Oh, love,' said Lily. 'Don't speak to me of love, Mr Fernon.'

'Be assured, Miss Macgregor, there is no prospect of my ever doing so.'

'How is it that you broke your leg while attempting to drown yourself?'

'Perhaps there wasn't any water in the moat that day.'

'I don't believe you.'

'As you wish. But you can have no idea of the effect that story has on some women.'

'What happened to your throat?'

'The razor slipped while I was shaving.'

'That was careless. Though they do say something similar happened to Queen Alexandra.'

'And all her loyal female subjects wear lace about their throats to this very day.'

'It spoils the look of you.'

'It's my look. I'll spoil it if I want to.'

'Why did you come to New Zealand?'

'I was an embarrassment to my family.'

'I'm sure you were. It's not hard to kill yourself if you're set on it.'

'I must have known enough to save myself for you.'

There was a lengthening silence. They'd run out of conversation. The tourists were preparing to come indoors; one spoke of rain, another of a stroll before dinner. Lily rose and began to dress. Mr Fernon lay watching her.

'What expression will you wear as you walk out of here?'

She glanced in the direction of the mantelshelf. 'A devout one, Mr Fernon.'

'You are a woman of unusual talents, Miss Macgregor. Would you like me to see if the coast is clear?'

His civility surprised her. 'I'm dressed and you're not. I'll risk it.' Jack would have gone home and she was unlikely to encounter a maid at this hour. She opened the door a crack. 'It's been unlocked all this while.'

‘Nobody came in.’

‘I might have.’

‘You did.’

The corridor was as empty as only hotel corridors can be. If she met anybody she knew on the stairs she would have to say she’d been looking for the Harraways and hope they believed her, but once in the lobby she could have come from any of the public rooms. How simple it had been after all, and how easily put behind her. The only thing that disturbed her on the walk home was the thought of those dusty boots on the clean counterpane.

Chapter 5

Bob settled on the Buick. It was the first private motorcar in the district and it created a sensation. Little boys and girls flocked about him with hope in their hearts, and their hands clasped behind their backs to show they weren't disposed to touch anything they shouldn't.

Lily was doing the ironing when her grandmother came in and said, 'Bobby Graham's here for you.'

'Bob, he's called Bob. Now that he's a grown-up.'

'That's only a rumour,' said Bob, who'd followed her grandmother into the kitchen. He cast a cautious eye in her direction, adding, 'Mrs Harraway sent me. She'd like you to keep her company while her husband and I play tennis.'

Lily took the waiting irons from the stove, half-expecting her grandmother to say: You needn't think you're going out, there's work to be done.

But all she said was, 'You wouldn't get me into one of those things. I hear it was in the river last night.' And, 'You can finish that later.'

Lily fetched a hat and veil, and she and Bob walked demurely down the drive to where the motorcar, all shining paint and gleaming brass, was waiting near the gate.

'This is ridiculous,' said Bob to the sky. 'Do you know, I nearly left the poor dear hidden up the side track where I used to tie the horse?'

'I don't think even my grandmother could say now that I'm too old to be running round the countryside with Bobby Graham and God only knows who else. There's some advantage in one's first grey hairs.'

'Have you grey hairs?'

'I'll have seven shortly, because I pulled one out this morning. How did the poor dear come to be in the river?'

'I drove round the bend before the little bridge too fast, and she slid on the gravel and went down the bank. She was only just in the water. I got out and lit a cigarette and thought: Now what.'

'Only now what?'

'A word to that effect. Then the Kelly boys came along. "Oi Bob," they said, "was the bridge a bit too quick for you?" We tried to push her out, but the bank was too slippery so we pulled her up this morning with one of the plough team. I don't suppose I'll ever hear the last of it.'

'Well, she looks lovely. There isn't a mark on her.' Lily gave her veil a tweak. 'Though maybe I should've put a pillowcase over my head so I won't see if you hit anything.'

'I won't hit anything,' said Bob sweetly, and opened the door with a flourish. All the same, he didn't seem in the sunniest of moods.

Perhaps she hadn't praised his motorcar sufficiently, but it was hard to be serious about anything that day. She turned to admire the interior, and saw on the back seat a heavy plaid rug with the initials RJG embroidered on one corner. 'Oh, I say, how absolutely splendid. You must have been sewing till all hours.'

Bob replied, rather absently, that it had been done in the shop where he bought it.

'I'd have done it for you, though the temptation to put BG might've been too much for me.'

Bob perked up a little. 'Oh, I say, that's awfully good of you. But it didn't cost any extra.'

She and Ruby lay on the rug to watch Bob and Nigel Harraway play. Bob was winning; that would put him in a better frame of mind. The day seemed almost too bright. The Grahams' house was sparkling after last night's rain, and the orange patches of self-seeding Californian poppies on the white shingle path made her eyes ache. She put her head on her arms and thought of a room filled with a kinder light, the sounds and stillness there.

Ruby said, 'You're not going to sleep, are you?'

'No,' said Lily with an effort. She seemed to have been woken from dreams of ivory and amber; the faint, elusive odours of his flesh teased her for an instant longer and were gone, leaving only the warm, dusty smell of the rug and the sharper one of grass crushed beneath it. 'I was thinking about the house, that's all. I haven't been here for ages.'

The Grahams' house was rather grand, though Bob was given to pointing out that the ground floor area wasn't much bigger than the Kellys' farmhouse, if you didn't count the ballroom, which had its own wing. 'That's not local whitestone it's built from. The original house was imported lock, stock and barrel about fifty years ago and hauled in by bullock teams, but it's had lots done to it since then.' Through her lashes the daisies on the lawn looked like streaks of melting snow. 'The first time I saw it was in winter. It was like visiting the Snow Queen's castle.'

She'd come crunching up the drive in a cocoon of warmth with her nose and cheeks stinging and her stomach fluttering too, for she'd felt unfriendly looks from every window. And at least one pair of eyes must have been watching her, because she'd no sooner reached the front door than Bob's big sister Connie flung it open. The house was warm and still, and smelt of roses. There were tiles in the hall, and rugs like church windows on the tiles. Connie told her how to find Bob's room, and she tiptoed up the wide stairs and along the landing, listening to the whisperers below.

'But it was only Phemie Davidson for Bobby.'

'Macgregor, dear. She's Phemie Macgregor now.'

Another low remonstrance, then Connie's muted snarl, 'But it was Phemie. Whoever. For Bob.'

Bobby lay in bed with the boys' papers he liked strewn over the eiderdown. His face was paler than usual, a perfect oval the colour of milky tea. His eyelashes made two sooty scallops on his cheeks, and she could see the fine blue veins in his eyelids. There was an orange cut into cradles on a little table by his bed. Lily wondered if that meant he was really ill and she'd be in trouble for waking him. She whispered, 'Bobby,' and his eyelids flew open.

'Phemie!' He smiled. 'You're so bundled up I nearly didn't know you.'

'Were you asleep?'

'I'm not sure. I might have been. Was I?'

'You look different when you're asleep.'

'How different?'

'Gooder.'

'Better.'

'No, just gooder.'

'I'm glad you came,' he said. 'I was bored. Take off your hat and things.'

'I never knew your house had battlements.'

'Crenellations. They look stupid.'

'They look nice, like blanket stitch. Your mother growled at Connie for opening the door.'

'I don't care about that stuff,' he'd said. 'I'm a socialist. Have that orange if you want. I haven't breathed germs on it.'

Funny she should remember that now.

She said to Ruby, 'Bob wasn't waiting for me at the gate one day, so I came here to find him. I went to the front door because I couldn't think where the back door might be, and Mrs Graham was annoyed because his sister Connie opened it.'

'Why?'

'Graham girls don't open doors to visitors — that's what maids are for. Though Connie's always done exactly as she pleases. She's very clever.'

'I don't see what's clever about opening a door.' Ruby was more interested in displaying the motoring coat she'd been using as a cushion than in hearing about the Grahams. 'I won't put it on,' she said, 'but I brought it because we're going to the Kellys' later, and Bob said it might be cool this evening.'

The coat was made of glove leather, and lined with a creamy, gold-tipped fur. Lily stroked it gently.

'God knows what it is. Pussycat, most likely. Mind you, I was lucky to get that. The chap who bought it for me was as tight as a duck's arse.'

Bob was retrieving a ball nearby and his head came up suddenly. Lily wondered if he'd overheard.

'Is Mr Fernon still here?'

'No, he went off this morning,' said Ruby. 'Though I daresay he'll be back again.'

'Is he on a bender?' Men who drank were often indiscreet.

'A bender? I hadn't thought of that. Why did you?'

'It's from working in hotels. We see men who for months'll be as sober as judges – well, that's no recommendation, one is a judge – and then they'll go on a bender for a week or two.'

'He's got some money right now,' said Ruby sagely, 'but I don't think drink's his demon. Bob'd had a skinful last night.'

'Where did you see him?'

'At the Grand. We went to play billiards with Joss, and Nige found him in the bar.'

'Did you know him in England?'

'Who, Bob? Course not.'

'Mr Fernon.'

'Not me, Nige did. They went to the same school, don't you know.'

'They're like that here too.'

'They're like it everywhere. I was born in India, did I tell you?'

Lily shook her head.

'Though at least I wasn't shunted off to boarding school as soon as I could walk on my hind legs and poke food in my mouth instead of my eye. And my parents would've had India as an excuse.'

'True,' said Lily, feeling some comment was called for.

'Then we went to the Cape, and then to Tasmania, but Mum hated it there. So we went home and Dad didn't like that. He got work in Chile, but we stayed put. Mum said she'd had enough of moving about and it wasn't as if I had a future as an engineer. But I'm like Dad, I love to travel, and Nige had to leave the army when he married me — you should've seen him in his uniform. So I said: Right, we'll go out to Australia. I'd been back there once on tour and I still liked it. But Nige wanted to come here so we did. He's got friends here.'

'Like Mr Fernon?'

'God, I hope not.'

'Why?'

Ruby made an impatient face. 'Nige has got his own life to lead. He's writing a column for a newspaper. "Our Colonial Correspondent." And he's going to write adventure books for boys. He can't run around after Joss forever.'

'Cathy Kelly says there's a title in his family.'

'A title? There's a baronetcy, if you can call that a title. I wouldn't. Nige always says that insofar as he can ascertain, it was awarded for sexual services to James I. And then his family had the cheek to turn their noses up at me! I felt like telling them that when my Dad'd had a few, he used to reckon there was a maharajah way back in our family tree, more elephants than you could spit at, and I bet he never had to bend over and touch his toes for anybody.'

This time Bob was safely out of earshot. 'Cathy meant in Mr Fernon's family.'

'Oh no, I don't think so. She's probably getting them mixed, but I suppose it all depends on how you look at things.' Ruby gave a snort of laughter. 'His mother is a famous beauty, so there'll have been a few titles in there if you know what I mean. Though I can't see Joss telling Cathy that.' She turned to watch the game. 'I wish they'd hurry up and finish. I'm getting bored.'

That left Lily little wiser about Mr Fernon or what the Harraways had to live on. Perhaps the bishop was sufficiently unsettled by his son's eccentric choice of bride to come up with a truly handsome wedding present, or maybe Nigel also received a remittance.

After the game they had tea on the porch with Alec Graham's

wife Ellen and the dowager Mrs Graham, cool-eyed and considering. Ruby retreated into statuesque silence, while Nigel admired the silver teakettle and asked no end of intelligent questions about farming and the district in general.

Mrs Graham mellowed before him. She spoke of the time when she was a young wife and thought nothing of travelling for days on horseback simply to attend spring balls. 'And whenever we had to ford a swollen river I was far more concerned for the safety of the horse carrying my hoops and gowns than I was for my own.' The railway had made a great difference, of course, though Ellen and Bob and Lily were too young to remember life without it. And now motorcars had replaced the mountain coach that used to thunder down High Street; that had been a sight to see.

Nigel was sorry to have missed it, 'for there's nothing like that in England now, you know.'

'I do,' said Mrs Graham.

'Lily and I were going to be highwaymen and hold it up,' said Bob.

'You were going to be a highwayman and hold it up,' said Lily. 'You told me girls couldn't be highwaymen, so I'd have to keep watch while you did it.'

'I had your welfare at heart. I thought that if they caught me they'd be sure to hang me, but you could've got away.'

'But it was my idea.'

'That's the prerogative of your sex,' said Nigel. 'Having the idea and then watching while we act on it.'

Ruby said, 'And if all goes well yours is the glory, and if it doesn't we're to blame, and that's the prerogative of yours,' but she said it very sweetly, and Mrs Graham offered to show her the gardens. She and Ellen went in to find her parasol, and a maid in cap and apron came to clear away.

'Do either of you blokes want the last sandwich?' she asked, and Lily, looking up, chanced to meet Nigel's shining eyes. He reddened slightly and turned away.

'I'll have it,' said Ruby, sparking into life. 'And after we've seen the gardens we'd better be off. Run and get the rug, Nige, and my coat — we left them under the oak tree.'

'I've seen the gardens,' said Lily. 'Bob can drive me home.'

'Won't you come to the Kellys'?'

'There's the ironing still to do.' Giving a little signal with her eyebrows, she rose and walked along the porch. When Bob came after her she asked, 'Will you lend me a book?'

'A book?'

'Well, I can read.'

'Sorry,' he said. 'Of course I will, if I have it. What did you want?'

'Nigel's going to write adventure books for boys. I want to see what they're like.'

'Oh, I've heaps of those. Come up and choose one now.'

His room was tidier than she remembered, but otherwise the same. The brown and white china dogs still sat beside the inlaid box that held his cuff and collar studs; there was the seahorse he'd found on one beach, and the stone adze he'd dug up on another, so smooth and sharp it was hard to believe it had been made by hand.

'Stop poking about and come and tell me which one you want,' he said, squatting in front of the bookshelves.

'All your old things are here.'

'I know. My mother kept writing to say I ought to take what I still wanted, but I never did. I'll sort things out this summer. What are you doing to my seahorse?'

'Wiping the dust off it.'

'Do you like it? You can have it.'

'Don't you want it?'

'Not if you do.'

She liked it because it was his; she liked all his things. Her grandfather owned nothing that was not purely useful. 'It lives here,' she said.

'Look, I think this is my favourite. I inherited it from Alec and it was the first I read, so perhaps that's why I liked it best.'

The title was incomprehensible. 'What's a . . .'

'*Franc-Tireur*? Read it and find out. I shall ask you next week.'

Written inside in ink was: *To Alec, with Love from his Father, Xmas 1887*. Underneath a much younger Bob had printed very neatly in pencil: *Ex libris R. J. Graham*. The plates were full of soldiers in strange uniforms, and had captions like: *In an instant one had garrotted him with a choking grip* and *The officer fell off his horse, shot through the heart*. 'Are there any girls in it?'

'Sisters, I think. They don't count. Do you want one with a girl in it? Let's see.'

'No, this'll do. I just want to see what they're like.'

'They're ripping, though if I were to read one now I might think otherwise. I was always offering them to you at school, but you never wanted one then.'

'I expect I thought you'd want to ask me questions to test my comprehension.'

A fly buzzed against the windowpane. Lily could see the three women moving through the lavender: Mrs Graham like a bantam hen, trim and bosomy in bronze; Ruby stalking beside her, an hourglass filled with stripes of cream and yellow sand; pale Ellen drooping after. They entered the walled enclosure with the sundial, and sat on the stone seat beneath an arch of roses. Nigel was playing with Ellen's pug on a bright square of lawn. They all seemed separated from her by more than glass and distance; she'd had enough of people for one day.

Bob said, 'I was lying here this morning thinking I've completed a revolution, and nothing's changed.'

'A revolution about what?'

'I mean a circle, I've come full circle. I'm back where I started and everything's the same. The bed's a little smaller, but that's all. It was an awful feeling.'

'Things'll change. They always do.'

'Don't you ever feel that life's passing you by?'

'Sometimes.'

'Then do things change for you?'

'Oh, yes.'

'How do they change?'

'They just do, that's all.' Lily went out to the landing and hung over the balustrade. 'Your house is always so quiet.'

'Isn't yours?' He came and stood beside her.

'No. At night, if you listen hard enough, you can hear the furniture bickering.'

'What about?'

'Oh, who's ungrateful, who's been spoiled. You know what furniture's like.'

'Indeed I do,' Bob sighed. Then he spun round, hoisted himself onto the banister and slid away, calling back, 'I've wanted to do this ever since I came home. Don't you try — you might fall and damage my book.'

'I wouldn't,' said Lily, but came sedately down the stairs. 'Are you sure this morning's mood wasn't brought on by your evening at the Grand?'

'How do you know where I was last night?'

'You've been away so long you've forgotten there are no secrets here.' Though hers seemed safe enough for the present. 'That might also explain why your motorcar was in the river.'

Bob looked knowing. 'Ruby told you. But I thought a barmaid would be sympathetic to such lapses.'

'I'm only a barmaid in winter. In spring I —'

'Turn temperate and vote prohibition.'

'Come home and make myself useful.'

Bob didn't ask why. She supposed he thought she did so out of duty. That was true in a way, but it was also true that she was drawn by tiny memories so remote they seemed lodged in her stomach rather than her head: the kindly black curves of the kettle, the monkey faces hidden in the rug, the clock's bolder tick when her grandparents were in bed. Those things didn't change, even if they were never quite as she'd expected them to be.

Lily made herself useful. She wiped the walls and cleaned the windows and had the curtains down to wash them; she made soap and jam. And all the while her thoughts crept back to Mr Fernon. At times he seemed so featureless she feared that if they were to meet by chance in the street she mightn't know him; at others he consumed her. Then all sense of task and time slipped from her, and she sat like a statue until her grandmother called to know if the gooseberries were top-and-tailed, or Ruby, entrusted with the Buick, came roaring up the drive to see if her skirt was ready.

'Almost,' said Lily guiltily, applying herself to the hem.

'I want to take it with me today, because this one I'm wearing's too tight. Perhaps you could let it out a bit? I seem to be getting very broad in the beam.'

Ah, thought Lily, glad of something new to occupy her mind, but when she made their tea she forgot to put leaves in the pot.

Her grandmother was infuriated. 'I don't know what's got into you lately. It's not funny, I'm parched. You must be sickening for something.'

'Perhaps she's in love,' suggested Ruby.

'That'll be the day.'

'Then if she's not, she ought to be.'

'With whom?' asked Lily coolly, and Ruby mouthed, 'Bob Graham.' So that was all right.

After Ruby had gone her grandmother struck up again about how useless she'd become.

'I can't sleep these hot nights,' said Lily. 'Dad keeps me awake with his snoring.'

'If you went to bed at a decent hour you'd be asleep before he started. And if you got a bit more sleep you mightn't be so scrawny. Have you taken a good look at yourself lately? You're nothing but skin and bone. Men like women with a bit of meat on them.'

'I think I'll move into the little room,' said Lily. She and her grandparents slept on the same side of the house, but the little room was off the front room and had been built at a later date to take in part of the verandah and open onto it. Her mother had slept there, but in spite of that Lily liked the room, and the calm that settled on her whenever she went in.

'Why do you want that room? You don't want to move in there.'

'It's further away from yours. I won't disturb you when I go to bed.'

'You don't disturb us.'

'Then how do you know what hours I keep?'

'Some people are too clever to live,' observed her grandmother. 'The window in that room sticks. You'll never get it open, so if you're too hot in your own room you'll be even hotter in there.'

'I'll open the door to the verandah.'

'The night air'll make you wheeze.'

'I haven't wheezed in years.'

Her grandmother gave in. 'Well, you'll have to get the Kelly boys to shift the furniture. Dad's too old to be hauling things around for you.'

'I'll use what's in there.'

'You don't want that big bed in there. You won't have room to swing a cat.'

'It doesn't matter.'

'But that's our old bed. That's a double bed.'

So that was it. A spinster had no business with a double bed. It was an affront to all married women, who'd paid so dear for theirs.

'Now what are you smirking about?'

'The thought of swinging cats,' said Lily.

Chapter 6

To Mrs Kelly's mind, her family's most disturbing acquisition was a tall Dresden fruit stand in tints of pastel touched with gold. The bowl was made to resemble a basket strewn with flowers, and more flowers wreathed its pedestal. Their delicate clusters of petals charmed her youngest children, for they looked very like cake decorations, though they yielded no sweetness to inquisitive tongues. A pair of plump cherubs stood against the pedestal; their wings were too small for flight, but they had sturdy little legs to trot about on. Knotted round their middles were draperies painted to resemble sprigged muslin, and these led to endless speculation as to each cherub's sex. Her children didn't believe her when she said cherubs had no sex at all; if that were true, there'd be no need for concealment.

Cathy had won it in a skating competition. At least, she'd won the prize donated for the most graceful lady skater and brought the fruit stand home. Then they heard that the shop had sent the wrong piece to the competition, and Cathy had carried off somebody's special order. Mrs Kelly rewrapped it tenderly and she and Cathy hastened into town, but the shop's manager wouldn't take it back.

'It was our mistake,' he said handsomely, 'and we'll simply have to order in another. It would be unfair to Miss Kelly to do otherwise.'

Honour on both sides was satisfied, but Mrs Kelly felt something other than honour had been at work here. The fruit stand was proof, if she'd needed any, that her husband was now also reckoned to be somebody, and the manager would sooner placate a well-heeled customer than disappoint his daughter. And with that proof came her guilty knowledge that if Mrs Dennehy's girl had won the prize and returned it, she'd have come away with a cheaper thing.

So the fruit stand stayed, reward and reproach, on the dining-room table until it came to be broken. That was the night Lily Macgregor brought back Pat's clothes all neatly named for high school, and Father O'Reilly dropped in to enquire about the possibility of a donation towards jerseys for the school's football team.

Both were asked to stay for a bite of supper, which Father O'Reilly hoped would be substantial. Cathy, who'd already put out cold meat, bread, and pickle in the kitchen, was redirected to the dining room: rather more, she thought, than Father O'Reilly and Lily Macgregor deserved. She seized the fruit stand by its pedestal and went towards the mantelshelf.

'Oh, do be careful,' said Lily, entering with a dish of teatime's leftover potatoes, sliced and nicely browned in butter. 'It looks so fragile.'

'Well, it's mine,' said Cathy, then wished she hadn't, because she wanted Lily to make her an evening blouse, and now it wouldn't be the right time to ask. Then everybody was round the table and her mother was slapping the little ones' hands away from the food while — 'if you wouldn't mind, Father' — the old idjit gabbled through grace.

'No boys tonight?' he asked. He meant their uncles, Frank and Gerald.

'They went to see a man,' murmured Michael.

'About a dog,' added Pat.

'Ah,' said Father O'Reilly on a mild note of regret, and turned his attention to Cathy, who'd refused the potatoes. Meals with all the children present tended to the riotous and Father O'Reilly wasn't above stirring things up a little. 'Those were all your ancestors had to keep them from starvation,' he told her.

'All the more reason why I shouldn't have to eat them twice in one day then.'

'Cathy!'

'She's right, Mum,' said Pat. 'There's no point in having your house burnt over your head and sheltering in churches and dying in ditches and the rest of that stuff on your way to the coast if all you're going to do when you get to the other side of the world is keep on eating potatoes.'

'That makes sense,' said Mr Kelly.

'Might as well stay stuck in a bog lamenting your lot for another three hundred years,' continued Pat.

'It must be wonderful to be a genius,' said Cathy.

'I'm on your side.'

'Seven hundred years,' said Father O'Reilly.

'She doesn't want you on her side,' said Michael. 'You're a know-all.' Pat was the apple of their father's eye, so he and Cathy never missed a chance to cut him down to size.

'Nine hundred years,' said Mr Kelly, who held that Ireland was a priest-ridden country and Brian Boru was to blame.

Father O'Reilly trimmed the fat from his mutton and sought to change the subject. 'Where's Oedipus?'

'Swolfoot,' said Michael, with a sly look at Cathy.

'Shut up.'

'He's in disgrace,' said Kevin.

'He done a poo under Daddy's bed,' whispered Theresa.

'Did a poo, thank you.'

'Don't thank him for it,' said Lily. 'He'll think you want another one.'

'Father O'Reilly doesn't want to hear . . .' began Mrs Kelly hopelessly.

'No, for it was he who put him up to it.'

'. . . the scatological details,' concluded Pat.

'I did, and you'll get no respite till I see you on a Sunday.'

'Well now, and there's a name for the foal,' said Michael.

'You don't even know what it means.'

'That'll be enough from you,' said Mrs Kelly. 'The Scatterwhatsit might do very well.'

'No, Mum. It wouldn't do at all.'

'And in the meantime we can call him Scatty,' said Mr Kelly peaceably, 'to save him from getting too big for his boots. And since all creation save myself is disposed to lend an ear to you, Father, we'd better step out to the paddock so you can let him know what's to be required of him.'

'Don't do it, Father, till you see him on a Sunday.'

'Oh, Mrs Kelly, would you deny me the chance of ever winning enough to buy a motorcar like Bob Graham's?'

The men went off and the boys trailed after them. Mrs Kelly breathed a sigh of relief. She and Lily began to clear away.

Cathy hurried Danny and Theresa into the bath, where they splashed each other and her till Danny wailed there was soap in his eyes. When she lifted him out he slipped from her grasp and ran giggling down the passage and onto the verandah, to be caught by Bob Graham, who'd just come up the steps with the Harraways. And Mr Fernon.

Cathy's face was hot, her sleeves up, her skirt wet; she knew she looked just like an Irish washerwoman, and she could have wrung Danny's neck.

'Isn't he adorable!' cried Mrs Harraway. 'Oh, Bob, give him to me, let me hold him.'

But Danny, who was not accustomed to being spoken of in this fashion, gave her a very cool look and tightened his grip on Bob.

Cathy shrank away. Lily came to unhook Danny from Bob, while Mrs Kelly offered cups of tea or something stronger and exclaimed to see Mr Fernon back again.

'I've some unfinished business here,' he said airily, though it seemed they'd been doing nothing more exciting than play tennis at the Grahams'. Mr Harraway assured Mrs Kelly that they'd had an absolutely splendid tea there, but they trailed through to the dining room anyway.

Mr Kelly wanted to know where Mr Fernon had been all this while.

'In Christchurch, visiting friends.' He mentioned the street. 'Do you know Christchurch, Miss Kelly?'

'Is their house quite near the cathedral?' asked Cathy, pushing unhappily at her wet hair.

Mr Fernon treated her to a smile like a benediction. 'By the bells of the church adjoining I am daily reminded of my burial.'

'It's *remembered*,' said Mr Kelly. 'From the bells of the church adjoining I am daily remembered of my burial.'

'In the funerals of others,' added Father O'Reilly, who didn't care to be thought a narrow man. 'I am daily remembered of my burial in the funerals of others.'

'Oh, well done,' said Mr Fernon, as if he were helping Pat with his Latin.

Mr Kelly and Father O'Reilly sniggered and made for the sideboard where the whisky decanter stood. Nigel Harraway enquired after the foal, and then praised Alec Graham's hunter whose acquaintance he'd made that day. The men went on to talk of bloodlines, of Traducer and the great Carbine; Cathy returned to the bathroom where Lily had taken Danny. Bob Graham, who liked babies in the soppy way that comes of never having had anything to do with them, followed her.

He said, 'We hardly ever see you. You ought to come out more.'

'I've been busy at home,' said Lily.

'So have I. Look!' He held up his hands. 'Blisters.'

'Is that from playing tennis?'

'Oh, very droll.'

'Who won?'

'I did.' He added glumly, 'Fernon's tennis is on a par with your arithmetic.'

'Dreadful,' she said.

'Disingenuous.'

'You must tell Mr Kelly that. He wants a name for the foal.'

'It's a pity Ruby's not keen on tennis,' persisted Bob. 'If we four were to play, she wouldn't let him lose to us.'

'I suppose not.'

'Or Cathy could partner him.'

'I could,' said Cathy, brightening.

'But I don't want to play tennis with him,' said Lily.

'Oh, he's all right,' said Bob.

Danny was in his pyjamas, but Theresa seemed unwilling to relinquish her towel in front of Bob. 'Come along to the bedroom, then,' said Cathy and sighed, for if she were to tidy her hair and change her wet skirt, which was only sensible and what she would have done if there hadn't been visitors, everybody would think she wanted to impress someone. If they noticed her at all, that was.

'Are the others still in the dining room?' asked Lily.

'Wait,' said Bob, and stooped to brush a streak of talcum powder from her skirt. He looked a little anxious. 'Did you mean what you said the other day?'

'What other day? I've said a lot of things, other days.'

'That you never wanted to borrow my books because you thought I'd test you on them.'

'I was teasing you, that's all. I hope it hasn't kept you awake at night.'

'Alec's working me so hard nothing could do that.'

Bob took a seat near the empty fireplace where Ruby sat and Mr Fernon stood; Danny, now in the mood for dalliance with the exotic stranger, sidled after him. Kevin and Theresa summoned Lily to the table, wanting her to draw pictures for them. 'A hawk,' suggested Theresa.

'No, a horse,' said Kevin.

'Please,' Mrs Kelly reminded them.

'A dog, please, Miss Macgregor.'

Her pencil flew over the paper: hawk, horse and dog arranged themselves beneath her hand. Father O'Reilly was lost in admiration. 'That's a rare talent you have there, Miss Macgregor, a God-given talent.'

'Watch him,' called Mr Kelly, 'he's out for what he can get. He'll have you drawing holy pictures next, or embroidering an altar cloth.' But he was disposed to pay for the jerseys. As Father O'Reilly had said, it would be one in the eye for the Grahams, who fitted out the opposition.

'Think of something hard,' said Kevin.

'Draw the fruit stand,' cried Theresa.

'Please,' sighed Mrs Kelly, looking about her, and so chanced to see it cast itself upon the air. After that everything happened very slowly and in perfect silence. Ruby Harraway was extending a long and graceful arm, but rather as if to have it admired than intercept the fruit stand's fall, and Bob seemed to float up from his chair, gathering Danny to him with one hand as he reached out with the other. He must have touched the fruit stand as it drifted by, for it missed the hearth and landed on the rug, where it bounced a little. The bowl came off without breaking, but the pedestal snapped behind the cherubs' wings.

Then there was a rush of speech, the Harraways asking each other how it had happened and Bob deploring his dropped catch. 'But I just couldn't have moved any faster,' he said, bemused by failure.

'You nearly got it, you almost did,' cried Ruby. 'I had to reach round Joss, I was too far away.'

'Did I do that?' asked Mr Fernon of nobody in particular. He added humbly, 'Then I'm sorry.'

'We'll buy you another,' said Nigel.

'It was Cathy's,' said Mrs Kelly.

'I gave it to you,' said Cathy with a shrug.

'I'm getting old and slow,' mourned Bob.

'You had Danny on your knee.' Ruby bent to pick up the bowl and broken pedestal, and exclaimed in sorrow that scarcely any of the flowers remained whole. Lily put her drawings aside and went to help her, wondering aloud about the possibility of gluing everything together again. Mr Kelly said that would be an interminable task, and Nigel repeated his offer of a replacement.

'It was my fault,' said Cathy, who thought Mr Fernon had dislodged it. He'd been standing with his elbow resting on the mantelshelf, and his sleeve could have brushed the pedestal at an angle sufficient to topple it. 'I must have put it too near the edge. Lily told me to be careful, but I wasn't.'

Mr Fernon said nothing. Then Cathy heard him murmur, 'You came back,' and Lily, who was kneeling at his feet with her eyes on the little heap of petals in her hand, said very low, 'I haven't been away.' After that, the fruit stand ceased to matter at all.

Bob and Ruby had lost interest in it too. He was coaxing her to sing. 'I'll play for you,' he said.

'Why don't you and Lily entertain us? You're a double act.'

'Mrs Harraway is afraid of disgracing herself socially,' said Mr Fernon. 'Even though I have told her that's an extraordinarily difficult thing to do in New Zealand.'

'Well, you'd know all about that,' said Ruby.

Mrs Kelly shooed them away and gathered up the hearth rug. Her nerves were frayed. 'It was only a matter of time,' she said, 'before Oedipus broke it.'

Nobody seemed to have heard her. She wondered if she'd spoken aloud, or merely thought she had. Father O'Reilly was urging Gerald and Frank to sing. She hadn't seen them come in but there they were, scrubbed and shining and looking very pleased with themselves.

'We will if Mrs Harraway will,' called Frank, rolling a bold blue eye in her direction. He had a little cut above one eyebrow.

'What happened to you, then?' asked Lily.

'I'm getting old and slow,' smiled Frank.

So there must have been a fight on, thought Mrs Kelly. No wonder the men were so chirpy, and Mrs Harraway too. They were knocking back the whisky like there'd be no tomorrow. Just tennis at the Grahams' indeed.

And there was no chance Father O'Reilly would ever say a word against grown men battering each other for their own and others' amusement; he'd be sorry to have missed it. She would have to talk to Dan, who'd spoken often enough of financing the boys onto farms of their own. Then they could marry and settle down and not be trapped like Lily and now poor Bob, and Father

O'Reilly himself, in the perpetual childhood of the celibate.

That last thought shocked her. The air was prickly with mischief; perhaps that alone had caused the fruit stand's fall. Maybe a thunderstorm was on its way. 'The piano is in the parlour,' she cried. 'You must all go into the parlour!' But really, she wished they'd all go home.

'A pity,' whispered Mr Fernon to Lily, 'about the ornament.'

'Did it fall, or was it pushed?'

'I think it may have jumped.'

'What some will do for a little attention.'

'The pretty thing knew it was admired, but not much loved. It must have found life burdensome. You heard Mrs Kelly: it was only a matter of time before Oedipus granted its release. Where is he, by the way?'

'He's in disgrace. He did something unmentionable under Mr Kelly's bed.'

'I should like to do something unmentionable to you.'

'If I leave now, how quickly can you follow?'

'Five minutes.'

'They'll notice.'

'No, I'll prevail on Mrs Harraway to sing.'

'When you leave here, don't walk across the paddocks. I'll go that way. Go down Kellys Road to High Street and turn in the direction of town, then left at the crossroads. I'll meet you by the bridge.'

Bob and Ruby were already at the piano. She needed no more persuasion: the pleas were all for Bill Bailey.

'I'll do the cooking, darling . . .'

'Now there's an inducement for him,' murmured Mr Fernon as Lily slipped past him into the hall.

She waited for him by the river, never doubting he would come. He caught her in his arms and put his mouth to her throat, and she thought she would sink into the long grass if he released her.

'Shall we do it here? Or would you prefer it indoors?'

'Somebody might come along,' she said.

His lips were against her ear. He was asking what the ground was like beneath the bridge.

'It'll be dry enough. Bob and I used to build dams there each summer.'

Mr Fernon took her hand and stepped down the bank, pulling her after him. The dark bridge was above her and the shingle slid underfoot; she lost her balance and lay where she fell. He tore off her drawers so easily she might have had no legs at all, and then knelt over her, tugging at his own clothing.

'My frock will be ruined,' she said, with a last flicker of wonder at herself.

'I'll buy you another.' His tone was impatient; he gripped her under the knees and jerked her towards him. She felt something prodding at her like a blunt finger that was having trouble locating the exact point of entry, then there was an odd, stretching sensation as his weight came down on her. Drawing back a little, he thrust into her again, and she threw out her arms in a vain attempt to brace herself. He seemed bent on driving every breath from her body, and his own. 'Hold on to me,' he said, but that was scarcely possible. The night was splintering around her; it was as if she were being flung between him and the stones on which she lay, and she had no idea how long this onslaught would last or how it might end. Then his body stiffened and just as suddenly relaxed, and all was quiet. He lay heavy on her, strands of his hair sticking to her mouth and cheek, and his chest rising and falling against hers.

From some way off came the scrape of men's boots on the road. Farmhands. Their voices were low and contented, but Lily caught Frank Kelly's name. They had been at the fight, they'd bet on him and won, and must have gone drinking afterwards. That, and the long walk home in the warm night air, had tired them. Their footsteps echoed above her, and there they stopped.

She heard a match flare as one man lit a cigarette. Another tossed something into the water. They spoke of the breaking-up of the last great estate of its kind and the land that had been auctioned — a leisurely, disjointed conversation of statements and assenting silences. Some lots were still available at seven to ten pounds an acre; the prices were beyond their means.

Mr Fernon raised his head, and she saw a faint, conspiratorial gleam in his eyes. He pressed his mouth against hers and she traced the outline of his lips with her tongue. At last the men moved on, their voices fading on the night, and Mr Fernon eased himself off her.

'They might have heard us as they came along,' she said.

'We weren't making much noise.'

Lily didn't see how he could be sure of that. She couldn't have said if her own gulps of air had been expelled in sighs or screams.

Mr Fernon retrieved her drawers and tossed them to her. She held his cock while he urinated in the river; she wrote 'Lily' with a flourish on the water.

He said, 'Those stones were rather hard on my knees.'

'And my back,' said Lily, not to be outdone.

'Shall I return to the Kellys' now?'

She thought of him sitting sad-eyed in their parlour, while the boys sang of endearing young charms and Cathy tried to coax a smile from that bitter mouth. His cock was hardening in her hand. It nudged against her palm like some eager little animal, a solitary creature of dim, determined habits which craved human touch.

'You can come with me,' she said. 'We'll go to my room. Or to the barn, if the thought of my uncle's ghost doesn't bother you.'

'I'd prefer your room,' he said, but hesitated, looking in the direction of town.

'Would you rather just go back to the Grand?'

'Too far away.'

Lily followed him up the bank and across the bridge. How simple it was when divorced from the nonsense of dances and sulks and chocolates, and how long she'd had to wait to be sure of that. Suppose she'd turned, that rainy evening years ago, and gone to the bright, sour young man sheltering in the doorway and said: Shall we do it here or would you prefer it indoors? But she'd never have done that, she couldn't do it now. Women didn't do that sort of thing. They had to wait for men like Mr Fernon to circle them, to soothe them with their indifference, to draw them on.

He asked, 'What's that sound I can hear?'

'A sheep,' said Lily very kindly, for one had lifted her head as they passed and given a small, sociable bleat.

'No. It's a continual sound.'

'They're eating.'

'No.'

'The creek, then.'

'No.'

'Somebody else at it under a bridge.'

'I think it's some sort of cricket,' he said. 'You're probably so accustomed to it you don't hear it at all.'

'Probably.'

'Is that scent from the lupins?'

'I suppose so.' Lily could hear nothing, smell nothing. All her senses were fastened on him.

The house was in darkness, as she'd known it would be. She felt about for matches to light her candle, but then drew back the curtain to have what light there might be from the cloudy sky.

He didn't look around him or ask if her grandparents were in the house or away, but sat on the edge of her bed and began to take off his clothes. His manner struck her as too docile, or too trusting.

We could be robbers, she thought, we might be murderers. I might've been sent out to lure him here. We could take his things and throw his body in a sheep pit, and who would find him there? Who would even bother to look long for a remittance man? Then the idea of her grandparents lurking in the front room with wolfish grins and sharpened knives made her smile, though if Mr Fernon noticed he didn't ask what she was thinking.

Chapter 7

Mrs Kelly thought it a pity Lily hadn't stayed to hear Ruby Harraway sing. And, after giving due consideration to the cut of Ruby's clothes, she also thought her own good skirt might look even better slimmed down a bit. She said as much as she toiled up the Davidsons' verandah steps to where Lily lay reclining in a wicker chair.

'Just the skirt?' asked Lily, shading her eyes with a lazy hand.

Mrs Kelly wasn't sure what to make of that. Lily didn't seem quite herself. An open book lay face down on her lap, and Mrs Kelly hadn't thought her one for reading. 'What's the book?'

'You wouldn't like it.'

'I don't have time to sit around and read all day.'

'That's exactly what my grandmother would say.'

'Has Mrs Davidson gone out?' asked Mrs Kelly, knowing what the answer would be, and held up the skirt. 'Shall I put it on so you can see what I mean?'

'Use the little room,' said Lily, indicating the end of the verandah, but then she rose and led the way. 'This is my room now.' She went to the window and jerked the curtain half-across, then back again. 'There's nobody about. I'll need to see what I'm doing.'

Mr Fernon had stood there that morning. The sky was already bleached by the light that meant a scorching day, but his skin had looked cool and moist to the touch. She'd thought of powdery cheese rinds, and of the dead-white fungi that grow in dank and secret places. Distasteful comparisons, yet the effect had not been distasteful.

'That's a big bed for a little room,' observed Mrs Kelly.

'It was easier to use it than take it down and move it.' Lily knelt beside her.

'Mr Fernon left not long after you.'

'He must've decided to walk back to town,' said Lily through a mouthful of pins.

'Walk?'

'It's no great distance. I know farmers never walk where they can ride, but I do it often enough.'

She had said, 'You'll have to go. My grandfather'll soon be up, and the first thing he does is go to the pump and fill the kitchen buckets. We only use the tank water for washing. He'll walk past that window.'

'What day is it?' he'd asked, combing his hair with his fingers.

'Sunday, but cows and farmers don't sleep in. They've eyes in their toenails round here, and they'll wonder what's brought you out from town so early.'

'The cows or the farmers?'

'Both. If anybody sees you, you'll have to pretend you walked out from town to call on Mr Kelly.'

'At this hour? Have you a book I can return?'

'No.'

'Whose is this?'

'Bob Graham's.'

'Now why does that not surprise me?'

'What do you think the unfinished business Mr Fernon spoke of might be?' asked Mrs Kelly of the top of Lily's head.

Lily's shoulders rose and fell. 'I think he likes to be mysterious, that's all. Perhaps he lost money at billiards and wants to win it back. Bob Graham might know. Shall I ask him?'

'Oh no,' said Mrs Kelly hastily, for it would be like Lily to say it was she who'd wondered, and then Bob might think she suspected him of playing billiards for money.

'Stop fidgeting, or it won't be even.'

'It feels rather tight. Will you get enough out of the sides to put a bit in at the bottom?'

Lily sat back on her heels. 'Are you thinking I could open the back seam and put in a frill, or do you want a low pleat in each seam?'

'I'm not sure what I'm thinking,' sighed Mrs Kelly. 'It must be the heat.'

'You can take it off now,' said Lily. 'I'll do you a drawing so you can see what I mean.' She went for a pencil and paper.

She had said, 'I'd like to draw you.'

'You may hang me, Miss Macgregor, you may quarter me, I am yours to command.' He came from the window and lay close beside her, his eyelids drooping like a drowsy child's.

'Don't go back to sleep.' He'd fallen asleep almost instantly that night, and she'd found it disconcerting that he should lie so easy in a stranger's bed.

'I can sleep in the grave,' he said, and rose yawning to gather his clothes from the floor. 'Why don't you come and live with me in Christchurch, Miss Macgregor?'

That was sudden. 'I live here.'

'For the summer.'

'And for the rest of the year I live at my father's hotel. You must go.'

He yawned again. 'Mrs Kelly and the young Kellys will be haring off to Mass in their hebdomadal glory.'

'Not yet.' Then she'd added carelessly, 'And if you're going to make a habit of visiting me, I shall have to buy a dictionary.'

'But I am not going to make a habit of visiting you, Miss Macgregor.'

The snub lay in his voice, not his words, and she felt it like a blow — the desire to cause trouble where there'd been none.

'As you wish, Mr Fernon.'

Mrs Kelly wished for a frill.

'That'll be easier,' said Lily, 'and fashionable too.' She gave one of her sudden, inward smiles. 'That's what's called a mermaid frill. Ruby had one in the skirt she wore to dinner, remember?'

'Is Mr Fernon staying on here for a while?'

'I don't know. You'll have to ask the Harraways.'

'And what do you think of him, now that you've seen more of him?'

'His manners aren't the best.'

Pots and kettles, thought Mrs Kelly.

There was a silence. Then Lily began to flutter; she trailed a wing. 'Come through to the front room, it's cooler,' she said. And, 'Shall I make some tea or would you like a glass of lemon-barley water?'

Mrs Kelly favoured tea.

'When I finished Ruby's skirt,' called Lily from the kitchen, 'she wanted me to let another out a bit. She says she's getting very broad in the beam.'

Mrs Kelly made haste to join her. 'Should she be gadding about the way she does? She's no spring chicken. I've even seen her start that motorcar.'

'How old do you think she is?'

'Oh, late thirties? She could give him a good few years.'

'As old as that?' exclaimed Lily.

As if she herself were just out of her teens, thought Mrs Kelly. 'There's hope for you yet,' she said. Somehow she felt she owed Lily one.

They were on familiar ground again.

The Harraways became frequent visitors. Nigel shot rabbits for Lily's grandfather and Mr Kelly. Michael Kelly was grateful, for shooting rabbits was his idea of work, not fun. By way of return he made it his business to let Mr Harraway know when and where fights were to be held and how he should bet, on the strict understanding that these manly pursuits were never to be mentioned in front of his mother.

Bob and Ruby revived their interest in the haunted house and drove off to prowl about its overgrown yard by twilight. Later they came back to the Davidsons', where Nigel had stayed to clean the shotgun and then help Lily bottle chutney, and suggested a spot of table-tapping. Bob's mother was keen on spiritualism, in a high-minded sort of way, and the young Grahams had had wonderful fun with a card table whenever their parents went out at night. 'It used to rear up and bang away like anything till Connie started asking it questions none of us knew the answer to, and then of course it stopped.'

'You'll wake my grandparents,' said Lily uneasily.

'Tell Ruby about the murderer who used to work for your grandfather,' said Bob. 'I like that story.'

'You tell it. You've heard it often enough.'

'I'll get it wrong.'

'I'll tell you if you do.'

'Right, then. The Fatal Farmhand. When Phemie was a little girl —'

'Lily. My name's Lily.'

'You were Phemie then.'

'Only to those who knew no better.'

'When Lily was a little girl her grandfather hired a man the animals all hated.'

'They didn't hate him, they just saw something in him we didn't, that's all. You're not doing very well, are you?'

'When Lily was a little girl her grandfather hired a man in whom the animals saw something we didn't that's all. He was pleasant enough, and he said he had farm experience, but the cows held their milk and the dog wouldn't work for him.'

'That was Frisky,' said Lily, relenting, 'and she was the easiest dog in the world to work. When I was only two or three I could go out and say, "Getaway Frisky," and she'd round up the ducks for me and drive them to the top of the hill. Then they'd rise in the air and fly back to the dam. She was a lovely dog, Frisky. It was a sorry day for my grandfather when he had to shoot her.'

'Why'd he do that?' asked Ruby.

'She got old. She couldn't work, and work was all she knew.'

'Now who's not doing very well? Stick to the story.'

'One day when the man was ploughing, the team bolted. They

came thundering down the hill and straight into the gate, and smashed it to smithereens. That was the last straw, and my grandfather gave him the sack. Years later we heard a man of the same name had been hanged up north for murder, and Bob and I were sure that it was him. But it probably wasn't.'

'We could ask your hall table,' said Bob in her ear.

'It never knew him, so I don't suppose it cares.'

'You can put that in your book, Nige. Is it all right if he puts it in his book, Lily? Make the man a foreign spy and our heroes can hang him themselves.'

'I don't think our heroes ever hang people,' said Nigel. 'They watch attentively while more tarnished souls do the deed.'

'They might as well be girls, then,' said Ruby.

'Sacrilege,' said Bob. 'I used to love those books.'

'My dear lad, so did I. I had one every Christmas.'

It was easy to imagine Ruby as a leggy tomboy, reading books for boys. 'They hanged a spy in the one I've got,' said Lily, and saw Bob look uneasy; he was afraid she'd say something silly. 'Not our heroes, other people. He was a schoolmaster.'

'A schoolmaster!' said Nigel, smiling kindly on her. 'Did the craven wretch fall on his knees and beg for mercy?'

'He did.'

'That would have brought joy to the hearts of little readers everywhere.'

When Bob and the Harraways did anything together they started asking Lily along. That made a foursome for games and expeditions and Saturdays at the Bay, where they lunched at her father's new hotel and sat in matinees until Nigel said he'd had his surfeit of cinematographic revelations. Then they looked for what Nigel called 'winter quarters' and Ruby 'digs', because the Harraways were now not going north till spring. 'Though I can't imagine anything worse than a seaside town in winter,' sighed Ruby.

'Nor can I,' said Bob, and teased her with tales of all the excitement she'd miss if they didn't stay put. Snow as high as the fences, and ice everywhere: the train sliding on its rails and taking days to reach its destination, her washing freezing solid as she pegged it on the line, and more crystals dangling from their outhouse roof than from a chandelier.

They bounded along, chattering like starlings. Ruby hung on Bob's every word, and on every word of Lily's when she spoke at his command. Lily walked with Nigel, who smiled at everything but no longer bothered to say much. She was coming to quite like him.

As they went past the bowling club Bob bent to peer through a crack in the fence.

'What's to see?' asked Ruby.

'Nothing out of the ordinary, but whenever we came here as kids and Alec saw me looking, he'd give me an almighty whack between the shoulder blades and tell me to mind my own business. He had a wicked whack, did Alec. So now I look to celebrate my liberty.'

They picnicked in the park that day. 'It's been years since I was here,' Bob announced happily, and while the Harraways took their crusts to the ducks and Lily repacked the hamper he lay back on the rug and reminded her of his first taste of freedom, 'that weekend we went to stay at your father's hotel. You bet me half a crown I wouldn't be allowed to, then you never paid me. And I'd planned to spend it all on frosted caramels.'

'But you didn't ask permission — you just sneaked away.' He'd come fairly flying past the train's long tail of wagons to throw his bag and then himself on where somebody opened a carriage gate for him. 'You shouldn't jump onto moving trains,' she'd said as he dropped into the seat opposite hers, grinning triumphantly. 'You might slip underneath and be ground to mash.'

'And you shouldn't hang out carriage windows,' he replied, clapping on his straw hat at a rakish angle. 'The train'll go into a tunnel and cut off your head.' Then he spoiled his effect with an attack of the fidgets when the train jolted to an unexpected stop, and that was how she'd known he wasn't meant to be there.

But he'd been different away from home. Ordering for her in teashops, buying her a parasol to match her dress, looking smug when men stared after her. And always touching her. Taking her arm to hurry her past the flyblown postcards in the tobacconist's, and her hand when they heard a train and ran like mad things to stand on the footbridge in a cloud of smoke and steam; brushing a smut from her cheek with a fingertip. She'd told herself then that boys of Bobby's age did that sort of thing. It made them feel grown-up. It was all part of being decent and honourable and superior, just as girls put up their hair, crossed their legs at the ankle instead of the knee, and pretended not to understand certain jokes and allusions. As if she'd gone about the farm blindfold, and not even known how to make sure of pumpkins. Which was all part of what?

'I left a note,' said Bob suddenly. 'That counts.'

'I thought you were asleep.'

'No, I was watching the light through the leaves. Do you still have that frock?'

'Which frock?'

'The very pale green one. You wore it here that weekend. It was like some white flowers are when they've just hatched out.'

'Hatched out?' exclaimed Lily severely. She didn't often have a chance like that with Bob.

'Unbudded then,' he said dreamily. 'With a hint of green in the petals. You have to keep looking to make sure it's not just a reflection from the leaves. I thought you were well named.'

'I was named Euphemia, which means fair-spoken, not greeny-white. And that wasn't a frock, it was a summer costume. I'm sure I made it after I started working for my father, so I couldn't have worn it that weekend.'

'You did, I can see you in it now. With the green parasol I bought you, remember?' He put his arm across his eyes. 'The skirt's quite full, with greenish shadows in the folds, and the jacket has one of those frills on it.'

'A peplum — that frill's called a peplum. I can see this isn't one of your better days.'

'The fabric had a pattern in it. It was damask! And you told me you'd made it from old tablecloths.'

He was right, he knew he was, and Lily gave in. 'There was a pile of them at the hotel. I had to do the cutting out so carefully, all around the food stains.' One of the maids had said the green dye she made might have taken better if she'd peed in it, but she wouldn't have told Bob that, not the way he'd been that weekend, and she didn't feel like telling him now. 'Anyway, it's long gone. I can't remember if I gave it away or cut it up for dusters.'

'Was that the last time we saw each other?' he asked.

'I don't know. It might have been.'

Mr Fernon had gone no further than the Bay, but he never joined their outings. That kept things simple. Lily saw him by chance one weekday she went there alone to buy paints and brushes. He was wearing a white linen suit and looked like any other well-to-do holidaymaker. She ducked into a doorway, but he called to her from across the street as if they knew each other well, then came cheerfully towards her. This was all so unexpected she was tongue-tied.

'And what have you been buying?' He tweaked her package out of her hands and squeezed it gently. 'Shall I guess?'

His guesses would be calculated to annoy her. 'Watercolours and some brushes,' she said.

'Oh, what a pretty pastime. What will you paint, Miss Macgregor? Walled gardens and stone seats wreathed all about with roses?'

'There was a dead sparrow on the verandah this morning. I thought I might try that.'

He smiled at some private thought, but kept her parcel. 'Will you walk?' he asked, and they walked.

'You look so . . .' began Lily, then caught herself. She'd been about to say 'happy', but remembering his snub she said '. . . white,' lest he should think she was vain enough to believe his happiness was occasioned by the sight of her and so deliver another.

'Oh, I shan't stay white for long.' He drew his sleeve along a row of iron railings. 'There. Grime. Is that more to your liking, my fair-spoken one?'

People will see, she thought, though there was no reason they shouldn't be seen together. He was a friend of the Kellys and he'd played tennis with Bob; to be with him now was no more than mannerly. Yet she felt false, walking there beside him. She looked at each house they passed and told him what she knew of its occupants; she found something to say about almost every garden. She chattered, and was relieved to see that he wasn't listening.

At length he said, 'Miss Macgregor, I have not the slightest interest in this dull little town and its even duller inhabitants.'

'Then why are you here?'

'I stayed to meet and then farewell a friend. I had just come from the railway station when I saw you.'

Lily wondered if the friend were male or female. 'And will your friend be back?'

'I do hope not. He has my best interests at heart.'

That made her laugh. They were approaching the cemetery, and they walked the last stretch of road in silence, then wandered among the graves.

'No commentary now, Miss Macgregor? No breathless enumeration of the pleasures of death? Why do you not point out the proximity of the hospital, the splendid sea views to be had from here, the handsome corpse gate where the thankful dead might shelter from the rain?' He put his arm around her waist and his mouth against her ear. 'For if a man knew the gain of death, the ease of death, what might he not do to provoke it? To solicit it by any hand that he might use?'

Lily shrugged him off. 'Did you read that somewhere or make it up?'

'I read it somewhere, and fortunately Mr Kelly is not here to correct my misremembrance. Why don't you remove your hat?'

'I can't. Not here.'

'Then where, Miss Macgregor?'

By unspoken accord they crossed the road and turned into the park, but this proved merely tantalising. 'There are people here,' she said.

'Live ones, alas.'

They stood together under a tree, but he made no move to touch her. Lily leaned back against the trunk to gaze into its sunlit canopy and wonder how it would be if he were to hoist her skirt and pay her the compliment of a few quick thrusts before they went on. All sense of falseness left her then. She took his hands in hers, slipping her fingers beneath his cuffs to feel his wrists; she pictured the fine line of hair that ran down his belly like a trickle of gold in the pan. *There is gold in the mouth, gold in the south, gold in the morning sun*, she thought and knew who'd said it: the buttercups, though there were none left now.

The dimness of the little room and her eagerness to see him gone had combined to cheat her of him, but there'd be light enough in her room at the hotel, and time too. Tonight she could absorb him; his image would be sealed beneath her eyelids. Every scent would linger on her skin, in her nostrils, in the soft tissues of her throat; already she could taste him there.

'We should go back.' She looked towards the town.

'I think you'll miss your train,' he said as they strolled on.

'I know.'

'Then where will you sleep tonight?'

'At my father's hotel. Where will you?'

He named a house built by a settler who'd made and lost his fortune before Lily was born. Its present owner was a Mrs Morton, a sea-captain's widow fond of entertaining. She took as lodgers only single gentlemen of carefree disposition who would not complain of noise or dawdle in the bathroom. 'I have a very pleasant room,' he said.

'Oh, no, that won't do.'

'Won't do as what, Miss Macgregor?'

'As winter quarters for the Harraways,' she said blithely, for they were on easy terms again. 'Have dinner at the hotel tonight, though not with me. When I walk through the dining room, ask me if you can have port or coffee in the lounge. I'll show you to the guest lounge and bring it to you there. With your bill, but you needn't think about that, and I'll tell you how to find my room.' She paused, then clapped her hands. 'No! I'll write it on the bill so we won't be seen talking together at all. But you must promise not to leave it lying about.'

'I'll cram it in my mouth and endeavour to swallow it. Would you like me bound as well as gagged?'

'Oh!' Lily glanced at his hands, then her own. 'Where are my paints and brushes?'

'I think I must have left them on a headstone,' he said, with the smile of one to whom such things were trifles.

It was the merest pinprick, but a pinprick none the less. Lily hesitated, not wanting him to see his carelessness disturbed her.

Mr Fernon contrived to look both repentant and reproachful. 'Are you about to make me go and find them?'

'I'm not about to make you do anything. They'll still be there tomorrow.' Then it struck her as odd that he hadn't suggested they return together, and now neither could she.

Yet despite Mr Fernon's occasional displays of a lack of application far greater than her own, Lily was happy. Her life had more shape and purpose than she'd ever known. The regular excursions to the Bay made it easy to meet Mr Fernon there; she had only to tell the others she was needed at the hotel and would return on Sunday's train. He came late to dinner or the bar and then went alone to her room, and to open the door and find him on her bed was a pleasure as keen as any he gave her.

Sometimes he visited the Harraways, and then she would lie waiting by candlelight for his step on the verandah, her every sense sharpened by apprehension. She felt less assured at the farm, a thing she suspected Mr Fernon knew, for it was then that he was inclined to be moody and talk of moving on, though it was always only to be 'sometime soon, Miss Macgregor'.

In the brief times afterwards, before he rose to dress and they became strangers again, they lay and talked of nothing. Lily liked the way he talked, now.

'I still want to draw you,' she said. 'Though I don't think I could do you justice. I took drawing lessons for a while, but I never learnt to draw people.'

'You dislike people.'

'You don't have to like people to draw them, you just have to look at them. But I expect if I'd learnt to draw people, they would've been fat women. Artists draw fat women all the time.'

He smiled. 'You should visit Greece. Or Italy.'

'Well, I don't want to go to Greece or Italy. Bob's been to Italy, and it's nothing but museums and churches and things.'

'Is that what he said?'

'It's all I've ever heard him talk about.'

'That's probably all he wanted to see. There are people, of course, rather more than there are here, but I'm sure you could avoid them. You'd like the galleries and the gardens. And there are lakes and mountains too. You might like those.'

'There's only one lake,' she said. 'There's only one mountain. There's only ever one of anything. Only one horse and that was Prince, only one sheep and that was Nancy, only one cat and that was Soot, only one dog and that was Frisky. The rest are just their shadows.'

'What boring names you give your animals.'

'They were farm animals. They wouldn't have known themselves with better ones. Anyway, names mean nothing. I've three of them.'

'And is there only one man for you, Miss Macgregor?'

'You may have that honour, Mr Fernon.'

'That is not what I want, Miss Macgregor.'

'The mountain doesn't want it, but he has it.'

Such nonsense they talked.

Chapter 8

Lily went over to the Kellys' with the evening blouse she'd made for Cathy. Her grandmother came too, so they went by the road, which was an easier walk for her. 'Oh my God,' she cried as they turned up the drive. 'What can she be thinking of now?'

'Why?'

'The table! Just look at the kitchen table!'

'What's wrong with it?'

'It's on the front lawn.'

And it was true that it didn't look at ease there. 'They must've had it out to scrub it.'

'I scrub mine every day of the week, but I don't have to do it on the front lawn.'

'I suppose there's a reason for it.'

'I suppose there is. And if she had a pig she'd keep it in the kitchen and there'd be a reason for that too.'

'Should people who have pigs keep them on the front lawn, then?'

'Did I say that?'

'Perhaps they're planning to eat alfresco. That means in the open air,' Lily added in a tone calculated to annoy her grandmother. 'Shall I ask?'

'No, you shan't. You'll mind your own business.'

And Mrs Kelly provided tea and scones on the dining-room

table without a word of explanation.

'Now, Mrs Kelly,' said Mrs Davidson, leaping up and laying brisk hands on the china, 'it won't take us a minute to get these dishes done.'

But Mrs Kelly didn't move. She had been in service as a girl; she'd learnt to cook in crumbling halls. She'd risen shivering in the dark to see through tears of pride the thoroughbreds being led out to their boxes while the scrawny young devils that were to ride them swaggered, and shivered too. She'd helped prepare dinners without number — joyful dinners, dismal dinners — and passing strange had been the things the girls who stood in cap and cuffs against the sideboard saw and heard from there. But they had never, ever told of a guest who sprang out of her chair to bawl at the hostess, 'Now it won't take us a minute to get these dishes done.'

So she sat tight, and dreamed of the days when The Scatterling, or whatever he might live to be called, would unwind his run at Riccarton, at Trentham, at Ellerslie and Flemington, and she could confound her neighbour by snatching the dishes from her hands and hurling them through the window.

Which was where Lily stood now, watching the Buick come bouncing down the back road. Father O'Reilly was driving, and stopped just short of a poplar. Out came Theresa, Kevin, two more little boys, and Bob. Someone threw a football into the paddock and they all dashed after it.

'What's out there?' asked her grandmother, back from the sink.

'They're home from school,' said Lily. 'Father O'Reilly and Bob Graham are playing football with them.' Father O'Reilly jogged about as if his knees were troubling him, but Bob broke in and out of movement as easily as one of Mr Kelly's horses, all the while holding himself in check, although his small opponents would have noticed nothing that wasn't flattering to themselves as he chased or evaded them.

'Poor Bob,' said Mrs Kelly. 'Have you ever heard what it was his wife died of?'

'No,' said Lily, but her grandmother made a little movement

that must have been a sign of sorts, for it was followed by a quick intake of breath from Mrs Kelly. Something below the waist, then. And something that wasn't to be spoken of too freely in front of an unmarried woman lest it prevent her coming to a proper appreciation of her own sorry plight. Lily tilted her head back, the better to hear what might be said behind her.

There was a cagey silence. Then a single syllable dropped from her grandmother's lips and hissed on the air like a wet finger on a hot iron.

Mrs Kelly's tongue clicked against her teeth.

'The result of a fall,' said Mrs Davidson more ordinarily. 'She was alone in the house when it happened. The maid had the afternoon off, and found her dead when she came in that evening. I heard it from a woman whose cousin used to work next door.'

'Oh, what a dreadful thing,' sighed Mrs Kelly. 'Poor Bob.'

'He wasn't there,' said Mrs Davidson. 'He'd gone away on business.'

The game in the paddock had ended. Lily, turning from the window, happened to catch her grandmother's eye, as scornful as a gull's. For an uncanny instant they formed a hitherto undreamt of confederacy, attuned to the ways of a world far beyond the ken of an ignorant Irish biddy who would summon the priest ahead of a doctor.

Then her grandmother snapped, 'You can get along home and start Dad's tea.'

'It's too soon,' said Lily.

Father O'Reilly and the small visitors had taken the ball and set off for the road, but Bob was making for the house.

Mrs Kelly's mind was now set on things medical. She'd heard Connie Graham was wanting to come home, 'and then we'd have our own doctor here.'

'Hoo,' said Mrs Davidson, 'Connie Graham. The men won't like that. It'll only be the women and children who go near her, and precious few of those. I wouldn't myself.'

Bob was on the back steps.

'I've said it before and I'll say it again, some folk've got —'

Lily sprang across the room, calling, 'Mrs Kelly, why's the kitchen table on the front lawn?'

'Lily,' said her grandmother heavily, 'Mrs Kelly and I are talking. And you've got altogether too much of what the cat licks its bum with.'

And Bob heard that at least, but when he looked at Lily his face was perfectly serious. 'I was going to drive on to your place, but then I thought you might be here. Why's the table on the lawn?'

'Bobby,' said Lily severely, 'Mrs Kelly and my grandmother are talking. And you have got . . .' she paused just long enough to sow a seed of discomfort in her grandmother, '. . . to help me bring it in again.'

'Ah!' Bob spun round and disappeared, with Lily close behind him. There were giggles in the hall and a yip on the verandah.

'They're as silly as they were when they were twelve,' observed Mrs Davidson, as if she were in no way to blame for this latest outburst.

From the lawn came the sounds of an argument over who was to take which end of the table.

'Just do as you're told,' said Bob, for Lily didn't want to be the one who went backwards up the steps. 'Otherwise you'll be lifting most of the weight.'

'But if I have to go backwards I'll trip on my skirt.'

'Hitch it up.' Then a whistle. 'Talk about a poppy show.'

'There's no pleasing you, is there?'

'I wouldn't say that.'

There was a shriek and a thud. Lily had sat down on a step. 'The legs caught.'

'It's too heavy for you.'

'If I had your end, I could get further underneath it.'

'All right, I give in. We'll do it your way.'

'It's too heavy for her,' said Mrs Kelly anxiously, because Lily was still complaining.

'Don't go so fast. My arms are coming out of their sockets.'

'Lift it higher! Brace it against your chest!'

'I can't, you idjit, there're things in the way.'

Mrs Kelly blinked, but said, 'I do think she's a great deal fonder of him than she lets on.'

'She could do a lot worse,' said Mrs Davidson. 'I can't say much for the rest of the family, but Bobby's nice enough. Dad was saying just the other day that no matter who drops in at the Grahams', Bob'll act like they're the very ones he most wanted to see.'

'To be sure, Mrs Davidson, and it's a great talent he has, a great talent for pleasing,' cried Mrs Kelly like a stage Irishwoman. She owed her one for that business with the dishes.

The table, with some help from Kevin, was in at last. Mrs Kelly told Bob that Cathy had washed her hair and asked the boys to take the table outside so she could scrub it while her hair dried in the sun. Then they'd all gone off and left it there.

'So,' said Lily to her grandmother. 'And now I'll go and put Dad's tea on.'

'Do you want a lift?' asked Bob.

'I think I'll walk.'

'I'll walk with you, then.'

'We'll come too,' called Theresa, trotting after them.

'We're not motoring,' said Bob. 'We're walking the long way round.'

'We'll come anyway,' said Kevin, and Bob looked resigned.

'Tell us about the naughty things you used to do when you were a little girl, Miss Macgregor,' said Theresa. 'Tell us what the dominie said when he caught you playing truant.'

'Phemie Macgrrregor! Jamie Macpherrrson!' trilled the dominie obediently. 'Why are ye nae in school?' The barely comprehensible homily saw Kellys Road out.

Then Kevin spotted a young couple walking hand-in-hand, and gave Theresa a swift nudge with his elbow. 'Look,' he said, 'lovers.'

They cupped their hands over their mouths and chortled into them. Their thin shoulders heaved, and their cheeks and necks turned rosy. It was all too much for Theresa; she had to run away.

'I'll race you, Kevin, I'll race you to the bridge.' She darted off, calling back, 'But you have to give me a start.'

Kevin counted slowly to five and went after her, his country boy's boots clopping on the road.

Bob was unusually quiet. Thinking of the pleasure he took in talking over old times, Lily asked, 'Can you still run as fast as you could when we were at school?' He'd won all his races on sports days, his bare brown feet scarcely seeming to touch the ground. Then he would flop panting on the grass beside her, his eyes as light and empty as a resting collie's. Whatever troubled him in calmer moments was always lost in action.

'I doubt it. Are you offering to race me to the bridge? How much of a start will you give me?'

'It was you who used to give me starts. And if I couldn't catch you then, I don't think I could do so now.'

'Oh, I think you could,' said Bob, and something in his voice stopped her from looking at him.

After a little, he said, 'I never know what you're thinking.'

'Don't start that again.'

'Start what again?'

Lily hesitated, then replied, 'Always wanting to know what I'm thinking all the time.'

'That's not what you meant.'

'Well, since you know so much there's no reason to ask me anything at all.'

It wasn't only Bob who was being tiresome. Lily heard the Kellys were fed up with Mr Fernon. Some business about the foal, Scatty by name and now it seemed by nature, running into wire and being badly cut about the knees. They could all only hope that there'd be no infection.

'And it might've been worse,' said Mr Kelly, wiping iodine from his fingers. 'He might have been frightened by Bob Graham in that bloody motorcar. What would have happened then?'

He rarely used a word like 'bloody'. It was the thought of his darling struggling against the wire.

'It's nothing to do with Bob,' said Mrs Kelly. 'Your precious Mr Fernon must have forgotten to shut the paddock gate.'

'He didn't forget to shut it,' said Mr Kelly bleakly. He'd inspected the gate and decided Scatty had nudged his way out. To close a gate but not secure it struck him as a peculiar piece of negligence, unexpected yet oddly typical of their visitor. It was limp-wristed; it was unmanly. 'And he's not my precious Mr Fernon. I only put up with him for the Harraways' sake.'

'Well, once they're gone we shan't have to see him,' said Mrs Kelly. 'And that'll be that.'

But it gnawed at her too. It put her in mind of a former acquaintance, a half-mad old woman at odds with her neighbours who'd tossed scraps of bad meat and mouldy bread over the fence in hopes that their turkey cock would find them, eat them, and so die. A haphazard route from helplessness to harm. Mr Fernon wasn't helpless, nor was he at odds with them, but his was an action that also said: I'll do this much and see what comes of it.

She remembered him sitting in her kitchen with the eyes of an unwelcome child, while Oedipus sought his lap and Pat leaned against his shoulder, and sighed. 'He's out to get attention. That sort can never have enough, and they don't care how it comes. Best ignore him.'

'I'm sorry I gave him his books back,' said Dan. 'We could've kept them as compensation.' He spoke with an air of conscious pettiness, for it was a petty thing that Mr Fernon had done. Yet it had darkened his horizons as he trudged about the farm, for thus were tragedies contrived by schemers and by cowards: the tap left trickling in a drought, the plank that barred a rotting bridge kicked carelessly aside, the stranger misdirected through the snow.

He attempted a lighter note. 'I'd find it easier to forgive him if he'd run off with you or young Cathy.'

Mrs Kelly saw no harm in settling Mr Fernon's hash entirely. 'He's already succeeded in turning Cathy's head. There's been no living with her since she first clapped eyes on him.'

'Why can't she want to be a nun like any other foolish girl her age?'

'Because it's not my side of the family she takes after. None of them do.'

'I'm delighted to hear it. I'd hate to have to start marking the whisky decanter.'

Both laughed then, but drearily. There was no real cheering them just now.

So there it was: another little accident that might have been no accident at all. Lily felt a twinge of shame on Mr Fernon's account, though he said nothing of it when he appeared at the farm. 'Why are you always in bed when I arrive?' he asked as he flung off his clothes.

'Because you come so late. When I'm living at the Bay you can see me out of bed, though I'm not sure we'll find much to say to each other.'

'I can't find much to say to you at all, but you're more available than most.'

'As are you, Mr Fernon.'

'You do understand,' he said later, 'that we can have no future together?' He spoke with a tragical air and she laughed, for it sounded like a line from a silly play where the women were all impossibly pure, and the men weren't and made a great to do about it from the very best of motives.

'I hadn't thought so far ahead. Why do you? Are you about to tell me you're not fit to kiss the hem of my gown, and rush off to join the Foreign Legion?'

His exertions hadn't lightened his mood. 'I would not wish to cause you any unhappiness, Miss Macgregor.'

That was nonsense. He didn't care what became of her, and not long ago she'd taken courage from that thought. He never pestered her with questions or laid claim to her with gifts; he set no store on being clean and doing things properly. He relieved her of the need to be useful, and his fits of dislike, real or feigned, were far easier to live with than earned goodwill. 'Unhappiness!' she said, rising to open the door to the verandah.

The mountain caps were lit by starlight, and the newest of

autumn moons floated like a soap bubble against the sky. There were the faint stirrings in the house and yard that meant the approach of day. Soon he would go and she would drift from ease through restlessness to bitter craving before they met again, but for now she had her temporary release. 'Well, I expect I will be unhappy when you go away for good and I have to learn to do without you.'

That pleased him. Perhaps he'd hoped to wound her, and believed that he'd succeeded. He caught her in his arms as if he sought forgiveness. When he fell away from her again, she put her lips against his ear and whispered, 'Why did you let Scatty out of his paddock?'

'Did I do that?'

'Somebody didn't fasten the gate. It could only have been you.'

He smiled as if he found his own absence of mind endearing. 'I did think, as I came away, that I might not have done so.'

'There was no great harm done,' she said easily.

'And were the Kellys much put out?'

She could have told him they were, but some dark instinct warned against it.

'Ought I to apologise?'

'I wouldn't worry about it if I were you.'

'You're too kind to me, Miss Macgregor.'

'Why shouldn't I be kind to you?'

'Perhaps I'd like you better if you caused me pain.'

'Oh, don't ask me to do that. I could never hurt anybody.'

'I'm sure you hurt Bob Graham almost daily.'

'That's different. He's lonely.'

Her answer delighted him. 'I'm lonely. Why will you hurt him and not me? I took you for a *femme fatale*. You disappoint me, Miss Macgregor.'

'Stop making fun of me. Bob ought to marry again. He needs a wife, he wants some babies.'

'And don't you want babies, Miss Macgregor?'

'I'd rather have a train set.'

'A train set?'

'Mmm. You take it out of its box and join the lines, you hook the carriages together and wind up the engine, and away it goes. Then when you're tired of it you put it back in its box, and it doesn't mind a bit. Train sets are convenient. Why don't you introduce Bob to some nice young ladies?'

'I don't know any nice young ladies. If I did, I would not be here with you. You will die a sad old spinster, Miss Macgregor.'

'But I shall have you to remember, Mr Fernon.'

'Then what can I do to make you hurt me?'

'Nothing at all.'

Chapter 9

Ruby lost patience with the men's polite inspections of possible lodgings at the Bay, and ordered them off to the beach to watch the lady bathers.

'It's too cold for swimming now,' said Bob.

'So there won't be any there,' Nigel said.

'Speaking as connoisseurs of same,' said Ruby, arch but immoveable, and they seemed to find this flattering and went to shiver on the sand while she haggled over two bedrooms and the exclusive use of a drawing room in a house not far from the hotel, all meals provided.

'Old bat,' she said to Lily, 'we're doing her a favour at this time of year. And did you hear me say Nige'd cut the hedge for her? He likes to do that kind of thing.'

The Harraways' departure from the district did not go unnoticed. Mrs Davidson quoted a sharp-eyed acquaintance who'd watched them board the train. '"And if that Mrs Harraway comes back with a baby — *well*. It won't be hers."' Then she waited to see what Lily would make of that.

Lily made very little of it. 'I don't think Ruby's the sort to want anybody else's,' she said, and went on fitting things into her bag. Her grandmother had derived a certain satisfaction from her intimacy with the Harraways, praising Ruby's figure and her lack of side. She'd drawn Ruby's attention to the fact that Mrs Graham had no grandchildren, what with Jean and Bertie Frasers' stated aim of waiting a while, 'though it's been a fair while now,' and nothing in that department from Alec and Ellen either. And when Ruby said, 'That Alec Graham looks to me like he thinks it's for stirring his tea with,' she'd cackled with delight. But she believed Ruby to be Lily's friend, so there was also pleasure to be found in what might be said of her.

'And she won't be coming back,' Lily added. 'The Harraways are going north in spring.'

'So he's given up that nonsense about buying a farm? Well, they'll be company for you at the Bay.'

'So it seems,' said Lily.

Bob was company as well. He'd moved, not quite to the Bay, but near enough. Some Graham friends had gone to a newly widowed daughter, and he was looking after their farm while they were away.

Their outings continued. They all went to the theatre and sat in a box and were stared at, for Ruby had painted her eyes and lips as though she meant to go on stage herself. During the interval a couple of Bob's friends came up to have a word with him and stayed to smirk at her. Mr Fernon joined them too, and when Nigel excused himself and left the box he slipped into his seat beside Lily.

For a moment she felt fearful, but he scarcely acknowledged her. He sat with his knees apart and his hands loosely clasped on the box's padded leather rim, gazing innocently about him. He looked very pure in a dinner jacket, and might have been no more than a well brought-up young man ensuring she didn't sit alone and unattended while the bolder spirits present slavered over Ruby.

Nobody could know how it is with us, thought Lily and wanted to laugh aloud.

'When shall I see you alone?' he asked, leaning back to contemplate the painted roof.

'It won't be so easy to meet at the hotel. I'll be working, and the others might very well be there.'

'In your room?' His leg came to rest against hers, but he continued to study the ceiling.

'No, but if you see them in the dining room or the bar you'll have to talk to them.'

'Not all night, I trust. You did say I'd see more of you once you were here.'

'And you didn't seem keen on the idea, so I haven't given it much thought. Anyway, I quite forgot about the Harraways and Bob.'

'Ah yes, the ever-present Bob. You are wonderfully solicitous of him.'

Lily sat fiddling with the tassel on her evening bag. 'He's an old friend, that's all. I've known him for twenty years.'

'And not so very long ago I heard you and he agree you hadn't met in ten. Isn't there something else you'd rather play with?' He took her hand and placed it on his thigh as if to see where it might wander of its own accord.

'Not here.' She glanced over her shoulder, but saw only the backs of Bob's friends. 'Though if we were alone and the lights were low . . .'

'I'd prefer somewhere more secluded. Perhaps you could come to my room?'

He smiled at her expression. 'Do you fear for your reputation, Miss Macgregor? You need not.' He rose, then stooped to pick up her evening bag, which had fallen from her lap to the floor. 'My landlady has several very dull little nieces who are always dropping by. You could pass unnoticed amongst them.'

His superior manner irked her, for still she understood the circles they were moving in better than he. 'I'll meet you by the steps to the beach after ten tomorrow night, then.'

Lily had thought that would be easy, because in all but the very worst weather there were strollers by the sea, but when she paused by the steps it occurred to her that he might find it amusing to keep her waiting there alone. She walked on until she drew level with Stella Morton's house, which looked scarcely occupied. The upper floor was in darkness, and only a faint light showed through the coloured glass panels by the front door. Deciding she wouldn't wait at all, she turned back, but this time Mr Fernon came up from the beach and fell into step beside her. She hoped that nobody was looking after them as they went through the gateway into a drab courtyard where high trees grew among paving stones made slippery by their leaves.

Mr Fernon tried the door, then felt for his key. 'I think I must have left it in my room,' he said. 'Perhaps we should go to the hotel.'

Having come so far, Lily felt let down. 'Can't you ring?'

'There will be people here. Are you quite prepared for them?'

'We can go to the hotel if you'd rather,' she said, sensing he too was uneasy about their being seen together, but he swung round and put his hand to the bell. A maid came, made polite noises, and disappeared. The entrance hall was half-filled by a gleaming mahogany staircase and a fireplace so tall Lily stood on tiptoe to see if she could reach the mantelshelf. 'I'd have to stand on a chair to dust it.'

'Try not to act like a housemaid, my dear. Run upstairs.'

Then a door to her left opened, revealing flickering patterns of fire and candlelight, and Mrs Morton came out in a sweep of full-skirted black silk and a waft of scent and smoky air. Her step was light and her waist narrow, but like her house she'd seen better days. Neither was old, but both were old-fashioned. She knew Lily by sight and by name, and they smiled upon each other now as if they'd never passed in the street unregarding. One of her large front teeth was quite discoloured.

'I see you know Miss Macgregor,' said Mr Fernon. 'She has consented to share my bed until we each find someone more to our liking. In my case that will probably be next week.'

Two could play at that game. 'Knowing all you require in a woman,' replied Lily sweetly, 'I'm surprised it should take you so long.'

Mrs Morton's mouth widened in a brief, bright acknowledgement of these pleasantries, but her heavy-lidded eyes did not leave Mr Fernon's face.

'What an apt pupil I have in you, my dear,' he said, turning to open the door to the room Mrs Morton had quitted. 'Wait for me in there.' He slapped her on the rear as she went by. 'I do believe that madam here is about to ask me for my rent money.'

The room glowed with more mahogany, and red and gold brocades. Several ships' officers were there, and four of Mrs Morton's nieces. Two sat whispering together on a sofa; one, dressed in the aesthetic manner and with fluffy hair of the yellowish white that owes more to peroxide than to nature, was arranging candlesticks in front of a gilt-framed mirror. Another slouched against the wall, smoking.

The men rose and introduced themselves by their Christian names or shortened versions of their surnames, and laughed a good deal at each other. The girls merely glanced at her through narrowed eyes and turned their heads away, in the manner of cats encountering another of their kind whose presence they resent but are not inclined to challenge.

A cat accorded such a welcome assumes a bland air and an unassailable position. So did Lily. She dropped into an armchair vacated by an officer, who perched comfortably enough on its arm and asked her where he might have seen her before. It did no harm to tell him; he wouldn't be a party to Bay gossip.

Mr Fernon came in. He drew up a dining chair, seated himself beside her and, addressing her as his dear again, asked if she fancied a drop of gin.

'No, I do not,' she said sharply, unsettled by his manner and the prompt departure of her protector.

Smiling to see he'd succeeded in provoking her, he took her hand. Lily remembered his gibe about her resemblance to the nieces, and looked at them again. They were all of average height and slender build, their hair was clean, their faces pale and slightly peaky, their dress elegant but inexpensive. And, apart from the head-duckings and shoulder-hunchings they were obliged to engage in to respond to the men around the room without once looking at her, there was nothing to them. They might have come from shops or the telephone office for an innocent evening party.

Perhaps they had. Lily had come from the bar and was dressed for it, but she wished again for the sort of clothes Ruby wore and the nerve to paint her face as boldly.

Mr Fernon appeared to have forgotten her. When one of the girls from the sofa crept over to whisper in his ear something certainly unflattering to Lily, he turned to look at her with mild surprise.

As if anyone who'd braved the Grahams' long drive and those interminable tennis parties could be seriously put out by such featherweights in the art of discomfiture. All the same, the excitement she'd felt when she turned through the gate was gone. Despite her stays her back was weary, and there was a dull pain in her forehead. The smoky atmosphere was making her eyes sting. Outside the night would be as bright and deep as velvet, the air brittle with its hints of salt and inland snow. To leave would look like petulance, but to sit there at his whim was silly. She looked down at their clasped hands, still resting on the glossy arm of her chair as though there were a kindness in their bodies that was altogether absent from their souls, and extracted hers from his.

He followed her into the hall. 'Where are you going?'

'To the hotel.'

'Do my friends bore you? I am very tolerant of yours.'

'They're not your friends.'

'Am I to have only such friends as you'd allow?'

'I meant the officers,' she said, bewildered. 'They'll be gone in a day or two. And you know I don't care what you do or who you see when you're not with me.'

'Then perhaps you should.'

'I'm tired, that's all. I was presiding over breakfasts at six o'clock this morning.'

'Come upstairs, then.'

Lily hesitated, for in her thoughts her hand was already on the rusting gate, but her leaving was inevitable; it could be postponed. They went up the carpeted stairs to a half landing almost the size of her room at the farm and thence to the upper landing, dimly lit and cluttered with plants and furniture. She stumbled against a little table, and its vase rocked alarmingly.

Mr Fernon opened a door and switched on the electric light, and his room sprang up before her, so ordinarily pleasant she was dazed. They might have been in any expensive boarding house or comfortable hotel. There was a double bed, a washstand, an oak tallboy and matching wardrobe, pictures of ships and steamers on the walls, large lattice windows that overlooked the sea. Then she thought of the late strollers, and shrank back against the door. 'Draw the curtains.'

'I'd prefer to switch off the light.' He did so. 'Don't you like my room?'

Lily sat down on an armchair to take off her shoes and stockings. 'It's not what I expected, that's all.'

And it lent a curious domesticity to their coupling, which was brief but cordial. Her arms felt numb and heavy on the pillow. A wind had risen and the sky was lighter; the swaying trees in the courtyard were casting wild shadows across the ceiling. She realised she had slept, but had no recollection of settling to do so. That surprised her. Mr Fernon might fall asleep in strange beds, but it was a new thing for her. She sat up, rubbing her arms.

His voice came from across the room. 'You may stay a little longer, Miss Macgregor. I shall not be so inhospitable as to turn you out before dawn for fear of giving scandal to chambermaids or farmers.' He was at the washstand, stirring something in a glass. 'I cannot sleep,' he added.

'Nor will I, now.'

'Have some of this, then.' He came and held the glass to her lips. She caught a sickly whiff of chloral and shook her head, which no longer ached.

'I want you to stay with me all night,' he said. 'I want you here beside me when I wake.' He put his arms around her, though it seemed that all he wanted now was to rest. She felt his body settling against hers.

An odd thought struck her. 'What if the police come?'

'Do they ever come here?'

'Not that I've heard.'

'Well, then. Theirs is not to impose chastity on the adult population. This is my room, and you're a respectable woman who lives with her stepfather and works in his hotel. Indeed, I think you run a greater risk entertaining me there.'

That was true. People were always ready to think the worst of barmaids, and the risk was to her father as well. 'But what of Mrs Morton and her nieces?'

'They are mermaids, Miss Macgregor. Mermaids of a lesser water than a certain lady of our acquaintance, but mermaids nonetheless. They can slip through any net set for them, leaving only the faintest of fishy odours behind.'

'I only wondered what we'd say.'

'I would say you're my fiancée, and we must go on like this until my family reconcile themselves to the notion of a barmaid in their midst and stop threatening to cut me off without a farthing. They'd believe that; it's the very stuff of fiction.'

'They'd tell you to find yourself a job and make an honest woman of me.'

'Are you not more honest as you are?' His voice was drowsy. 'Would you like a ring? Shall I buy you rubies?'

Lily wondered if he were half-asleep and dreaming. 'Are they so short of money she wants to sell hers?'

'Rubies plural, Miss Macgregor. Those pretty little red things that are vulgarly supposed to represent the asking price of a somewhat less than virtuous woman.' His hand between her thighs relaxed, his breathing grew deep and slow.

But Lily lay wide awake, gripped by a strange exhilaration. For all the silliness she'd had to endure that night, from now on things would be simpler still. She hadn't taken up with Mr Fernon because she wanted kindness; that wasn't what she'd hoped for when she saw him in the Kellys' yard. And if asked then, she'd have said it was more than likely he'd do all the things decent chaps weren't supposed to — at least no more than once.

Things which staider souls rewarded with grand names like vice and debauchery, but which seemed to her nothing more than a continuation of the same sort of naughtiness she'd engaged in with Jamie Macpherson, a scabby-mouthed little boy who'd smelt, not unpleasantly, of garden sheds and old machinery. Together they were often suspected of pulling up carrots or stealing eggs, and Jamie had evened the score by making up stories about their accusers, wherein they pitched tents and set about clearing their bits of land. Then a great wind blew, their tents were torn away, and they were set upon by fierce dogs and bulls maddened by the storm and chased howling through gorse and thistle.

She had done the illustrations. For her victims' greater humiliation she drew them naked, a state easily explained by the force of the gale and the teeth and horns of their tormentors. She gave the men thingies like horses', and udderlike bosoms to the women. And had the great good fortune to thrust these early examples of her God-given talent under her pinny as the dominie burst in on them.

Although she hadn't known this was art until years later, when a student asked her to an evening lecture and thence to his room to see some erotica — an interesting word that proved to mean no more than a book of dirty pictures drawn by a hand a hundred times surer than her own, but with an equally vengeful child's eye. So irresistibly did they remind her of her own early efforts, though without the dogs and bulls and the natural effects of extreme fear, that she giggled. Her companion's expression became both scornful and pitying, for he took her for a fearful prude. She tried to explain about herself and Jamie, laughed immoderately, and paused to wipe her eyes. Then it dawned on her that he'd hoped the pictures would make up for all he lacked in charms, and snatching up her coat she bolted into the street, sobbing with laughter. She had to lean against a wall to compose herself; passers-by were looking strangely at her.

Her student friend had come to such stuff late and saw meaning in it; she had left it far behind. But I was good at it, she thought as she lay smiling in the dark. It came naturally.

Mr Fernon seemed bent on showing her something too. His

desire to convince her of her unimportance and to teach her lessons she'd learnt long ago was tiresome, but no more than that — a small price to pay for her time with him. And his disregard for any feelings she might have freed her from having to think of his at all.

She eased herself away from him, drew the curtains, and switched on the electric light to dress by. He didn't stir. The hinged top of the tallboy lifted to reveal a speckled mirror above the shallow compartments that held combs and brushes, cuff links and collar studs. The face beneath her tangled hair was white and haggard, but exultant too, as if some older, buried self had risen in her and was clamouring for release.

The dim light still burned on the landing. She crept down the stairs, but the rooms below were quiet; the front door, no longer locked, opened soundlessly. And I'm good at this as well, she thought, it comes naturally to me. Like the trees whose wind-tossed branches had flung shadows on the ceiling she was shedding all her leaves, and she felt as light and free as they must do.

Chapter 10

Now they could use his room as a meeting place, Mr Fernon took to sending notes to the hotel. One, addressed to *Euphemia Davidson, Spinster of this Parish*, caused brief bewilderment but, 'That's me,' cried Lily cheerfully, snatching it from the porter's hand. 'It's from a girl I was at school with. She was the biggest dunce imaginable and never learnt my new name. What a scrawl! I suppose this is her way of letting me know she's married.'

She hadn't the nerve to write back to him. Her handwriting was better than his, but she knew he'd find much to amuse him in her spelling and punctuation. Instead she obeyed his summonses, even though there were times when she feared entering his room to find another woman there. He'd arrange that if he thought it held a lesson for her; she always went prepared to don a face to show him that it didn't. She'd be good at that too.

Ruby appeared at the hotel, imperious in a fur-trimmed Russian coat with deep cuffs and black frogging. She sat in the office drinking tea and displaying a signed photograph of herself, misty-eyed and tender-mouthed. 'That was me, Miss Ruby Ellis. Alice is my middle name, I thought it sounded nice. My maiden name was Gandy, that's Gandy spelt G-A-N-D-Y, though Nige's dear papa had doubts. Rags, the other kids used to call me. No, you keep it. Pin it up there with the other theatricals. Nice to have a bit of real talent round the place.' She reached into her glossy muff and drew out another photograph. 'Here, have a look at this one. The boy of your dreams.'

And of course that was also Ruby, crowned with ostrich feathers and standing hands on hips in the tights and boots of a principal boy. Lily and Bob had been right: she was magnificent, though scarcely decent. Her sequined satin tunic only just reached the top of her thighs. 'Those were the days,' she sighed.

'You must have looked about seven feet tall,' said Lily inadequately.

'I got a standing ovation before I opened my mouth. That was the night I met Nige — he couldn't get round to the stage door fast enough.'

'I'm not surprised.'

Then Ruby felt the need for exercise. She wanted to walk along to the cliffs and hear of shipwrecks and drownings.

'I've things to do,' said Lily, but her father, even pinker-faced than usual, clutched at the photographs and waved her away.

The tide was out, exposing ribbed sand and clumps of brown seaweed. Bored-looking seabirds stood about in clusters.

'That's what I'm going to come back as. I'd enjoy life as a bird,' said Ruby, squinting at the grey horizon. 'Just fly away whenever I felt like it.'

'You'd have to lay eggs all the time.'

'No, I'll come back as a cock.' Then, 'My God, you've got a dirty mind.'

'I was thinking of you in someone's hat, that's all.'

Ruby's hat that day was wonderful, a high toque with a black fur trim and a spray of oily green feathers. People stared at her, though not always with admiration. The men looked bemused or enlightened, and the pretty women calculating; their plainer sisters attempted derision or remained carefully blank. Perhaps admiration was too generous an impulse to be accommodated in a town the size of the Bay.

'Doesn't Joss live round here somewhere? I need to pee.'

'He mightn't be there.'

'I wasn't counting on him to hold my hand while I did it. I just want someone to show me where to go.'

Once upon a time the Bay had seemed quite large to Lily. Now it grew smaller by the minute. 'You shouldn't have drunk so much tea. You should've gone before we came out.'

'I didn't want to, then. It's this big house here, isn't it?'

'I think so.'

'Then we'll just ring and see, shall we?'

The maid opened the door. She was polite and incurious. Mr Fernon wasn't in.

'I've a letter for him,' said Ruby, feeling in her muff. 'A family matter. So I'd prefer to leave it in his room myself, if you don't mind.' She swept into the hall and began a slow turn, inspecting the plaster ceiling.

There was the familiar swish of unfashionably full skirts and Stella Morton appeared, dressed for the street in her customary black. She wore a pert little hat tilted over one eye, but there was a tiredness in her freckled skin and sandy hair that the kinder lights of evening concealed.

Ruby bore down on her and they whispered earnestly together. Ruby's hat and feather bobbed up and down; Mrs Morton's heavy eyelids rose and fell. Then Ruby turned and made for a door behind the stairs and Mrs Morton brushed past Lily, her pale lips parting in a murmured greeting. That front tooth was almost black, yet it served to draw attention to her wistful smile.

A dumpy woman with a bucket, pan and shovel came into the hall and knelt to clean the grate, sighing as she did so.

'That's that then,' called Ruby, emerging from behind the staircase. 'We'll just take up the letter and be off.'

'What were you talking about?'

'Maids,' said Ruby loftily, and began to mount the stairs. 'I thought she might know of a girl who has her own reasons for wanting to get out of this town for a while. Nige needn't think I'm looking after a baby on my own. Well, no painted Jezebel, she.'

Lily shushed her. 'You don't know who's about.'

However, the upper landing was deserted, with all the doors save Mr Fernon's left wide for airing.

'A game little woman making the best of her widowhood, alone and unprotected in a wicked world,' pronounced Ruby, stooping to admire an arrangement of dried flowers. 'No wonder the blokes like her. Nothing to frighten them there.'

'Do they like her?'

'Oh yes.' Now she had a languid air. 'There is something infinitely seductive about that disfigured mouth, and the hint of dissolution in her pallid flesh. I'm quoting, of course. I don't think I've got it quite right.'

That possibility had never entered Lily's head. *I see you know Miss Macgregor. She has consented to share my bed . . .* The quick smile, the eyes that hadn't left his face, that air of frail appeal. So strong was the image that for a moment she was blind. Then we can't go on, she thought. Not like this.

Ruby was watching her narrowly.

'How old do you think she is?'

'God knows,' said Ruby, as one might say: Who cares. 'Forties? Fifty? I can never tell.'

Too old then, surely. That must be Stella Morton's way with men, as Ruby's was to flatter and command. And to break with Mr Fernon now was unthinkable; she'd grown too used to him.

'Stop walking three paces behind me. I can't decide if I'm royalty or you're planning to stick a knife in my back. Which is his room?'

'I think the guest rooms are the ones along the front,' said Lily faintly. 'His must be the one with the door closed.' She'd even come to like sleeping with him there. Sometimes that was all they did, and she had no need of his morphine or chloral. He was her narcotic: he soothed her, he filled her, he made her complete, and the slow tides he caused to rise and fall swept all else away.

Ruby opened the door and peered inside. 'It's clean, I'll say that for it.' She sauntered along the landing, looking into each room she passed. 'Who comes here, exactly?'

'The rooms are let to travellers, single men. And ships' officers on shore leave. There're parties, all sorts of people come.' It was when she had to go too long without him that she couldn't rest. Then she'd leave the hotel and wander about the streets, though now if they met by chance she'd pretend not to know him and hurry by. It was easier that way. 'And sometimes girls come here to meet them, the officers that is, but there isn't anything you could put your finger on.'

'No, there never is. Ah, this's more like it. Come in here.'

That room was small and cramped, with dark red walls. A wide, gilt-framed mirror hung over a dressing table that was only a couple of feet from the end of the large bed.

'There's nothing to it,' said Lily, with a shrug. One day she and Mr Fernon would have to part, but not yet.

Ruby stretched out on the bed and surveyed herself in the mirror. 'Oh my God, think of the view you'd get.'

'How do you mean?' When drawn the plush curtains would cover the entire wall, but the window itself was small and grimy. The back yard was cluttered with crates and empty bottles.

'Well, you might lift up your head and take a look over his shoulder. A bloke's arse doesn't show to advantage when he's screwing. Here, help me up, I'm cast.'

Screwing. Lily had never heard it called that before. She thought of sending a note to Josselin Fernon, Esquire: *Dear Mr Fernon, A certain lady of our acquaintance has hinted that you have been screwing your landlady. If this is true, then I do not think it proper that you should use her house as a place for screwing me.*

'What's so funny?' asked Ruby.

'What you just said.'

Lily sent that note, signed by 'A Friend' in case he left it lying about, but Mr Fernon said nothing of it, even when she made the darker nights an excuse for asking him to come to the hotel. She summoned up the courage to sketch him there, though it put him in a restive mood.

‘How much longer do you intend to be?’

‘I’ve nearly finished. And I never said you weren’t allowed to move.’

‘Shall we go for a walk?’

‘It’s very cold.’

‘I’d put my clothes on first. And you like the cold.’

‘We might see somebody we know, and since you don’t like my friends and I don’t like yours, one of us is bound to suffer. There, that’s enough for now.’

‘Am I to be permitted to see any of these masterpieces?’

‘Oh no, you’d laugh at them. I don’t think I can do you justice — you’re much too beautiful.’

‘And you are much too kind. If you have it in you to be kind, why don’t you draw Bob Graham?’

‘I couldn’t do him justice either,’ said Lily, considering. ‘Nor do photographs. He always looks beady-eyed and very serious, which of course he’s not. I suppose it’s because he’s no good at staying still.’

‘Do you do anybody justice, Miss Macgregor?’

‘Probably not. Anyway, I couldn’t ask Bob to come up to my room and take off all his clothes for me.’

‘I should think he’d be delighted.’

‘I should think he’d be shocked.’

‘Is he easily shocked, then?’

‘Leave him,’ she said. ‘Why are you so interested in him?’

‘I think you and he would be happy together. And I’m very much afraid that I have been a bad influence on you.’

‘It’s too late for that, Mr Fernon. The day I looked through the Kellys’ kitchen window and saw you in the yard I felt the stove rake move inside me.’

‘You felt the what move inside you?’

‘The stove rake.’

‘And what is that?’

‘I suppose it’s a rake you use for cleaning out a stove, though I use a shovel, quite a small one.’

‘Then why have you one inside you?’

'I read that in a story.'

'You read of it. Was the story about an affair of the heart, then?'

'More an affair of the spine.'

'And not a tale of love?'

'Some might say it was. But really, it's about recognition.'

'Is there a difference? Tell me something more.'

He didn't know. That would teach him to laugh at her for thinking Italy was nothing but churches and museums. 'Everything's the wrong way round. It should have been in winter, not summer. I should have been in the yard and you in the kitchen, and I should have been male and you female, perhaps.'

'Such is life in the Antipodes.'

And I have broken through the window to lean against you and come away unharmed, she thought but didn't tell him so.

'You said male and female, not man and woman. Am I right in assuming the story's not about people?'

'No, they're not nearly interesting enough.'

'Animals, then.'

'There was a dog who had something to say.'

'Draw me a picture.'

'That'd make it too easy for you.'

He asked no more questions, but she could see his inability to solve the puzzle was annoying him. 'Perhaps you should run home and ask your friends the mermaids, Mr Fernon.'

'Mermaids have no souls, Miss Macgregor. They recognise nothing, and I'm sorry you are not more like them. You ask too much of me.'

'I ask nothing of you.'

He rose and began to dress with an elaborate air of disbelief.

'Oh!' cried Lily, stung, and kicked at the eiderdown he'd dropped across her feet. 'This is all because for once I know something you don't.'

'And you bore me with your childish games.'

'You started it,' she said, and could have bitten her tongue, for that was how she spoke to Bob. It didn't do for Mr Fernon.

'I don't believe you care for me at all.'

'So what are these?' she asked, brandishing her folder of sketches.

'Proof of your looks, not your liking.'

'Proof of your looks, I'd have thought,' retorted Lily, but knew she'd been caught out. Then what did he expect from her? Declarations of love that he could turn against her, hoping to reduce her to jealousy or tears? Or would he prefer the unkindness he'd spoken of, so that the tears and tantrums could be his? 'And it's you who asks too much of me, so don't expect to see me next Saturday night. I shall be otherwise engaged.'

'What a blessed relief, Miss Macgregor.'

Chapter 11

Bob often telephoned Lily at the hotel, but he never had much to say. He'd slipped on a muddy path and twisted an ankle, his nearest neighbours were a dour lot who kept themselves to themselves, there was a guitar in the house and he was teaching himself to play.

He made occasional visits, and then he and Lily called on the Harraways or squelched about the empty park through drifts of yellow leaves. Because of the shooting season there were many more ducks than usual. They flurried about on the pond and its banks and kept up an irritable quacking. Bob thought he might have heard a bellbird, but the combination of Scotch mist and squabbling ducks made it hard to hear much else at all.

'I think the usual residents have had enough of their visitors,' said Lily.

'I can understand that,' said Bob, still looking around for his bellbird.

'You're a visitor yourself, now.'

'No, I'm not. It's just that I was away for so long. When were we last here?'

'A couple of months ago, with the Harraways.'

'No, I meant just us. I'd forgotten what it's like in winter. In fact, I've forgotten what everything is like without the Harraways.' He went on to speak hopefully of a comedy at the theatre, though the author's name meant nothing to Lily.

'But we should go,' she said. 'Just us.'

'I thought you worked on Saturday nights.'

'Not always,' said Lily.

Bob came for dinner, but late because it was raining and the road was bad. They had to bolt their food, which turned into a competition of sorts over eating fast without making an exhibition of themselves to others in the dining room. There was no time for drinks, and when they ran out to the Buick and she remembered to ask after his ankle, he broke into an exaggerated limp and claimed to be in need of a medicinal whisky.

There were already several motorcars outside the theatre, and Bob asked if she would mind waiting alone in the foyer while he parked further up the street. Lily said she didn't mind at all, but as she stepped out of the car she knew that Mr Fernon was in there and it would be impossible to avoid him. The conviction was so strong she faltered on the pavement.

'What's wrong?' called Bob.

'Pins and needles,' Lily called back, and went on.

He was there; he might have been waiting for her. He came towards her through the crowd. 'Miss Macgregor,' he said. 'So lovely, and alone.'

'It's what I prefer, Mr Fernon.'

'Then I see you're not yourself tonight.'

Lily looked behind her. Bob had come in, and was greeting some friends. The girl with white hair appeared at Mr Fernon's side. She didn't acknowledge Lily, but caught at his arm and made reproachful eyes at him.

'Have you met my fiancée?' he asked of the air above their heads.

Well, then. She could play that game as well as he. Bob's voice was coming nearer; there was just time. 'Please accept my congratulations,' she said. 'Have you bought her rubies?'

'Hardly necessary in this instance, Miss Macgregor. A couple of gins and a squeeze of the tits should do the trick.'

The girl continued clinging to his arm with her face averted and a certain rigidity of manner, as if she didn't understand her part in this charade but was determined not to be deprived of it.

Bob smiled on her, and she ignored him even more pointedly. Mr Fernon did not proceed with the introductions.

'I think it's time to go in,' said Bob, as though nothing were amiss. And then, 'Did you know that girl?'

'No,' said Lily. 'Do you?'

'I should say not. I may be lonely, I'm not desperate.'

'Bob!'

'Well. She's not even common enough to be amusing. But I suppose I have to admire his cheek, turning up here with something like that.'

'Perhaps she felt a little out of her depth,' said Lily, then remembered Bob didn't know the joke about mermaids.

'Certainly, and even as we speak she's trotting back home to her mother.'

'She might be in love with him.'

This too was lost on Bob. 'Do I detect a hitherto unsuspected streak of sentimentality in your make-up?'

'If there are streaks in my make-up they were put there by the rain.'

'Every time I see him he's with a different woman. Though I notice he never picks a prettier face than his own.'

'He might find that rather difficult.'

Something of the surprise she felt must have sounded in her voice, for Bob opened his programme and hung his head over it. Yet he was right. It was impossible to imagine Mr Fernon with a splendid piece like Miss Ruby Ellis, more elephants than you could spit at, sweeping into Stella Morton's hall like a conquering hero.

'So you like his looks?' persisted Bob.

'I've never really thought about them. Yes, I suppose I do. Most women would.'

'I thought women didn't care about looks in a man.'

'A lot of men like to think that. You've no need to.'

'What do you mean?'

'Stop fishing for compliments. Don't you ever look in the mirror?'

'I'd rather look at you.'

The curtains were parting. 'You've paid to watch the play,' said Lily, and hoped they wouldn't see Mr Fernon as they left the theatre. Bob would want to make up for his little burst of spite by offering a lift, and Mr Fernon would make the most of that opportunity, while she'd be scarcely able to defend herself with Bob beside her.

She wondered where the girl lived. In a narrow little house in an ordinary street, very likely, with her father and mother and several brothers and sisters as well. No doubt she worked somewhere – in a bar perhaps, or the sort of shop where her hair wouldn't matter – and took her wages home. Her parents would be proud of her, and of the life they perceived to be hers. They'd have got used to her hair and fringed shawls, just as Lily's grandmother once had to her collars and ties. That girl might draw well too, or write poems and things, or even have some theatrical ambitions.

All the same, she should have known better than to snub Bob and let Mr Fernon see he was upsetting her.

Would he take her to his room? He had no reason not to. Unless, of course, she knew how things might be between him and Stella Morton. Lily pictured them crossing the slippery courtyard, the front door opening on the downstairs smell of patchouli and Turkish cigarettes which no amount of airing would dispel, the girl's clothes on the armchair where her own had hung. That particular scene caused her no pain; images of him with other women numbed her. The sickly appearance of their powdered faces and the flabby monotony of their flesh so deadened her senses that, by a strange reversal, what he did in that way to slight her merely strengthened her against him. When the time came for them to part she'd be glad of that.

'Let's rush off,' she said afterwards, 'or we might have to talk to Mr Fernon and his lady-friend.'

Bob seemed happy enough to do so, but outside there was a downpour.

'I'll run to your motorcar with you. I don't want to wait alone and unprotected in the foyer again.'

'Here, take my hand,' he said as they prepared to plunge into the street. 'No, on second thoughts, don't. A hand that's signed the pledge shall never hold mine.'

The things he remembered. 'I didn't really sign the pledge,' called Lily, splashing after him. 'I made that up to impress you.'

'Then don't disillusion me now.'

But once in the Buick he seemed incapable of dragging his thoughts away from Mr Fernon. She and Bob had been seated in the stalls, and during the interval Bob had spotted Mr Fernon in a box and been unable to identify his companions. Bob hated not knowing who people were. He said, 'Well, I hope they admired the little charmer on his arm.' And, 'He's a masterpiece of self-parody.'

Then he sighed. 'I must be turning sour with age. People talk about the value of first impressions, but I remember deciding as a kid that whenever we take an instant dislike to somebody it's usually an indication of what's wrong with us rather than with them — snobbery, or envy, or just not being able to accept anyone who's different from ourselves. So it's worth taking the trouble to get to know them; you might be in for a pleasant surprise.'

'I'm sure you're right,' said Lily, for he sounded almost embarrassed by his youthful tolerance. 'Did you take an instant dislike to Mr Fernon?'

'Not dislike,' said Bob hastily, 'that's far too strong a word. But there's something about him that bothers me. He's so . . .' They were at the hotel, and he stopped the motorcar. 'Irresponsible, somehow. And he seems to go out of his way to appeal to all our prejudices, including his lady-friend's. I could see she didn't think much of us. I wasn't rude to her, was I?'

'Not at all. I thought she was rude to you. Are you coming in for that medicinal whisky?'

'Wait,' he said. 'There's something I've been wanting to ask you.'

'Ask me inside.'

'No. If I don't do it now I never will.' He hesitated. 'Promise me you won't be shocked or upset?'

'Cross my heart and hope to die,' said Lily, as carelessly as she was able.

'Have you never wondered who your real father was?'

She laughed.

Bob looked surprised, but pressed on. 'Did you ever think it might have been your uncle?'

'My uncle? He shot himself before I was born.'

'Maybe not before you were conceived.'

'No, the colouring's wrong,' cried Lily gaily. 'My mother had fair hair and blue eyes and I've an idea he did too.'

Bob was unconvinced.

'Perhaps the man my mother married is my real father. He has ginger whiskers.'

'Why don't you ask him?' He was looking directly into her eyes, a thing that always made her uncomfortable.

'Why should I, after twenty-five years of behaving as if he were? I'd find it easier to ask my grandmother's hall table.'

Bob smiled, but not at her. He seemed to think he'd uncovered something she'd far rather have kept hidden. That was maddening.

'Listen. My mother ran away when she was thirteen or fourteen. She went south and worked in hotels, then she came home and had me. Later she married the unfortunate Mr Macgregor and took me to live with them. She ran off again, and he sent me back to the farm, but I kept his surname and when he got a hotel here I used to visit him. Now I work for him. That's all I know, and all I care to know. He might know where my mother is, but we never speak of her and only she could tell you who my real father was. I know it's a very dull story, but life is dull. It's only fools like you and my mother who think it can be made more interesting by dashing about here, there and everywhere.'

She had never spoken to Bob in quite that way before.

'I'm sorry,' he said. 'I didn't mean to upset you.'

'You don't upset me, you annoy me. There's a difference. Are you coming in for that drink or not?'

'Perhaps I'd better not,' he said, but did.

They took their whiskies to the empty guest lounge. There were two sofas at right angles to the fire and they might have had one each, but Bob sat beside her. He spoke of the inland weather. 'The other day I saw a mouse scurrying along on top of the snow. I couldn't think where it had come from, or where it could go, and then a hawk came out of the sky and took it.'

'Poor little thing.'

'I suppose the hawk was hungry.'

'They would both've been hungry, but the odds were all with the hawk.'

'Next time I see it I'll shoot it.'

'Don't do that.'

'It'll be after the lambs soon enough.'

'Wait till then.'

'If I wait, it might have young of its own. They'd starve.'

A young couple entered the lounge. Bob and Lily looked welcoming, but they made for a window seat and pulled back the curtain to see the ships at anchor in the bay. One of the maids brought in a tray with glasses and champagne, and winked at Lily as she passed.

The young man asked, 'What shall we drink to?' and the girl replied, 'To us.' They clinked glasses timidly. 'To us.'

'They were at the theatre,' mouthed Bob.

'I thought it'd be sweeter,' said the girl. 'I'm not sure I like it.'

'Well, it's on our bill now. Drink up.'

'Do you think he's bought the fizz so he can have his way with her?' whispered Bob.

'They've been here for a few days.'

'Oh, my dear, I do hope they're married.'

'If they are, it's only just. They're so polite to each other.'

'They might be foreign spies.'

'Nige could put them in his book.'

'You know,' said Bob in a normal tone, 'I can't for the life of me work out if it was the Oak or the Albion your father had last time he was here. They're almost side by side and they look so alike.'

'It was the Albion.' And because he still seemed subdued, she added, 'That's where you came to stay.'

'Your father was surprised to see me.'

'When he said to bring a friend, I think he meant a girl.'

'The place was full. I had to have your room.'

'And I had to share with one of the maids. An admirer came and whistled at the window and got told to bugger off.'

'Women can be so very cruel.'

'I thought it was because of me but she said no, he was a halfwit.'

'You win a bet, they never pay.'

'You cheated. But if you come to town next Saturday I'll treat you to some cinematographic revelations. And a bag of frosted caramels, of course.'

'Twice,' he said.

'That'll cost more than half a crown.'

'I stayed there twice.'

'Did you?'

'Yes. That summer I left school, and then a couple of years later in the autumn. You didn't like my moustache.'

Now she remembered too. He had come into the bar and she'd pretended not to know him. 'But don't you think it makes me look older, wiser, altogether more mature?' he'd asked.

She had thought it made him look as though he were stifling a belch, but tried to sound refined. 'I think it makes you look dypseptic.'

'Dypseptic! Now why didn't I see that? Oh, my dear, I should die, utterly die, if word were to get about that I was dypseptic.'

All the same, when he came down next morning the moustache was gone, and she felt a twinge of guilt because he'd been so proud of it.

Bob asked, 'Was that the last time we saw each other?'

She didn't say they'd seen each other in the park just a week ago, because they'd gone to the park then and he'd asked if she could tell him how long it took two men to dig that ditch.

'Let me picture it,' she'd said, closing her eyes. 'They're digging now. Oh Bob, something terrible is happening. One man just called to the other, "How is it that we've been digging this ditch all these years without a drink or a smoke or a bite to eat and Bob Graham on our backs day in and day out and you've never said a word to me?" And he's hit him with his shovel and killed him dead. Now he's pushed him into the hole and he's tramping down the earth on him. Oh, Bob, I fear that ditch'll never be digged.'

That was when he'd put both arms around her and his tongue into her mouth and she laughed and he stalked away, indignation in every lean line of him. By the time she got back to the hotel he'd packed and gone. Not long after, she and her father moved to Christchurch, and Bob never came to see her there. Which was just as well, because he wouldn't have liked the artistic friends she'd made. She hadn't liked them much herself, but that didn't bother her the way it would have bothered Bob.

And then she heard he was engaged to be married, and imagined him with his hair plastered down in some dim Dunedin parlour, accepting cups of tea from well-spoken women who could scarcely have known him, who'd never seen him sliding down the stairs on a tea tray or listened to him boast of all the different birds he'd spotted in one day. Her butterfly had been caught and pinned in his glass case, but it didn't make him happy.

She was sorry that she'd not more patience with him.

'Dypseptic,' said Bob reflectively.

'That was a test for foreign spies.'

'Did I pass?' His arm lay along the back of the sofa.

Sleety rain splattered against the windows, but the air around her was hot and still.

The other couple were preparing to leave. 'What shall we do with the bottle and glasses?' whispered the girl, and the young man said, 'Just leave them there.'

They murmured goodnight as they passed.

'Do you stay here often?' asked Bob.

They exchanged smiles as if daring each other to speak, then chorused shyly, 'We're on our honeymoon.'

Lily and Bob made sounds of pleasure and congratulation.

'But awful weather for a honeymoon,' said Bob sympathetically.

'It's the easiest time of year to get away,' said the young man.

'And we don't mind the weather,' said his wife. 'It's just so nice to be waited on.' She added in a burst of confidence, 'They even turn the bed down for you.' Then both went pink, repeated their goodnights, and fled.

'Told you,' said Lily, leaping up and flinging herself down on the sofa opposite. 'Did we have a bet on it?'

'Not that I recall.'

'Where did you go for your honeymoon?'

'When?'

The things he remembered, the things he chose to forget. 'When you were married, of course.' Still, she wished she hadn't asked.

'Oh, we didn't. We decided to go later, to Europe. Though we never did.' He took out his cigarette case and put a cigarette between his lips, but made no move to light it. After a moment he rose and tossed it into the fire. He seemed about to leave, then leaned against the mantelpiece and stared down into the coals.

Lily thought of him driving back to the farm over dark and slushy roads. The hotel was less than half full, and the ordinary thing would be to offer him a bed for the night, but a bed was not quite what he wanted. He wanted to spend the night with her, and he'd be incapable of suggesting that.

But she could, quite easily now. She could say: Stay here with me tonight, I'll even turn the bed down for you. And if he looked surprised at that, she'd add: Well, if you'd rather, I'll whistle at your window so you can tell me to bugger off.

It would be awkward and embarrassing at first, but it wouldn't matter if she laughed because surely Bob would too. And it would please everybody, even Mr Fernon. It was what they all expected of her.

By now the newlyweds would be snug in their room with the rain against the window. To stay in a hotel with someone, to dress for the theatre and drink champagne with him, to go upstairs to bed with him, and come down to breakfast with him, to walk with him, talk with him, eat with him and sleep with him, *this night, every night, each night and all* — the words thudded in her head, a half-remembered rhyme chanted at school — something something *candlelight and Christ preserve my soul.*

Never again to know the pleasure of her own company or the excitement of a stranger's. Never to lie in the dark straining to hear a soft footfall on the verandah, or to stand on a crackling night beneath a lighted window, daring herself to go in. Never to rise before dawn and dress and walk away, her own self again but with another's taste and smell in and all about her.

There was a tightening in her chest she hadn't felt in ages, and she put her hand to her throat. I would suffocate, she thought, I'd die.

Bob said, 'What is it you're afraid of?' His voice was low and urgent. 'I won't hurt you, I'll be careful. I wouldn't do anything to hurt you.'

'Afraid?' she said, pretending she'd only half-heard him. 'I'm not afraid of anything. What should I be afraid of?'

He didn't answer.

She began to ask him things: how much longer was he to manage the farm, and would he go home for the summer? Had he ever sorted out his belongings there as he'd said he would?

To her ears, her voice sounded strained and artificial, and Bob's answers were limited to two or three muttered words.

'And when are you going to be a lawyer again?'

'I'm not.'

Lily was surprised, and said nothing.

Bob read disapproval into her silence. 'I've seen enough mortgages to last me a lifetime. I wasn't cut out to be a lawyer — that was something else I got wrong.' Then he added in a dull, tight voice, 'Why all the questions?' and she felt a rush of fury at his tone. They'd had such fun together and he'd spoilt it, and here he was spoiling things again, as if there weren't dozens of women who would like nothing better than to have Bob Graham dancing attendance on them.

'Why not? You ask me questions all the time. I was wondering what you were going to do next, that's all.'

'I haven't decided,' he said unpleasantly. 'Though when I do you'll be the first to know. Thank you for the whisky. I can find my own way out.'

But she rose and trailed after him, hoping aloud that the road wouldn't be too bad and belatedly praising the play.

Chapter 12

There could now be no doubt that Ruby's was an interesting condition. She lay on the sofa before a blazing fire, wrapped in her motoring coat and complaining of the weather.

'Bracing, Nige calls it. I call it bloody freezing.' Nigel liked to sleep with the window open and their landlady's cat came in and climbed all over her. 'Mind you, that's the only thing that seems to want to nowadays. Isn't that right, Nige?'

Nigel had been busy finishing his column, and said he was going out to send it.

'Why can't you write something like *The Blue Lagoon* and make some real money?'

'Because I know what it is to live in a South Seas paradise, and there are limits to my powers of invention,' retorted Nigel, disappearing through the door.

Ruby rolled her eyes at Lily.

'Have you thought what you'll do when the baby comes?'

'Cathy Kelly's here. Mrs Kelly doesn't trust hirelings in these matters, so I've Cathy to advise me on the proper care of the newborn.'

'Cathy? Here?'

'Yes, she's out somewhere with Joss. You only just missed them.'

'I don't think her parents would approve of that.'

'She's a kid — he wouldn't be interested in her. She said to me, "I've got no figure." "Chin up," I said. "Till I was eighteen I was as flat as a Hobart Town paling, and look at me now!"' Ruby laid a sorrowful hand on her belly. 'Well, don't look now, but you know what I mean.'

'She is eighteen.'

'Is she really? High time she learnt to look after herself then. I had my first engagement at eighteen, did I tell you? There stood I in the chorus, ninon over none-on, with all the dinner-jackets in the stalls waving their programmes at me. Varsity chaps out on the rantan. Wave away, boys, I thought. My mother knows what I'm doing, does yours? Most of them were harmless.'

'I'm sure Cathy's mother doesn't know what she's doing. She wouldn't like it one little bit. I'm surprised they let her come, knowing he's still here.'

'Perhaps they don't know he's here. Perhaps someone, namely you, forgot to tell them.'

'Why would I tell them?'

'You're the one who thinks they ought to know.' Ruby began to buff fingernails that already shone like glass. 'I'll have a word with her,' she said sulkily, 'but she probably won't take any notice of me. No one else round here ever does.'

The front door banged. It was Nigel, sounding cheerful. 'Guess who I found loitering in the street?'

'Bob!' called Ruby.

'Ruby!' cried Bob, but then saw Lily and looked sad.

'I'm not staying long,' she said. 'I have to go back to work.'

'I can't stay long either,' he said to Ruby. 'I brought Jean into town and she'll call here for me when she's ready to go home.' He finished telling Nigel about a near accident at the farm with a new chum and a horse who was a kicker, and managed a smile for Lily. 'It reminded me of the time we wanted to cut a dash, and put that lovely new mare in the gig.'

'When was that?' asked Ruby.

'Years ago,' said Lily.

'I still want to hear about it. Take no notice of her, Bob — she got out of bed on the wrong side this morning.'

But Bob stood looking as if they were indeed a double act and he couldn't say his piece without her.

Lily gave in. 'You wanted to cut a dash. It was nothing to do with me.'

'I beg to differ. You said, "Put the damn thing in and see what happens."'

Ruby chortled.

'I'm sure I said darn. And I only said that because I could see how much you wanted to.'

'You said damn, and it thrilled me to the core. I thought, Ooh, how modern.'

'And what happened?' asked Ruby.

'She kicked the bottom out of the gig. My father was furious. "I'll pay for it," I squeaked. "You will," he said, "I'll take it out of your hide." I forget how many acres we ploughed that spring, but I had to walk behind the harrow day after day. My feet were covered in blisters and my legs felt like india-rubber, though I wasn't going to let him see I was suffering. The harrowing of hell, that was. And I had no sympathy from Lily.'

'I didn't see you for a while.'

'True. I was in bed and asleep by eight-thirty every night.' But it had left him in good shape for cricket and football.

'Rugger,' said Nigel happily. 'Where did you play?'

'At school,' said Lily. 'And at the university.'

'Three-quarter,' said Bob in a voice resonant with pity. 'Or sometimes centre.'

'Lily's was a good try,' chirped Ruby. She couldn't imagine why anyone would want to play rugby: the ball was wrong, for one thing. It bounced funny, and there was no point in making anything more difficult than it need be. Lily supported her because she knew Bob and Nigel enjoyed such feminine inanity, but it felt wrong. This game belonged to picnics on the beach or croquet on the Grahams' lawn, and the time for it was gone.

Jean came in, bright-faced from the cold, and exclaimed at the warmth of the room.

'Don't start taking things off,' said Bob. 'We're going now.'

'But you've time for a drink,' cried Ruby. 'We've some fizz in the meat-safe — I should've thought of it sooner. Lily, do you mind? I'd get it myself, but I've got these ankles. Nige, run and see if you can coax some glasses out of the old bat. Otherwise we'll make do with teacups.'

'Oh, what a treat,' said Jean, taking the bottle to examine the label. 'Who's going to open it? Shall I?'

'Here, I will,' said Bob. 'Stop waving it about like that. It'll squirt everywhere.'

'Hold it tight around the neck, and when you've eased —' began Lily.

'I wasn't brought up to pour drinks,' smiled Jean, handing the bottle to Bob.

'Would you care for a cigarette, Mrs Harraway?' called Ruby. 'Thanks, Mr Graham, don't mind if I do.'

'Sorry,' said Bob, putting down the bottle to take out his cigarette case, so Lily filled the glasses. They drank to coming events, Jean sipping her champagne with an air that suggested there might be good news in the offing for Mrs Graham. When she and Bob left Nigel went out too, this time to buy newspapers.

Ruby struck up as soon as the door had closed behind them. 'My God, Bob's the jewel in that family's crown, isn't he? Did you hear her? "I wasn't brought up to pour drinks." And what were you brought up to do, if you don't mind my asking? Other than act like Lady Muck, I mean. I nearly said it, it was on the tip of my tongue, but I didn't want to upset Bob. Nige wouldn't have liked it either. He says women like that can't help themselves.'

'She said it to Bob.'

'She meant it for you. I hate her sort. You walk away from them with a smile on your face and it's not until you're halfway home that you realise you've been insulted. I wish I had said it now. Men don't do that sort of thing to each other.'

'Oh, don't they!'

'Not unless they want a black eye they don't. Nige'd whack another bloke if he wanted to, but he's daft about women so I'm expected to be a bloody saint where they're concerned. I don't think much of Connie Graham, either. We saw her once with Bob. "You haven't met my sister Constance, have you?" he said. "How do you do, Miss Graham," I said, because I knew she wasn't married, it must've been something Bob had said. "*Doctor* Graham," she said. You never told me she was a doctor.'

'I told you she was clever.'

'You said she opened the door to you and her mother didn't like it, that's all you told me.' Ruby sat drumming her fingers on the arm of the sofa. 'You ought to stick up for yourself more.'

'I do stick up for myself.'

'No you don't, you let people walk all over you.'

'I never do anything I don't want to. Not really.'

'Says you. Well, make sure you get something decent out of Joss before he buggers off. Then you can marry Bob and settle down.'

So Ruby knew. Of course she did; she'd have known all along. Still, Lily could not look at her. 'How much should I ask Joss' — his name caught on her lips — 'Josselin for?'

'You can't ask for money, you never ask for *money*.'

'I've heard you ask Nigel for money often enough.'

'That's different, we're married, and a fair swag of it's mine. Tell Joss you're sick of having to make all your clothes. He'll know what you mean. Say how cold the winters are, and how you wish you had some furs. Next time he goes to Christchurch, you go with him. Take him shopping. If in doubt, try for pearls.'

The thought of shopping with Mr Fernon was laughable. They'd collide in doorways, they'd trip on the stairs. She wouldn't know what to say to him, or what he might say to the shopgirls. 'We don't go anywhere together.'

'Whose idea was that?'

'It's what we both prefer.' It was what she preferred, anyway, and Mr Fernon never seemed to expect anything different.

'Be a bit nicer to him.'

'I am nice to him.'

'He says the only time you're nice to him is when you're drawing him, and then you never show him what you've done.'

Lily felt her face change, and drew a careful breath. 'He did offer to buy me a frock once, and a ring. But I'd rather have the money. I could do things with it.' She'd have been content with a measure of gentlemanly discretion, but it was too late to hope for that.

'There you are then. Just think of a way to get it without asking. And I trust you're being careful.'

'Careful? I'm always careful.' It was Mr Fernon who'd been careless. 'What should I be careful about?'

'Jesus, don't you know anything? Do you want to finish up like me?'

In that respect Mr Fernon was careful, most times. She liked the feel of it, the little rush of warm fluid on her belly or between her thighs. 'That's different, you're married.'

'Oh, very clever. Then you've nothing to worry about, because there's no chance Joss'd ever marry you. Blokes like him are happy to muck about with girls like you, but they always marry their own kind.'

'What kind's that?' asked Lily, diverted by the thought of a female Mr Fernon: a melancholy temptress fit for frightening wayward boys.

'Look, the only person who cares about you is Bob, and the sooner you get that into your head the better.' Then Nigel came in with his papers, and Ruby changed the subject rather neatly. 'I never knew Bob'd been married,' she said.

Mr Fernon must have told her that too. 'His wife died a couple of years ago.'

'They can't have been married long.'

'They weren't. A year at most.'

'What did she die of?'

'I don't know.'

'Was she already ill when he married her?' Ruby's tone was sentimental.

'Oh no,' said Lily, and laughed.

'What's so funny?'

Nigel said, 'Somehow I can't see Bob sauntering down the

aisle with a moribund beauty.'

A moribund beauty. It sounded like a blighted rose. 'No,' said Lily, 'that's not the sort of thing he'd do.'

Ruby was peeved. 'Why didn't he marry you?'

'It wasn't like that.'

'Would you marry him now?'

'No, of course not.'

'What do you mean, of course not? He's in love with you.'

Love. Ruby should know better. This constant clamour about love from grown men and women was infantile. 'Well, I'm not in love with him.'

'You're different when you're with him.'

Ruby was a fine one to talk. Everyone was different in that way, including Mr Fernon. He went about with Nigel, and with Stella Morton's nieces; he gossiped with Ruby and he'd played tennis with Bob; he'd loaned books to Mr Kelly and mocked his eagerness to learn from them. He'd even slapped her on the backside and offered her a gin. He was different all the time. Too different. 'I've known Bob for ages, that's all.'

'You're always talking about him.'

'That's because you're always asking about him.'

'Well, I think he's gorgeous.'

'So does he,' said Lily, then felt disloyal.

'Lily is of the opinion that there are few who would have fallen in love if they'd never heard of it,' said Nigel from behind his newspaper.

'Oh, I am, I am!' cried Lily. 'How did you know that?' She hadn't known it herself, but it made perfect sense.

Nigel put his paper aside. He'd felt her gratitude; his cheeks were red. 'I'm not without a modicum of intelligence.'

'You've got a very funny side to you, Lily, if you don't mind my saying so.'

Lily supposed Ruby's nose was out of joint because Nigel had taken her part and blushed, and he'd probably done that only because Ruby thought Bob gorgeous. People were squalid, that's what they were. She was glad that now Ruby was staying indoors she wouldn't have to see so much of her. And when the Harraways went north Mr Fernon might go with them. Perhaps Bob would too. That would solve all her problems.

'Now what's so funny?' asked Ruby.

My side, thought Lily, but said, 'I just had an idea. I might go away next summer to Australia. I could work in hotels, or as a housekeeper on a farm.'

'You'll need money for the fare,' said Ruby slyly.

Lily went to Stella Morton's to speak severely to Mr Fernon, which also led to a quarrel of sorts. Because of the righteous nature of her business with him she went at an earlier hour than usual, and even though the door was unlocked she rang the bell. The maid showed her to the room where they'd sat on her first night there. It didn't look so grand under electric light. The curtains were faded, and the armchairs had the furtive air that comes of being too much sat upon by strangers. Mr Fernon was alone, reading by the fire. He pushed back his hair and looked up at her with a smile so appealing her heart sank.

'I want to talk to you.'

'And can you not curb this unnatural appetite? No, I see you can't. Some people may come in, so we'd best go upstairs.'

Lily spoke of Cathy Kelly. Mr Fernon pretended not to understand, then succeeded in making her feel quaint and old maidish.

'You flatter me, Miss Macgregor. You always do. All Miss Kelly sees in me is a sympathetic audience. You do not dream of a husband, house or children; neither does she. Indeed, she can scarcely remember a time when she didn't have the sticky hand of a little brother or sister clinging to hers. The tenderest joys of hearth and home which every proper young woman craves have been hers from infancy. Give her a plump little bunny, shot through the head: she will clean it and bone it and cook it to perfection. Show her an open wound and she'll dress it, point out a pool of vomit and she'll mop it up. And she finds it all very boring.'

That he should listen patiently while Cathy poured out her tale of youthful woe was so improbable Lily couldn't picture it. Yet even as she told him this, she found she could, and fell silent.

'When her mother was only a little older than Miss Kelly is now she set out alone for the other side of the world, knowing there'd be no going back if things weren't to her liking. Miss Kelly would like to do — well, not the same thing, but something. She longs for the liberty you regard as yours of right, Miss Macgregor.'

As if she hadn't spent her life in places earned by her ability to clean and cook and sew, serve drinks, amuse, and threaten no one's interest. 'You know nothing about me. Or what I've had to do to earn what you call my liberty.'

'Come now, Miss Macgregor, I think we know each other very well.' He stood before her and began unfastening her jacket.

She pulled away from him. 'I'm sure if Cathy wanted to stay and find work here nobody would say she couldn't. They just wouldn't want her going about with you, that's all.'

'They, Miss Macgregor? And who are they? More malevolent Irish fairies? Or can it be that you are jealous?'

Lily felt suddenly tired, and sat down on his bed. Was she jealous? And if so, why? Because it seemed he might be capable of kindness after all, though not to her?

'My dear, you look bemused.' Taking her face between his hands, he kissed her forehead. 'What a poor opinion you must have of me.' He pushed her gently back onto the bed. Her hat squashed sideways over one eye, but he held her there. 'Do you think I've failed to notice what a hard-working little soul you are? Trotting to and fro with Mrs Kelly's mending, presiding over breakfasts at, what was it, six in the morning? Drifting through the dining room with a word here and a smile there until you have me wondering just how many of us you've agreed to entertain in your room at a later hour?'

He caught her wrists in one hand, which gave him the advantage of having the other free, and pinned her arms above her head. The fabric of her blouse was straining against her upper arms, and a couple of stitches gave. She protested, but half-heartedly.

In another moment he would see how silly they were being, and stop.

Mr Fernon smiled down on her. 'For who would ever know what goes on behind those candid eyes? And who could possibly guess at what that pretty mouth can achieve? Oh, poor Euphemia, my unclaimed treasure.' He released her wrists, and as she twisted away she heard her blouse tear. Though old and worn thin, it had looked good and she was fond of it. She lost all patience then and made to rise, but he caught at her again. 'I'll kiss one work-weary little hand, shall I? Now, which is it be?'

There was a sharp sound, and her palm stung. Mr Fernon looked surprised, then laughed.

Her hands flew to her own face. 'I'm sorry,' she said. 'I'm so sorry.'

Putting two fingers in his mouth, he felt inside his cheek. When he brought his hand away there was a tinge of blood on his forefinger, and he went to the tallboy to inspect the damage in its mirror. 'My lower lip is cut against my teeth, but I don't think I shall have a bruise. What a pity. That's a very swift right you have there. Have you been taking lessons from Miss Kelly's famous uncle?'

'I'm sorry,' Lily repeated. 'I'll go.'

'No, Miss Macgregor, you must stay and make it better. There is something eminently kissable about a bleeding lip, don't you think?'

'Or a disfigured mouth,' she said.

'You are right, Miss Macgregor. You have been right about everything. Well, almost everything. You missed a C in acquaintance, and there is an E in the middle of Josselin.'

'Then it's best that I should go.'

'Because you misspelt my name?'

'You know very well why.'

'Ah. I must confess I found your late regard for the finer feelings of my landlady odd, to say the least.'

'I didn't come here to talk about her.'

'Oh, did you not? Stella is only too happy to talk about you.

She asks after you quite often.'

And what did he say on those occasions? Whatever would cause pain, of course.

He smiled. 'Even you must see that to the untutored eye you have much she lacks.'

He'd become the prize in a game where only he knew all the rules. 'I'm going,' said Lily hopelessly. 'Things used to be all right between us and now they're not, and I don't understand why.'

But that was a false note, petulant and dull. Things had never been all right between them. There'd always been mistrust and mockery, hints of cruelty, the risk of discovery and shame. Once she had enjoyed it; now it was beginning to weaken and worry her. 'I don't know what it is you want, that's all,' she said, and shrugged to signal nonchalance.

'I don't want you to go. I don't want you to leave me.' There'd been another lightning change of mood: his eyes were tragic, and there was a note of panic in his voice. It might have been he who'd hit her. She had the sudden presentiment that if she were to turn away he'd clutch at her, pleading; this was followed by an equally absurd vision of herself beating at him with both fists as she struggled to the door.

To stay seemed much more sensible. 'If you really don't want me to leave, then of course I won't. It's not as if I've anything planned for tonight.'

He sent her a savage look, and she knew that round at least was hers. However much he might talk of being rid of her, he wanted her to be the one to end it, the one who'd be to blame. She could deny him that at least, and find a perverse pleasure there.

When he went to the washstand to mix his customary nightcap, he was still in a sour mood. 'One of these days I shall take enough of this to kill myself,' he said, holding up the glass to admire its contents.

'See if I care,' said Lily, but took the glass to gulp a bitter mouthful as he got into bed.

He pulled at the covers and turned his back on her.

Lily dozed fitfully. The sounds of doors and voices disturbed her, seeming to come from just beside her pillow. She woke in fright, then decided she couldn't be awake, she must be dreaming, for there were people moving in slow procession through the room.

It's the dead, she thought, the thankful dead, sheltering from the rain. She tried to move to escape that thought and the shuffle of their feet on the floor, but her head was heavy and her limbs full of chaff, like a cheap doll's.

Mr Fernon's arm fell across her. 'I'm overtired,' she said, 'and I must either go to sleep, or wake up properly. I'll wake Mr Fernon and ask him to wake me.'

She put her hand on his shoulder and felt worn corduroy, a fabric she'd never known him wear. He was walking away from her with the unhurried stride of a farm boy, his hair lifting slightly on the breeze. Her own legs would scarcely move; she went down on her hands and knees to crawl after him. There were horses approaching and she knew they'd avoid her, but she was afraid of the motorcars. She watched their distant headlamps, hoping the drivers would see her kneeling on the road.

Then it was broad daylight and the farm was parched and brown. She took the copper-stick from the wash house, rapped the tank to hear if it held enough water for washing, and went in to the tub. The tap water looked rusty. Telling herself it would soon clear, she dropped an armful of shirts into the tub. The tap ran red and spattered her white skirt and blouse. There were dead and dying maggots among the clothes; they stuck to her arms, and then to her hands when she tried to brush them off. She wanted to wail with fear and disgust, but sought and found the steel within. The pipes were rusted, and something had got into the tank and died — a rat or bird, no more than that. All she had to do was lift the washing from the tub.

Through the wash house window she saw Bob coming towards her, and knew he wouldn't fail to see the blood and maggots; he'd take pleasure in pointing them out to her and hearing her attempt to explain.

'Are you still here?' asked Mr Fernon. 'Do you know, for a moment before I opened my eyes I hoped you were Miss Kelly?'

'Don't be so stupid,' said Lily, and wondered why she'd thought he would save her from her dreams.

When Lily took the baby clothes she'd made to the Harraways, it was Cathy who opened the door. 'Oh, it's you,' she said.

'Whom did you expect? I've brought some things for Ruby.'

'Keep your voice down. She's asleep.'

Lily's voice was never loud, nor did she think it likely an expectant mother would be aggrieved at being woken by a visitor bringing baby clothes. 'Then is Nigel here?'

Cathy shook her head. 'He found a stray dog yesterday, and he's out looking for its owner.'

'Good, because I want a word with you.'

'What about?' Cathy looked sullen and mistrustful, as well she might, but she stood aside to let Lily enter.

'Why are you seeing Mr Fernon?'

'I might ask the same of you.'

'Does your father know what you're up to?'

'Does yours? And I don't mean Mr Macgregor.'

Lily felt tempted to slap her too.

Cathy knew she'd overreached herself. 'As I've already told Ruby, we went for a walk along the beach, and had afternoon tea.'

'Where?'

'At the tearooms. Where else?'

'Then what?'

'Well, if you must know, a bandy-legged little Irishman stopped us in the street and asked me if I was Frank Kelly's niece. He said he'd been out to see Scatty, and while he was waiting for the train home he felt thirsty and went into the Grand. He bought a glass of raspberry because he daren't touch the hard stuff, he hasn't had a drop in years, and a big ugly fellow started laughing at him for an Irishman who didn't drink and tried to pick a fight with him, calling him a wowser and asking him outside. Then Uncle

Frank came up and said that if there was any fighting to be done he was the one to do it, and he'd be only too happy to meet the fellow outside. And so the little man stood there shaking my hand and saying it was an honour to make my acquaintance.'

'There's glory for you,' said Ruby, who'd appeared in the doorway. She shot a mocking look at Lily, then sat down on the sofa to unwrap the parcel of clothes.

Miss Kelly's famous uncle. Lily felt foolish, but not wrong. Mr Fernon's motives hadn't been innocent, and neither were Cathy's. There was an obstinacy in her down-dropped eyelids and the angle of her head which suggested that whatever Lily or Ruby might choose to think, she knew differently and better. You are old, said that bent and shining head, you are past it, and you don't know how things are any more.

It was Ruby's turn to pounce. 'Don't you go getting any ideas now,' she said quite cosily.

'What about?' asked Cathy.

'Joss Fernon.'

'I'm not getting ideas, and he was only being friendly. I think he's lonely.'

'Most blokes are when they're fully clad and vertical.'

Cathy looked earnest. 'I don't think he's very happy.'

'Happy? Jesus! Do you see anyone round here who is? I'm not happy, Lily's not happy, and when Nige flounced out this morning he didn't look too bloody happy. Come to think of it, neither did the dog.'

There was a thoughtful silence.

'Well,' continued Ruby, 'it might have been diseased. Here's me ready to drop any day, and he's bringing home stray dogs.'

Lily, rather taken with the idea of Nigel flouncing, would have liked to ask what sort of dog it was, but held her tongue. Ruby had the disconcerting habit of returning to the attack just as you smirked or stretched or otherwise got back to normal. Cathy made the mistake of huffing a little sigh.

'Listen, do you think that all Joss needs is you, wonderful you? Do you think he'll love you, marry you, and take you away to live happy ever after in some exalted pile?'

'Of course not,' said Cathy disdainfully, and Lily knew this was probably true. All the same, Cathy's cheeks were flushed. Ruby had touched a nerve.

'Saved,' Ruby warbled, 'by the love of a good woman.' She cast another glance over the little petticoats and gowns. 'I'm too tired to live so I'm going back to bed, which is the proper place for a bad one. You two can carry on without me. Just remember, if you break anything you have to pay for it. Rules of the house.'

'Satisfied?' asked Cathy of Lily.

'He's using you,' began Lily, then stopped. That dismal night had left her too tired to live as well.

Now Cathy was all ears. 'Using me? What's Joss using me for?'

To humiliate me, thought Lily, as he used me to humiliate Stella Morton and that white-haired girl. She said, 'All you offer Mr Fernon is another way of getting at your father.'

'What do you mean, getting at my father? Why would he want to upset my father?'

'Because that's the way he is.'

'The way he is,' echoed Cathy scornfully.

'Didn't he let Scatty out of his paddock?'

'That was an accident.'

'If you believe that you're even sillier than I think you are.'

'You're jealous,' said Cathy. Her expression was both furtive and triumphant. 'And what do you offer Mr Fernon?'

Contempt, thought Lily, which may be what he most desires. But she saw no need to say so.

Chapter 13

Ruby had a daughter. 'Look at her, just look at her! Isn't she lovely? Don't you wish she was yours?'

'No. I wouldn't mind a train set, though.'

'Ask Joss to buy you one.'

'What's her name?'

'We haven't decided. I liked Cecilia, but Nige said everyone'd call her Cissie. So I said Celia then, but he wouldn't have that. He and Joss know a rhyme about someone called Celia shitting, though Nige says now he's got to know her he thinks it'd do very well. I've had enough of those two. I've done three really good things in my life – I had that standing ovation in my first panto, I threw a brick through the window of a chap what done the dirty on me, and now I've got her. That's all I care about. They didn't think much of Lily for a name either.'

'No, they wouldn't.'

'I expect she'll be Julia after Nige's dear mama, but I'm not giving in too easily. Speaking of mothers, Mrs Graham came to visit me, did I tell you?'

Lily shook her head.

Thrusting out her bosom, Ruby cooed, '"Is your husband pleased?"' and then became herself again. 'Cheek! I said, "Why wouldn't he be?"' She pursed her lips. '"Wouldn't he have preferred the first to be a boy? I think all men do." So I said, "Well, if boys are what they bloody want, boys are what they can bloody marry" — except I left out the bloodies — "and I used to know a few I could've introduced him to, but he didn't seem that way inclined." That shut her up. God, I wish she'd told me that before I met *Doctor* Graham. I could've said: Listen, dearie, if your mother didn't think you worth a damn when you were born, she's not going to change her mind now you're pushing forty, doctor or no.'

'I'm sure you wouldn't have — it might've upset Bob. But I hope you're not expecting to play croquet at the Grahams' again.'

'Oh, isn't Bob allowed to play with naughty girls? That's just the sort who always want to, in my experience. Put the damn thing in and see what happens is all they ever hope to hear. Look, she's smiling!'

'Wind.'

'See the gown she's wearing?' Ruby used its hem to wipe the baby's bubbling mouth. 'Your Auntie Lily made you that. Anyway, we're going to Christchurch next month to visit our friends there. And you'll be pleased to know I've written to ask Mrs Kelly if Cathy can come with us.'

'Why will I be pleased to know?'

'It'll keep her away from Joss. And when you and he can tear yourselves apart you can come and stay.'

'Won't that make your friends' house rather crowded?'

'They won't mind, they've heaps of room, and they'd scarcely expect me to stay there on my own. Nige is going on to Wellington. "Enough of this scribble, scribble, scribble, Mr Harraway," I said. "You've got real responsibilities now." So he wants to see about a job there, and the others might go with him to have a look around. I'll need someone to talk to.'

Bob also wanted someone to talk to, and he was still inclined to talk about Mr Fernon. Lily encountered him in town one drizzly afternoon. As they struggled out of their coats in an overheated teashop she asked what he'd been up to lately, and he mentioned seeing Joss Fernon and the Harraways. His manner conveyed a lack of better company; he looked pale and preoccupied, which made Lily feel guilty and then rather cross. She was about to ask if he were sickening for something when their tea arrived, and he perked up enough to tell of going out to wet the baby's head with Nigel and Mr Fernon, and how very drunk the latter had become.

'Why do I have to hear about it?'

'You asked what I'd been doing. And I thought you liked him.'

'I said I liked his looks, as I recall. I've no interest in his drinking habits. Of course you and Nigel were sipping shandy all night long.'

'No, but we were capable of walking in a moderately straight line. In no time at all he was ready to fall over.' Now Bob was wearing the reflective little smile she was more used to seeing on his sister Jean. 'Some upset with a woman, apparently.'

'Who?' asked Lily. If that was Bob's game, best end it now.

'How should I know? He's probably not too sure himself. One of those little drabs he hangs about with, I suppose.'

'What did he say?'

'Oh, he yammered on about how women don't really like him and never stick with him for long. I was sitting there thinking: I hardly know the chap and he's telling me all this.'

'Try working in a bar.'

'No thanks, too embarrassing. After a bit Nigel managed to shut him up, and I had the distinct impression it was a tale he'd heard many times before.'

'I'm sure he has.'

'What makes you say that?'

'I was agreeing with you, that's all.'

'Wonders'll never cease. But don't you ever wonder about those two?'

'Why?'

Bob looked less comfortable. 'Well, they're very thick.'

'They were friends at school.'

He studied a thumbnail. 'I've some old schoolfriends too, but I don't think I'd take one along on my honeymoon.'

'Nigel didn't take Mr Fernon along — he was already here. They caught up with each other in Dunedin.'

'Yes, I've heard all about Our Exploits in Dunedin. They even managed to find an opium den.'

'That's not difficult.'

'It's a lot more difficult than it used to be.'

'Then I refuse to believe you've never set foot in one.'

'Not since I was at the university I haven't. And then the police came and we had to squeeze through an upstairs window, head first and backwards so as to grab at a tree branch and drop into the alley below. Believe me, there's nothing like seeing the stars from that angle to cure you of a taste for all things celestial.'

Lily would have liked to hear more, but Bob wasn't about to recall a past that did not include her. 'Anyway,' he said, 'by the time we got Fernon home he was practically unconscious. We balked at the prospect of hauling him up the stairs and left him in one of the lower rooms to the tender ministrations of that woman he lives with.'

'Do you mean his landlady?'

'If that's what you'd prefer to call her, then yes, I do. I feel sorry for her.'

'I don't. It's her house, and if she doesn't like the way he acts she should ask him to leave.'

'She might be afraid of him.'

'Why?'

'There was a bruise here.' Bob reached across the table and touched her face just below the corner of her eye. 'I'll bet he did it.'

Lily drew back from his hand. 'That house is so cluttered she probably fell over a piece of her furniture.'

'That's always possible. Or maybe she was chopping kindling and a bit flew up and hit her in the face. She could even have walked into a door. How do you know what that house is like?'

'I went there one day with Ruby. She had a letter for Mr Fernon, family business she said.'

'You went there?'

'Why not? Didn't you?'

He gave her a look. 'You can be incredibly naive at times.'

'Bob, I know what goes on that house. And so does all the Bay, though it pretends to think it only natural that a sea-captain's widow should like to entertain ships' officers. Perfectly respectable people go to her parties, and there's absolutely no reason why I shouldn't call in there with the Harraways.'

'I don't know why you have to see so much of them. They're not interested in you.'

'I never thought they were. They're different, that's all.'

'But don't you ever wonder what they see in you? A farm girl, a barmaid, who's always trotting after them lapping up everything they say and do?'

'Which of them told you that? It doesn't sound like Ruby. And it couldn't have been Nige or Mr Fernon — the words are all too short, for one thing.' She laughed, but a dull flush spread along Bob's cheekbones. He was lonely and that made him jealous, but it was sad to think he attacked her in this way because he wanted her to spend more time with him. Perhaps he hoped that if he weakened her enough she'd turn to him for consolation.

He asked, 'Will you meet me later?'

'I can't. I'm working in the bar tonight.'

'Shall I come and see you there, then?'

'I won't be able to talk to you. We're not allowed to spend too much time talking to particular men.'

'I'm not particular,' said Bob, brightening, but her expression couldn't have matched his, for his face fell again. 'You're angry with me.'

'No, I'm not. It's just that I can't see you for a few days.'

'How about next weekend? My friends'll be back by then so I won't have anything to do.'

'I'll be working.'

'Are you coming home this summer?'

'Yes, and sooner than usual, because my grandparents have decided to sell and there'll be double the amount of cleaning to do.'

'How soon?'

'I'm not sure.'

Bob looked quizzical.

'I might go away first, to stay with a friend for a week or two.'

'Oh, yes,' he said, as if accepting the feeblest of excuses.

Mr Fernon came into the bar a few evenings later. He was pleased the Harraways were leaving. 'Mrs Harraway has the distinction of being one of the most boring bitches in Christendom. Second only to your sweet self, in fact.'

'Then why did you talk to her about us?'

'Did I do that?'

'You know you did, and you shouldn't have. And if you're going to start getting drunk and making a fool of yourself I'd rather you didn't do it in front of Bob Graham. It seems that everywhere I go now, I have to hear about you. I don't like it.'

'My dear, I'm not much given to secrecy, nor do I care what others think of me. If their opinion is based on the truth then it's no more than I deserve, and if they are mistaken it's of no importance at all.'

'Oh, don't be so pompous,' said Lily, feeling that something of significance had been lost by his reply.

'You wanted me, Miss Macgregor, and now you have me. I'm sorry if I disappoint you.'

'I'm not disappointed,' said Lily. Nor had she been, when the only eyes to fear were those of other Bay residents whose interest, though malicious, would have been inconsequential. Cathy's resentment, Ruby's advice, and now Bob's jealous curiosity were much harder to bear. 'You're the one who's running round complaining. And it wasn't just yourself you were talking about to Ruby, it was me.'

'No, Miss Macgregor, I was talking about myself and how you bore me. I thought Mrs Harraway might know a way of communicating this that even you would understand. A way I could be rid of you.'

He wandered off. Lily thought it unlikely she'd find him in

her room that night, but when she went up after closing time he was underneath her eiderdown irreproachably asleep, or pretending to be.

She felt the familiar stirrings of desire, and then pleasure with herself for having stayed to drink port and discuss the cut of a plump barmaid's wedding gown while he grew bored alone. His face was turned slightly from her; she pressed her lips against his temple, and the corner of his unresponsive mouth, then raised the eiderdown to run her fingers down his body to where the best-natured part of him was wakeful on its own account even as he lay unawares. It responded to her touch, then shrank back into her hand, disliking the cool air. But there was no doubting Mr Fernon slept, and Lily, seeing in his presence a wish to make amends for the recent savagery between them, was seized by an unaccustomed tenderness. She longed to cover him with chaste, conciliatory kisses, but it felt wrong to wake him now. She switched off the light, undressed quickly and returned to the bed, where there was scarcely room beneath the eiderdown for two. With some idea of encouraging him to turn on his side so she could creep under the blankets, she lifted his outstretched arm and was placing it across his chest when something about this arranging of so unresisting a body alarmed her.

She hastened to the light switch, called him 'Joss' and 'Josselin', shook him and slid her arm beneath his shoulders; his head fell back, exposing the scar on his throat. Rage and fear lent her strength. She slapped him hard, earning a resentful frown, and managed to raise his upper body enough to pull him forward. There was a gurgling sound as his head dropped onto his chest, and dark liquid dribbled from his mouth. Then his shoulders heaved, she flung the eiderdown clear, and another mouthful spurted onto the bedspread. Wedging herself behind him, she pummelled his back — a cure for choking rather than an encouragement to throw up, but since she dared not leave him even to go to the washstand for the basin in case he fell sideways and was sick in the bed, there was no hope of running to the kitchen for mustard and warm water. However, his doubled-over position seemed to be doing the trick; he was now folded almost in half, puking between his knees.

Her bedspread was made of wool; she had crocheted it and tacked on a blanket for backing, and she always washed it herself. Failing the basin, it was the best recipient of sick, and nobody would be surprised when they saw she had it in the tub. And Mr Fernon did not seem to have had so very much in his stomach; he couldn't have lingered in the bar after leaving her, but gone home to drink one of his concoctions instead. She thought again of a liberal dose of mustard and water, just to be on the safe side and to teach him a lesson as well.

At length he raised his head, sighing, and sank back against her, but she dragged him out of bed and endeavoured to make him walk across the room to the chair. His legs gave and he slumped to the floor, where he curled into an obdurate ball.

'Stay there, then,' said Lily, and bundled the bedspread into a corner of the room. A sheet and pillowcase were splattered, and to have to strip and remake her bed at this hour seemed an intolerable imposition. She berated him for his selfishness, the scandal if he'd died in her bed, his reliance on the goodwill of those who owed him none, 'though at least Bob Graham can be thankful you didn't spew in his motorcar, and next time I see him I shall tell him so.'

Mr Fernon had uncurled slightly and seemed insensible again. His hair had sticky strands in it, and his face and body were streaked with sick and spittle. There was drinking water in the bottle on her washstand; she poured some into the ewer and set about wiping him down. One insult or another must have penetrated his brain for he gasped and tried to speak, though his lips emitted only faint hissing sounds, and then with her help managed to stand. He pushed at her and lurched away to lean, head hanging, against the door.

'I'm sure I don't want you here, but you're in no fit state to go,' said Lily. 'Now you're clean you can get back to bed.'

He began to urinate on the floor. The ewer was to hand; she caught it and fell on her knees at his feet. Fortunately his bladder was no fuller than his stomach had been, but there was a wet patch on the rug now. Lily retrieved the soiled pillowcase from the pile of bedding in the corner, and used it to soak up the moisture and smear a little sick there to disguise the smell of pee in case she had to ask for help to get the rug clean. She could blame the mark on herself, a bout of nausea.

'I hope there was a fair amount of opium in whatever it was you took so this'll be the last spill I have to contend with,' she said, rising, and suddenly turned dizzy, as if she too would fall. 'Stand there if you must — I'm going to bed.'

But sleep was out of the question. She was fearful he'd take it into his head to leave, and be found on the stairs in the morning. After some minutes she heard him stumble towards her, and then felt his weight on the foot of the bed.

'You can't sleep there. Get under the covers,' she said, but he muttered that he thought it best to stay where he was.

'Then do, and freeze,' snapped Lily, infuriated by this new desire to lie at her feet like a dog — no, like something much less than a dog: a shivering, dribbling, blotchy-faced thing fit only for harsh words and blows. In a frenzy of disgust she thrust out her bent legs, which somehow dislodged him. He slid to the floor and lay quiet.

Lily closed her eyes, but soon conscience got the better of her. This time Mr Fernon was more co-operative and let her help him into bed, and since she was up she thought she might as well go to the bathroom and empty her ewer and basin. When she returned he was snoring, a thing she'd never heard him do, but it sounded very normal. She fell into bed and slept as soundly as she usually did beside him; in the morning it was he who woke her.

'I thought you might have to start work early,' he said virtuously. He admitted to a slight headache, but looked remarkably refreshed and cheerful. She supposed such nights were commonplace to him.

Yet even though she knew how much he would enjoy her reproaches, it was only a matter of days before she gave in to the temptation to lecture him again on the trouble he might have made for her father, and his lack of regard for all who had to earn their livings.

'It is entirely possible that I would have recovered without your attentions,' he said mildly.

Indeed it was, but her attentions were exactly what he'd wanted, or why go to her room? He knew she'd try to wake him — if not for *love*, then for space to lie down. Just as he'd wanted Bob's attentions the night they went drinking with Nigel, and for all the scorn Bob had displayed to her he'd be quite capable of commiserating man to man on the fickleness of women. Those two must have left poor Nigel wondering why he'd ever thought they would want to celebrate his daughter.

'Your little performances might win you sympathy from some, but they don't impress me. The other night I felt tempted to pick up a pillow and finish the job myself.' That wasn't true — far from true in fact, because it made light of the surge of sheer loathing she'd felt for him — but it served to make her point. 'Put it over your face and sit on it.'

'Mean-spirited to the last. A woman of true feeling would dispense with the pillow.'

'I don't find that funny,' said Lily, and fell to grumbling about the mess he'd made of her bedspread.

Mr Fernon listened with an expression of undisguised glee, and she could see there was something comic in her anger. She was reminded of an entertaining episode she and Bob had witnessed years ago at the Albion, where the husband of one of the chambermaids had come to the desk drunk and quarrelsome, and sworn at her father. That was too much for the maid, who'd been hiding in the office; she flew out screeching, 'This is my work! You keep away from my work or I'll break both your skinny little legs.'

But that was life among the lower orders and, while doubtless instructive to a socialist like Bob, of little use to her. Mr Fernon's legs could not be described as skinny, nor was he averse to having them broken. All the same, she found herself saying, 'Next time you decide to poison yourself, I suggest you do it here.' They were at Stella Morton's, where she'd gone to prevent his coming to the hotel. 'I don't care what you do — hang yourself if you must, since you don't seem to care how you look to anyone — but keep away from my family and my friends.'

Which shouldn't be hard, because she had almost no family and very few friends.

'I will understand if you don't wish to see me again,' he said to her sudden silence.

'Not seeing you will be rather difficult in a town the size of this one. But if you're bored here you don't have to stay. I never asked you to.'

'True. And if I remain, it will not be because of you.' He paused for effect. 'I'm no longer in love with you.'

Once upon a time that would have made her laugh. Even now she snorted with amusement. 'That's beside the point, because you never were. It doesn't matter.'

'I'm sorry, my dear, but it does. It matters to me.'

And he really did sound sorry. Sorry for her.

'But we agreed! Ages ago. You said you'd never speak to me of love.'

'Then I was wrong. And I'm sorry for that too.'

Surely he knew better than to believe she was pleading with him, like one who'd been seduced and was now to be abandoned, but his voice was grave and his expression full of self-reproach. He was playing with her as he'd always done, and he'd changed the rules again.

'Listen to me,' said Lily very carefully. 'You don't have to pretend you're sorry because you want it to end. You can go away at any time.'

'So could you.'

She had an inspiration. 'Then here's a way of getting rid of me that even you will understand. You can pay me to stay away from you. Not a regular remittance, of course. A lump sum will do very well.'

'I'm disappointed in you, Miss Macgregor. If money was all

you wanted of me, you should have asked much sooner.' He indicated the tallboy. 'There's plenty in the top of that. Take what you want.'

'I will. And just remember this was your idea, so don't start complaining.' Springing out of bed, she went to the tallboy. There were ten rolls of fivers beneath the speckled mirror. She guessed each held twenty notes, and picked one up.

Her caution amused him. 'Come, my dear, do you think I would rate my pleasure so low?'

Lily took another and smiled to think what a figure she must cut, standing naked with a roll of fivers in each hand. Yet it all felt very ordinary too. What had begun across the Kellys' dinner table as a sharp exchange, ostensibly about an idle cat, was ending here quite naturally over a thousand pounds, one hundred good acres, crammed into dusty little compartments with cuff links and collar studs. Something made her say, 'You shouldn't keep so much money in your room. You should put it in the bank.'

'I withdrew it from the bank. I do intend to go away, you see.'

'Where?'

'That can now be of no interest to you. Take what you want. Have it all, if you must.'

'I shouldn't like to see you starve.'

'You underestimate me. Have you forgotten how often I dined at your stepfather's expense?'

'Why, so you did.' She scooped up two more rolls, but his expression didn't alter. 'I think the pleasure was all mine,' she said, 'and in a way I'll miss you. But I'll keep my side of the bargain. This time I hope you'll keep yours.'

Chapter 14

At first, Lily's trip to Christchurch did not promise much respite from Mr Fernon. Ruby was possessed of a choice piece of gossip she'd winkled out of Nigel about another of his affairs. 'With a married woman, three or four years ago in England. She had a son close to his age, and she was nothing to write home about, Nige said. When her husband found out and threatened divorce, she broke with Joss.'

'I suppose she did.'

'He tried to cut his throat, did you know?'

'He stood a safe distance from the razor while he did it,' said Lily. Ruby was not the first woman she'd known to be captivated by the notion that men might fling themselves about like headless chooks merely because women were capable of rejecting them; the wonder was that men, with all their unfair advantages, were prepared to feed such vanity. 'Was this before or after he broke his leg while drowning himself in the moat that hadn't any water in it? Or all at the same time?'

Ruby's face darkened. 'I never said anything about a moat.'

'No, he told me that.'

'Not everything Joss says is true, of course,' said Ruby, reclaiming him effortlessly.

'Perhaps it was another day. And a different woman.'

Ruby ignored that. 'His father was threatening to have him

put away, but Nige got dear Papa to intervene. What a scandal! Joss must've been in love with her.'

'Did he go and tell her husband so? Or just discuss her failure to be nice to him with a mutual friend?'

There was an awful silence. Then Ruby said, 'You can be very disparaging, if you don't mind my saying so.'

Lily didn't mind. She'd learnt such habits early, and had kept them close; they were part of that buried self Mr Fernon laid bare. But there was no point in quarrelling with Ruby now. 'Can I?' she asked. 'I'm sure I don't mean to be.'

'After all,' continued Ruby, 'it's not as if you've had much of a life.'

'That depends on what you call a life. At least it's one I can manage on my own.'

'What do you mean?'

'Joss and I have agreed to part,' said Lily meekly.

'Whose idea was that?'

'His. He said I was the most boring bitch in Christendom.'

Ruby mellowed visibly. 'Oh, well, we're none of us perfect.'

'Should I chuck a brick through his window?'

'That's a high window — you'd need a good throw. And then you'd probably hit madam while she was grovelling by his bed.'

'Bob says he hits her.'

'Nonsense,' said Ruby indulgently. 'He wouldn't hurt a fly.'

Yet he'd hurt quite a few people, or tried to, thought Lily. Barbed remarks, too light a hand on a farm gate, attentions to a silly girl who'd heard too much of love. And he would have liked to hurt her, though it was she who'd done the hitting.

'And you can tell Bob not to fret about madam. Her sort always know exactly what they're up to. Though I can't say I ever really liked Joss,' Ruby went on, with a magnanimous air. 'I only put up with him because he's one of Nige's friends. Nige doesn't have many friends.'

'Doesn't he?'

'Well, not like me — I make friends wherever I go. Nige likes to keep an eye on him.'

‘Why?’

‘Oh, he always has done. He used to take him home for the holidays and things, and they stuck together at school. You can imagine what sort of life a boy with those girlie looks would’ve led, though Nige says by the time they left everyone was scared of him. I said to Nige, “And were they scared of you?” “You learn how to take it, you learn how to hand it out,” says Nige. The army was the same. So’s life, if you ask me.’

‘Surely Joss wasn’t in the army?’

‘No, Nige was. Don’t you ever hear a word I say? He had to leave when he married me, but he’s thinking of joining up again. He says they mightn’t be so squeamish here.’

I wouldn’t count on it, thought Lily but said, ‘Anyway, Joss gave me some money.’

‘How much?’

‘Four hundred pounds.’

‘Jesus! You’re well set up.’

‘I thought I’d go shopping. I’d like some new clothes.’

‘I’ll come with you,’ said Ruby, her eyes lighting up at the prospect of a jaunt around the expensive shops. ‘You don’t mind if I come with you?’

‘Not at all. Who’ll mind the baby?’

‘Julia, she’s called. Cathy will, of course. She’s taken Nige’s dog out for a walk, but we can go tomorrow.’

And as if to prove she was harbouring no hard feelings of any kind, Ruby struck up about Bob. ‘I’ll miss him,’ she said. ‘If we decide to live in Wellington, you and he’ll have to visit us.’ And, ‘He doesn’t seem too bothered about finding a proper job. He must have plenty of money.’

‘He and his sisters would’ve had some from his father.’

‘How much?’

‘I don’t know. You’d have to ask him.’

‘I will. I’ll write and say I’m making enquiries on your behalf. We want to be assured that his intentions are honourable.’

‘You dare.’

‘Think of the life you could have!’

'Think of the in-laws I would have.'

'You mightn't have to see much of them. Bob told me he wouldn't mind going abroad again. He has friends in the Argentine. You can live there, and we'll come and see you.'

Ruby was quite her old self again. There was something reassuring in that, and in being led around the shops and told what to buy. 'Now don't ask how much anything costs. If you need to ask, you can't afford it.'

'What if I can't?'

'You can, but let me do the talking. I'll say we're shopping for your trousseau. Just as well we've got a swanky address for them to send things to!'

Lily ordered a tailored costume with a longish jacket and a slim skirt, a hat, shoes, and a large leather purse on a long chain to hang from her shoulder because the costume was so lean she could put nothing in its pockets without spoiling the line. 'And anyway, you'll need your hands free to fend off the blokes.' Talk of hands led to gloves, and gloves to silk stockings, and silk to underwear — *lingerie* — and so back to outerwear. Lily drew the line at a teagown, pretty as they were. Her grandmother would have a fit if she wore one at the farm. A filmy summer frock then, in melting shades of blue and green, another hat, more shoes. And there had to be an evening gown. Lily favoured midnight blue, but Ruby insisted on plum.

'Well, it's cherry really. Black cherry's what I'd call that colour. It'll do wonders with your skin and hair, though you'll have to slap the war paint on a bit thicker than you do.' A braided evening cape, long gloves, a matching evening bag and shoes, and very nearly another huge hat. 'For the theatre, you can wear it there.'

'People'll poke me in the back and tell me to take it off.'

'Bob'll just have to fork out for a box,' said Ruby, but gave in. 'And now I want some cream cakes and a cup of tea.'

'I'd like to look at jewellery,' said Lily. 'I think I'll buy some chocolates, and I want a train set as well.'

'And we'd better get something nice for Cathy so she doesn't start asking where the money came from. Do you think her mother'd let me take her on to Wellington?'

Lily wore her new costume to travel back to the farm. It wasn't until she and all her luggage were on the railway station platform that she remembered she'd meant to arrange for someone to collect her. Once the train was gone she would ask the station master to telephone to the Grahams' and see if Bob was there. Or perhaps not. It might be better to leave her things at the Grand and walk if no one offered a ride.

She stood irresolute, her baskets and boxes beside her, and a well-dressed man turned and barked, 'I'd keep a close eye on those if I were you.'

For a moment she thought he was threatening her, which was absurd. Then she realised he had troubles of his own. He was about to board the train and some piece of his wife's luggage had disappeared.

Several of the children who hung about the station were scurrying to and fro with helpful suggestions: maybe it had been put into the carriage, or might it have been left in the hotel? It was a hatbox and no, it wasn't there, nor in the carriage, so it could only have been loaded into the luggage van.

Nothing would do for his wife but to have it out again; she wanted it with her on the train. The guard was unwilling to see the van unloaded. Theirs had been among the first luggage on because they were going all the way to the Bay. The woman grew fretful, fearing that the hatbox had been crushed by a trunk. By several trunks. She took out a handkerchief for a dab at her eyes. The man was flustered. He wanted to climb into the van and hunt for the hatbox himself.

'If it can be found at all,' added his wife significantly.

The man looked at Lily and snapped something she didn't catch, but she knew she was supposed to share his indignation. It was because of her get-up and her own pile of luggage. He took her for a tourist like himself.

'It'll be in the van,' she said. 'Nothing's ever stolen round here.'

This time it was he who didn't hear. 'That's what I hate about this blasted country,' he announced, and advanced on Jack Dennehy, who'd just emerged from the van scarlet-faced and empty-handed. He blustered, 'I'll have your job.'

Of all the things he might have said, that was the silliest. Boys as smart as Jack were hard to find. Lily was about to say, Take no notice of him. She was going to add, My father would give you a job any day. She even thought of telling Jack, Bob Graham's coming to collect me and if anyone makes trouble for you he'll have something to say.

The man looked at her with eyes like damp pebbles and repeated, 'I'll have his job,' and something clicked in her head. The tiniest of clicks, like the tick of a clock in a very large room, but for the merest instant it was deafening. Then she heard herself saying, in an accent not unlike Mr Fernon's, 'I do not think you would be capable of doing it.'

'What?' he said. 'What did you say?'

'His job. You may have it, in fact you're very welcome to it, but I am quite sure that it would be beyond you. It requires a pleasant and obliging nature. And a modicum of intelligence.'

He stood goggling, but her little speech hadn't cleared her head. She felt consumed by hatred for him, and everybody like him who lived to bully, to criticise, or even just make fun of those weaker than themselves who failed to behave exactly as they thought they should. There was fire in her veins; she was bursting into flame.

Who were these people, anyway? They'd come, they'd go, but Jack had spent all his meagre, dissatisfied life here and would very likely die here, enduring the rudeness of red-faced fools for no better reason than that they had money and he did not. Money made everything possible.

She opened her purse and took out a wad of notes. 'How much was the hat worth? Five pounds?' She peeled one off and flicked it at the man, aiming for his chest, but it fell short and fluttered to the ground. 'Ten?' This one reached him, then floated down to join its fellow. Such power she felt, and her fury left her. It would be funny to see him stoop for them, and scrabble at her feet. 'Twenty?' she asked, and dropped two more notes into the space between them. The hat she had on cost close to that. She'd been scarcely able to believe it, but Ruby reckoned that was nothing. Once a bloke had bought her one for thirty. 'Forty? Fifty?'

The fivers swirled in an eddy, and the man stood watching them as if he hadn't quite grasped what they were. Then he said, in a very reasonable way, 'You know I cannot possibly take your money.'

'But I'm not only paying for the hat,' said Lily, 'I'm paying you to shut up. You may keep the money or you may leave the money, but either way you will shut up. You have nothing to complain of now.'

He turned abruptly and stalked towards the train, and for the first time she noticed the knot of people staring.

His wife's voice carried to her, as it was meant to do. 'Obviously,' she said, 'a lady of the town.'

And she was out of reach, beyond retaliation. Oh, the cowardice of good women. Where would they be without their husbands to live off, to harry, to hide behind? He at least had stood his ground for as long as he was able.

Jack Dennehy was gathering up the notes. She'd have let them lie there, as proof of her scorn for that man and all his kind, but Jack held them out to her and would have been offended if she'd told him to keep them.

'Can you take my things into the hotel? I'll arrange for somebody to collect them tomorrow.'

He grinned. 'Do you trust me not to lose them?' The little crowd was dispersing, but a few heard and rewarded him with laughter.

'Most of them,' said Lily, 'were on our side.'

There was a small, delicate silence. Then Jack said, 'And the rest would've been wondering how you came by all those fivers, Miss Macgregor.'

Chapter 15

Lily's grandmother eyed her hat and costume, but all she said was, 'Bobby Graham called in just this morning.'

'What did he want?'

'One of their bulls was loose, and the men were going round the farms telling people not to let the children leave for school.' Her tone was almost deferential.

Oh, the men, thought Lily, then everything is as it should be. 'Anyone can get on a horse and ride around a few farms, bull or no bull. I could do it myself.'

'You weren't here,' said her grandfather.

'Fancy that.' To conceal her irritation she took refuge in the habits of childhood, cutting her bread into neat cubes to drop one at a time in her soup, holding each under with the bowl of her spoon till it was soggy enough to be eaten. 'Anyway, that can't have been the reason why Bob called here.'

'He was passing, so he looked in to ask if you were home yet.'

'And I suppose you told him I wasn't?'

'You weren't,' said her grandfather patiently.

'You and he always used to get on so well together,' said her grandmother.

'We still do.'

'He's even better looking now than he was when he was a little fellow.'

'Yes, he is.'

'He seems very fond of you.'

'We've known each other for a long time. It would be strange if he wasn't.'

'I mean . . .' began her grandmother.

'I know what you mean and it's out of the question.'

Her grandmother's cheeks took on the ruddy-veined appearance of a late gooseberry, but all she said was, 'You could do a lot worse.'

'I could hardly do better, but I'm not doing anything.'

'That'll make a nice change.'

Then it started, missing Mr Fernon. There hadn't been time for it before, or perhaps the time had been too soon, but it came on her whenever she went to the room she'd occupied for his sake and where she used to lie counting off the nights until they'd meet again. Lily was glad then that her grandparents were quitting the farm and she wouldn't have to lie there alone for much longer.

She tried to remember all that had passed between them, to find a spot, the turning point, where things had first gone wrong. Her inability to call him by his Christian name; his first, undeserved snub; those startling twists and turns of mood, her willingness to meet and match them. She shuffled pictures in her head like playing cards, but they did nothing more than raise the phantom of missed opportunities: the hours wasted in sleeping, the mornings she'd risen early to dress and walk away.

By day it didn't matter, for he'd never been a part of her days, but at night she was racked by feelings too deep and unfamiliar to be judged as pain. It was as if every drop and grain of her had recognised its loss and was crying out in protest on its own account. Once, she'd believed her safety lay in his indifference to her; now it seemed she'd always had too little of him, while he'd possessed her entirely. But she'd given him up and he was gone, and she must learn to live without him.

⚜

There was much to do in the house, so much that Mrs Kelly was surprised to see her come for the mending.

'When will you find the time?'

'I can't sleep,' said Lily, leaning against the bench to gaze into the empty yard. 'I never can when it's warm. I'll do it once my grandmother's in bed.'

'You'll ruin your eyesight,' said Mrs Kelly, but lost no time in bringing out the basket.

I've completed a revolution, thought Lily, just like Bob said he'd done, but for me everything has changed.

'I was thinking we mightn't be seeing you again,' said Mrs Kelly.

'Why ever not?'

'With your grandparents gone, you'll be living year round with your stepfather.' Mrs Kelly selected a sock. 'I think this one's gone beyond recall — it's all darn now.' She passed it to Lily for inspection. 'Or you might be off somewhere else, as the case may be.' She was thinking of Bob Graham, and his talk of the Argentine.

'I have such dreams,' said Lily to the sock. Then added disappointingly, 'I dreamt there was a drought.'

'I thought you said you weren't sleeping.'

'No, this was weeks ago at the Bay. I dreamt I was doing the washing.'

'With pump water?'

'No, there was water in the tank. It was such a silly dream. I was dressed all in white, like for a summer party, and the water was red.'

'Will you have a cup of tea?' asked Mrs Kelly, rising.

'Yes, if you're making one. The tub was full of blood.'

Mrs Kelly's neck went cold, but she said very steadily, 'Well, what was it you were washing?'

'Shirts, white shirts. First of all I thought the water was rusty, and then I knew it was blood.'

'God help us,' said Mrs Kelly faintly. Her eyes had filled with tears of fright, though they at least were warm.

'I tried to keep calm, I told myself that all I had to do was take the shirts out of the tub, but I was wailing inside.' Lily paused, remembering Bob among the scorched paddocks: somehow it didn't seem right to speak of his part in this. There was silence from the scullery, and she peeked through the door to see Mrs Kelly standing chalk-faced by the sink with the kettle in one hand and the other frozen on the tap as if she too feared the water. 'It was only a dream,' she said.

'Some dreams are not fit to be told.' Mrs Kelly turned the tap, and they listened to the homely sound of the kettle filling. 'We'll talk about something more cheerful, shall we?'

And she plunged into a rambling account of a misfortune that had befallen the two half-wild cats who lived under the verandah and did everything together. Dan had been dipping the dogs for fleas, and seeing the cats loitering nearby he'd seized White Nose by the scruff and dunked him too. 'Black Nose made himself scarce, which was as well for him, because poor White Nose's fur fell out and his skin was so cracked he could scarcely move at all.' They couldn't go after rabbits, and had been reduced to catching the sparrows that flew in and out of the shed where the sacks of grain were stored. 'Black Nose jumped about on the sacks to frighten the birds, and White Nose stayed on the ground and swatted them down as they swooped past him out the door.'

'That's not a cheerful tale. Poor White Nose! And those poor sparrows.'

'Well, his fur's growing back and he's much better now. I told Dan to think himself lucky he didn't dip Oedipus.'

'Would Oedipus notice if he couldn't move?' asked Lily, picking fur from the mending.

'The tea's made,' said Mrs Kelly flatly. 'And now you can tell me just what went on at the railway station.'

'When?' asked Lily, and Mrs Kelly sighed. Some things never changed, and Lily Macgregor was one of them.

Bob appeared at the Davidsons' a couple of days later. He'd ridden over, and he hitched his horse to the verandah rail and sat waiting for Lily there.

She dawdled over dressing. 'And my hair's wet,' she told her grandmother.

'He must've seen you with wet hair before. Put a towel over your shoulders. It'll dry in the sun.'

Bob asked, 'Have you only just got out of bed?'

'No, of course not.' Her grandmother was always up at what she called sparrow-fart; there was small chance Lily would be allowed to lie in bed much past it. 'What makes you think that?'

'Your grandmother said you were getting dressed.'

'We spent the morning packing things and cleaning. I felt so hot and grimy I went to have a bath.'

'Oh, yes,' he said.

That's how it was now. Questions that scarcely merited an answer, the air of disbelief when she gave one. 'My grandmother told me you looked in the other day.'

'Have you been taking lessons from Frank Kelly?'

For a moment Lily was blind. 'What do you mean?'

His expression was speculative. He'd sensed her panic.

'Look, Bob, if you've something to say, just say it. I've work to do and I'm sure you have as well. You can't intend to spend the day sitting here asking me silly questions.'

'I heard you went several rounds with a fellow at the railway station.' Now he sounded hurt.

'Oh, that. Mrs Kelly asked about it too. He was being nasty to Jack Dennehy, and I hate that sort of thing.'

'They say he fled from a hail of fivers.'

'My life's savings, no less, so I'm glad Jack retrieved them for me. I drew them out to have a costume made, but my father said he'd pay for it.'

'I should think so. He's not oversupplied with daughters.' Bob smiled, then added, 'There was something I wanted to tell you.'

And she knew it was something he hoped she'd rather not hear. 'What was it?'

'I thought you might be interested to know your uncle didn't die before you were born. You must have been about eighteen months old when he killed himself.'

'How did you find that out?'

'Easily. I went to the cemetery and looked for his grave. I'm surprised you never thought of doing so.'

'Why would I want to? Anyway, you told me he'd be buried at the crossroads with a stake through him so he couldn't come back to haunt us.'

'That was years ago, and I believed it myself then. He was only seventeen when he shot himself. Of course it doesn't say that on the headstone. It says *Departed this life*.'

'I suppose that's more tactful than *Done a very silly thing in the ba-arn*. Not as much fun, though.'

'You can be really unpleasant at times, do you know that?'

'*I* can be unpleasant?' Bob's sneers and gibes were less contrived than Mr Fernon's, but the more wearing because they sprang from a need to win affection, not disclaim it. He wasn't faultless; his family was something less than charming, and there were things in his past she could quiz him about but chose not to, for reasons she didn't quite understand. She knew Bob better than he knew her; perhaps that made her the stronger, and some sense of fairness, or even honour, prevented her from retaliating in kind. But Bob was wrong to rely on that in quite the way he did. 'And is all this interest in my uncle just because you think he might have been my father?'

He had the grace to look abashed. 'I don't, now. And I —'

'Good, because it's just as likely to have been yours. They say he was a lady-killer in his day, and we know my mother was common enough to be amusing. Dark-haired people often have red-headed kids. You might be my half-brother, think of that! We could make up another song about it.'

'Now it's you who's being silly.'

'Listen, I've nearly got it. He was a lady-killer, he was hung beyond compare, he went down to the cowshed and he sprung it on her there. Come here, my pretty maid, he said, and gave an evil laugh. It's the bull what gets the glory and the cow what gets the calf. The cows sing that last bit, very low and sorrowful.'

'That's not funny, Phemie.'

'Well, I never thought it was funny to have you going on about my uncle all the time. It's none of your business.'

He said shamefacedly, 'I just thought it might explain things.'

Explain things. 'What things?' asked Lily, but he didn't answer. Which didn't matter, because she knew. She learnt nothing at school, and heard the furniture whispering, and laughed at things only she could see; she even threw fivers at tourists. Now the veils and masks of a lifetime's caution had fallen away, that very funny side to her was bare for all to see.

Or perhaps not. Perhaps it was only that Bob never knew what she was thinking, but he knew she didn't love him in the way he wanted her to. 'Oh, Bobby, just forget it. All we ever do nowadays is argue.'

'And whose fault's that?'

'It's nobody's fault. We just do, that's all.'

'I'm sorry,' he said, 'it's my fault. I'm tired, and I'm always irritable when I'm tired. And I still haven't asked you to the ball. That's why I looked in the other day.'

'What ball is that?'

'It's my mother's birthday on Friday, and it's been years since we put the ballroom to its proper use, so Alec said three score years and ten are worth a ball.'

'I'm not sure I want to go out just now. They'll all have heard about the scene at the railway station.'

'True, but they'll either regard you as the heroine of the hour or be too polite to mention it. Don't worry, I'll look after you. And if you don't feel safe with me you can stick close to the Kelly boys. Nobody will dare look sideways at you then.'

It wasn't the men she was afraid of, but the women. By now they'd have priced her costume and made an attempt on her hat; they'd have asked each other what the dress-baskets and boxes might contain. And the wife's parting shot would have carried to more ears than hers and Jack's. That last little morsel would have been pressed and sucked behind pursed lips for every drop of juice it could be made to yield.

'I'd have spoken up for Jack if I'd been there,' said Bob, then laughed. 'Not in quite the same way perhaps, but I would've.'

'I know you would,' said Lily, with the rare luxury of perfect truthfulness. 'It was thinking of you that made me do it.'

'And it's not as if you've done anything to be ashamed of. Not really.'

'No, I haven't, not ever. Not really.' But still she hesitated.

'Now don't tell me you've nothing to wear.'

'Oh, no! I've something to wear.'

'That's settled then. I'll pick you up at seven-thirty.'

'I thought you said I was to come with Frank and Gerald.'

'Don't you trust me to protect you?' Then he spoilt it all again. As he settled himself in the saddle he asked, 'By the way, how was your friend?'

'What friend?'

His smile was indulgent, but there was a glint of triumph in his eyes. 'Why, the one you told me you were going to stay with for a while.'

'Oh, you mean Ruby Harraway. She and little Julia are both very well, thank you. I thought you'd have known that already. How's your bull?'

'My bull?'

'The one you were looking for when you came by the other day.'

'He's safe at home again and thanks you for your interest.'

And it was too late now to say she wasn't going to the ball.

Chapter 16

Lily wore her new evening gown. She rouged her lips, and darkened her eyelids and lashes with a judicious mix of candle soot and castor oil.

'Oh, my God,' said her grandmother, 'the things you see when you haven't got a gun.' She was busy at the kitchen cupboards. There was a pile of old newspapers on the table, and some stray bits and bobs waiting to be packed: a ball of twine, the oyster knife, horn buttons cut from an old coat, a chipped basin.

'Ruby Harraway chose it for me.'

That name still had power to charm. 'You'll put Mrs Kelly's nose out of joint.'

'Why?'

'I hear she's been living on rabbit food for a month, and was off to a dressmaker at the Bay. She's come a long way if anyone has. Well, I daresay the Grahams will've thought to include a jig in the programme.'

Lily felt a sudden urge to kick her grandmother in the backside as she knelt there at the cupboards. She never missed a chance to pick at other people's lives, but she let her own lie quiet enough. 'Why is there nothing of my uncle in the house?'

Her grandmother sat back on her heels. 'Your uncle?' Her tone was mild, enquiring.

'Yes. My uncle, your son.'

'Why, what on earth would there be?' It was as if they spoke of him every other day and the topic had been well and truly exhausted.

He wouldn't have had Bob's store of toys and books and treasures, but in all her cleaning Lily had come across nothing a mother might have kept: no cracked little boots or envelope of baby curls tucked at the back of a drawer. She'd found marbles and the knucklebones, and once there'd been a pet sheep and a creaking swing, though they'd all been hers until her mother laid her claims to them. Apart from the grave Bob spoke of, her uncle might never have lived at all.

'A photograph,' said Lily feebly. There'd been one of her mother, as sweet and soulful as a Jersey cow.

'We're not the Grahams, you know. We couldn't be rushing our kids off to a photographer every time they grew another inch or changed their partings.' Her grandmother looked considering. 'We'll have to get a photograph of you done up the way you are. It'd do to keep the hawks away. That'll be Bobby now.'

Lily shrank from the thought of facing Bob under her grandmother's implacable eye. 'I'll meet him outside,' she said, clutching her new cape round her. Indeed, she felt monstrous beside those hopeful, harmless oddments on the table: garish, half-naked, hobbled by her skirt and unsteady on her heels.

'I hope you've got some smelling salts handy. He wouldn't see a sight like you every day of the week.'

But Bob scarcely glanced at her when she joined him at the gate, and in the Buick he kept his eyes on the road. Sheep lifted their heads to watch them pass, but only those near the fence bounded away. 'See that?' he said. 'They're used to it. It didn't take them long.'

'The two sitting down didn't move at all.'

'I saw them on the way over and stopped to have a better look. One's sick — I don't think it'll last much longer. The other'll be its friend. You see that with sheep sometimes. Having friends.'

After a little he said, 'You're very quiet tonight.'

The night had barely started. 'It's been a long day.'

'For me too.' He yawned to prove it. 'I was up and out by five this morning. But a few drinks'll see me right.'

'They might have the opposite effect.'

'Not in your company.'

'And how many have you had already?'

'Oh, here we go. Two. One while I was waiting for the bathroom and another while I was dressing, all right?' Then he added, 'And if you're afraid you'll find my company soporific, you'll be pleased to know another of your friends is coming.'

'Who?'

'Joss Fernon.'

Something leapt in Lily's side, but there was a sickness there too, as if the spasms of loss she'd felt had done some lasting harm. 'You invited him?'

'Well, I couldn't not. He's back at the Grand and he'd have heard about it.'

'You don't even like him.'

'I don't dislike him,' said Bob carefully. 'I just don't like the way he acts at times. Didn't you know he was here?'

'No.'

'Then you haven't seen him?'

'Of course not. I've been busy at home.'

'Oh, yes,' he said.

If in one way Lily was sick of Mr Fernon, in another she was getting very sick of Bob. She tried flippancy. 'He might bring one of his lady-friends.'

Bob was not to be won over. 'No, he won't. He can behave well enough when he chooses.'

'Mr and Mrs Kelly won't be pleased to see him. You should've heard them when Scatty got out of his paddock.'

'If the only people coming to the ball were those that you, I and the Kellys could agree on,' said Bob, 'we could hold it in the card room. What's wrong with you tonight? It won't kill you to be civil to him.'

Yet if Mr Fernon was here it could only be because of her. He wasn't keeping his side of the bargain.

There were three motorcars on the sweep of drive in front of the Grahams' porch. Bob parked his, then stepped back to admire the effect, telling her what and whose the others were with the natural pride of one who leads a fashion among friends. He seemed more cheerful, but as she emerged from the guest cloakroom and went to join him in the hall he stood watching her with his head slightly on one side and something like the old expression, both shy and calculating, that he'd worn when they first came to know each other.

'What's the matter? It is too bare? Should we go back so I can change?'

'No, it's fine. It's just that I've never seen you in that colour before.'

'I've never worn it before.'

'You didn't make it yourself.'

'No, I'm fed up with sewing all the time. I told you, remember? My father gave me money for new clothes.'

'You said you'd bought a costume.'

'I had this made as well. Isn't it suitable?'

'It's entirely suitable. You'll be the best-dressed woman here.' He offered his arm, then smiled as though he'd just remembered something that had been evading him. 'You're the colour of milk and blood.'

'What a memory you have, Mr Graham.'

'A better one than yours, Miss Macgregor.'

I should go home now, she thought, but let him lead her on. The ballroom was lit by candles, not electric light — another example of the Graham tact, for not all the female guests would have new gowns for the occasion. Candlelight made hers less conspicuous, although several people were looking curiously at her. Bob stayed close, smiling as sweetly as ever. He took her card. 'Just the one, I think. I'd better not monopolise you.'

There were too many men, but it scarcely mattered. Some would be happy to spend the night upstairs in the billiard room, or smoking and telling dirty stories in the garden. Frank and Gerald Kelly were hovering, and Bob passed them her card. They looked bullishly handsome in evening dress, and smoothed their white gloves as if afraid they'd split. Gerald had acquired a ripple in his nose.

'Is there someone in particular you're hoping to see?' Bob asked silkily, and Lily felt unutterably weary.

She had come only to please him, and it was he who'd invited Mr Fernon, not she. The prospect of an evening where each could take his turn at taunting her was intolerable, but her face felt too stiff to fall. There was much to be said for war paint, as there was something to be said for stays. 'I was looking for the Kellys, that's all. My grandmother said Mrs Kelly has a new gown too.'

'They haven't arrived yet.'

'I wish I'd come later. I'm tired already.'

'We shan't have to stay very late,' he said as if he didn't live there. 'My mother's friends won't, and I'm not in the mood for the rout that'll ensue once our elders have departed.'

Mrs Graham made a huge fuss of her. What she'd heard of the incident on the railway station she must have chosen to ignore. Still, Lily didn't know why she was being so very pleasant. Perhaps it was only that she was cheered by the sight of Jean's thickening figure, though of course she didn't draw Lily's attention to that. She was full of Bob's plans to go to the Argentine. 'His mind is quite made up — he's written to our friends there. Has he said nothing to you?' She hesitated, then pressed on. 'I blame Nigel Harraway! And that other friend of Bob's, Mr Fernon. They've unsettled all the young men with their talk of the places they've been and where they'll go next.'

And there was Mr Fernon with Connie Graham. Lily might have been watching him through a sheet of glass, as she'd done that day in Kellys' kitchen till the late sun blinded her, and she turned away to question Mrs Kelly, idly, deceitfully, with the darning in her hands and that terrible longing deep within her. But she felt nothing of that now.

Then it must be over, she thought, it's gone. I felt it go. Everything changes, and this has too.

He came up to her and wrote his name in her programme

with the air of one who does no more than his social duty.

'Do you know him?' asked Mrs Graham.

'Slightly,' said Lily. 'I met him one evening at the Kellys'. Mr Kelly was quite matey with him for a while.'

'Oh, Mr Kelly,' said Mrs Graham with a fleeting smile.

'And I've seen him with Bob and the Harraways at the Bay. He came into our box at the theatre one night.'

'He's been here to play tennis with Bob, but I must have been in town when he came. I did see him early one morning, after I'd had a particularly bad night.'

Mrs Graham was given to bad nights, and the district had noted long since that the death of her randy husband didn't seem to have alleviated this unhappy condition. 'I rose and dressed at first light and went out on Hector, but I soon regretted it because it came on to rain so very heavily. Then I saw him standing quite still under the tree by the crossroads. Such a fright he gave me. I thought, he has no reason to wait there. I rode up to him, and of course . . .' She smiled. 'So silly. He told me he'd woken early and walked out from town, only to be caught by the rain.'

She seemed about to say something more and then to decide against it. Instead she put her hand on Lily's arm. 'I don't really mind what my children do as long as they're happy. In the end, that's all that matters.' Her face was bright and hopeful. Whatever she had nearly said, it could have nothing to do with Mr Fernon.

When he came to claim his dance he asked, 'Would it be precipitate of me to wish you and Bob every happiness for the future?'

'Bob and I are friends, that's all.'

'Does he know that?'

'I don't know what he knows. He's not in the best of moods tonight.' Bob was watching them now, but when his eyes met hers over Mr Fernon's shoulder he sent her an encouraging smile.

'Is this the first time we have danced together, Miss Macgregor?'

'It is.'

'And I have never seen you look so charming. Did I pay for all that you have on?'

'You did. But you haven't kept your side of the bargain.'

'Perhaps I cannot live without you.'

'I think you live without me very well.'

'There you are wrong, Miss Macgregor. I'm tired of being unhappy and alone. I should very much prefer to be unhappy and with you.'

All our lives, she thought, we will be able to dance like this and talk like this, but the other thing has gone. Bob was right. Mr Fernon could behave well enough when he chose, and now that it was over there was nothing left to fear. She wondered how things might have been if he'd had Nigel's easy and accommodating temper. Could she then have felt for him what others called love? But if he'd been so very different, they wouldn't have met at all. Or he too might have had an unsettling wife in tow.

'Were you not my fiancée once?'

'There was a brief engagement.'

'To my lasting sorrow. Shall we try again? Those are garnets at your throat and ears; I think I offered rubies.'

'Are you speaking of a proper engagement, Mr Fernon?'

'A very proper one, Miss Macgregor. I should not so much as put my hand upon your knee, and you would maintain to perfection the frosty demeanour you have now, in order to ensure that I remained in no doubt as to the honour you did me. In view of the disparities between our faces, families and fortunes the greater honour would be yours, but I would be too generous to remind you of that, and you would be in too sweet a state of delusion over the triumph of true love to perceive it at all.'

'You do me too much honour now, Mr Fernon. And if it is face, family and fortune you seek in a bride, I think the best the district has to offer is clever Connie Graham. Why don't you try for her?'

'That thought did cross my mind, I must confess, but after a few minutes' conversation with her I found myself quite lost. Though not in the manner I could lose myself with you, Miss Macgregor.'

The music ended, they separated, Lily felt a momentary lack, and then Bertie Fraser came for her. Bertie told her she looked stunning and held her close, much too close, but Bob was whirling about with Mrs Kelly and had given up watching her. He seemed happy enough, although when they spoke at supper she noticed a slight slurring in his speech. That may have been no more than tiredness.

The night was not so bad, but at length grew tedious. Every other man she danced with spoke of a leaking roof or mended harness, and wondered if she'd any fivers to chuck at him. She had been enjoying herself and now she wasn't, that was all, but she couldn't slip away from here as easily as from the Kellys'. There were thank yous and farewells to be made, and that would lead to a kerfuffle about how she was to get home. She couldn't see Bob anywhere. Neither, it seemed, could Mrs Graham, who was also preparing to withdraw and had started sending eye signals to her children scattered round the room.

None of the Kellys looked ready to leave, but there was pleasure in the thought of hastening down the drive alone. So much pleasure, in fact, that she felt she could postpone it and stay a little longer. Then Bob reappeared and when she told him she was going he did nothing to dissuade her, but insisted on driving her.

'What will people think of me if I don't?' he argued, reasonably enough. 'Someone's sure to pass you on the road and offer you a lift, and ask why you were walking.'

'I'll tell them I like it.'

'Then they'll want to know why you always have to flit about on your own.'

Lily sighed, and felt the old tightening in her chest as Bob followed her down the front steps. Together they cast a long, lumpish moon shadow on the white shingle drive. On such a night as this she'd walked home with Mr Fernon; if they'd done a little better she might be walking with him now. 'As soon as I can I'll cut across the paddocks. It's light enough.'

'Dressed the way you are?'

'It'll give the sheep something new to talk about.' She remembered the one that had stayed by the roadside with its sick friend, and wondered if it would make another friend or go on with whatever was left of its short life alone.

'Look, people think you're odd enough already. Anyway, your shoes aren't suitable.'

And to prove him right a pebble turned under her heel.

'See?' He took her elbow to steady her, and held her until they reached the Buick. As he opened the door he ran his fingers up her arm to where it was bare above her glove.

'Don't,' she said, and drew her cape about her, but he pushed it back and pressed his lips against her shoulder.

'I've been wanting to do that all night.'

'Well, don't.'

'Sorry, I forgot. One may look but one mustn't touch. That's how it is with you, isn't it?'

Lily got into the motorcar and sat listening to the faint music of each breath. This time it wasn't only Bob who was stifling her; there was still some baffled thing inside that wanted to be free.

The Buick was slow to start, but even when Bob joined her she hadn't thought what to say. After a while she asked, 'Did you know the Harraways are definitely going away? I think Nigel has a job in Wellington.'

'Well, of course.'

'Why of course?'

'That sort always do.'

'What? What do they do?'

'Go away.'

'You sound as if you don't like them.'

'I don't.' Then he added, 'Nigel's not too bad.'

'He's nice. He said such a clever thing once.'

'I'm sure he'd be immensely flattered to hear you say that.'

His slight emphasis on the word 'you' made that sound more offensive than it need have, but perhaps it came out wrong because he'd been drinking.

'Ruby's all right,' she said.

'She's a tart.'

Lily stopped watching for the sheep and looked at Bob.

The side of his face was growing steadily superior. 'And when can we expect that other shit to depart?'

Lily said nothing.

'I'm sorry if my language offends you,' he said.

'It doesn't.'

'No, I didn't think it would.'

'If you mean Mr Fernon, you'll have to ask him.'

'If you mean Mr Fernon,' he mimicked her, 'we can do without his sort around here as well.'

'Did you tell him so tonight? Is that why you invited him?'

'I wouldn't tell him the time.'

Somehow that brought them to safer ground. Bob seemed to relax a little. 'Well, that's not strictly true. I had quite a chat with him in the garden.'

'That's nice.'

'Don't you want to know what we were talking about?'

'Not particularly.'

'We were talking about you.'

'How very dull.' They were approaching the gate. It was shut, which meant she would be able to get out of the motorcar. 'I'll walk from here. You don't need to see me to the house.'

He caught her wrist and leaned towards her. Thinking he meant to kiss her, she turned her face away.

'No, it wasn't dull at all. He asked me . . .' Bob began, then seemed to be having trouble remembering the question. 'He was interested in learning if I had ever . . .' and now she understood that he was choosing his words very carefully and wanted her to know it. 'Enjoyed your favours,' he said.

Lily was glad he couldn't see her face. 'What a strange thing to do. But I thought you said it was a long conversation.'

'You sound rather short of breath.'

'The night air doesn't always agree with me. May I get out now?'

Bob let go her wrist.

'Thank you for a pleasant evening,' she said, and walked unhurriedly towards the gate. Behind her she heard the motorcar turning on the gravel.

Chapter 17

Once Lily was inside, her breathing eased. She put on her silk wrapper and undid her hair, and sat at the dressing table to study her unfamiliar face, bleached by the moonlight in her room. It might be best to wear that new mask a little longer, in case Mr Fernon called.

She would say: Why did you ask Bob about me? Don't you know anything? The slow turn of his head, the corners of his mouth lifting. Did I do that? And what was Bob's reply?

He will not come, she thought, but listened for his step on the verandah. Instead she heard his hand against the door. She would say it, then. She would say: Why do you do these things? Why do you want to make everybody hate you? And what is it that you really want of me? Come now, Miss Macgregor, I am sure you know the answer to that question.

Perhaps her ears had deceived her; the door remained closed. She rose, opened it and saw that it was Bob who stood there. He looked dazed. Ill, almost. 'Bob?' she said, and drew back. 'I didn't hear the motorcar.'

'You didn't hear the motorcar.' He made her admission sound like proof of some particular piece of stupidity on her part or cleverness on his.

'No, I didn't. But then I wasn't listening for it. I thought you'd be at home by now.'

'Yes, I'm sure you did.' His lips parted and he seemed about to say something more, but no sound came. He lowered his head, looked briefly at the floor, and stepped into the room.

'What's happened?'

He pushed the door shut behind him. His eyes were like jet in the moonlight.

'You don't look well. Have you had an accident? Did you hit a cow in the dark?'

'A cow in the dark.' Bob smiled at and past her as though he had more audience than her alone, then gave his head a little shake. 'It's not dark.' He came nearer, rubbing at his forehead. 'What have you done to your face?'

For a moment she thought his eyes were troubling him. 'My face? Nothing. I haven't washed it yet, that's all. What's wrong?'

'You look like the bloody whore you are.'

The only way out was onto the verandah, and he was a hundred times faster than she. He was now halfway between that door and the door to the front room, which was locked. She'd turned the key before she sat down at her dressing table, as she always did, but Bob wouldn't know that.

She said, 'Well, you don't have to tell me what's going on if you don't want to. Shall I make you some tea?' And moved towards the locked door.

Bob slid in front of her and nearer, with perfect concentration. 'Nothing,' he said, 'is going on,' and glanced around again as if he wanted someone else to share his exasperation. He was still pale, but his expression was more familiar: that wary regard, the judicious calculation of the odds for mischief. His eyes had lightened and there was a softening about his mouth and jaw, though his thoughts were inward still. She'd seen that expression earlier, in the Grahams' hall, and hadn't understood it then.

But he was further from the verandah door than she was now. 'Bob, you must stop this strange behaviour. I don't understand what you want.'

'Don't you? You're unusually slow tonight.' He smiled, then added, 'But it's not tea.'

Lily made a sound of amusement and turned idly from him. To go to the window would take her nearer the bed, but if he stayed by the locked door there was the slimmest chance she could reach the verandah ahead of him. She began to drift towards the window.

Bob took off his coat and dropped it on the floor. 'You won't get that open. Your grandmother asked me to try the other day. It's stuck fast.'

'I know.' She glanced back; he was taking off his shoes. 'It always has been. I was going to look out, that's all.'

'Do you think there might be someone out there? Somebody you'd rather like to see?'

'No,' she said, and leant forward eagerly. 'Should there be?' For the first time he took his eyes off her, and she spun round and tried to dive past him. That was a mistake. While she'd remained in her old sphere of slow evasions he was hesitant too, but her sudden movement swept him into action. This was what he understood. He caught her easily by one arm and threw her against the wall, pinning her there with the weight of his body. He needed no other audience now. All his attention was for her. Putting one hand around her throat, he forced her head back. 'Do you like violence, then?' he whispered. 'Is that how it is with him? Is that what excites you?'

'No. No, of course not.'

Bob stepped back, but didn't take his hand from her throat. 'Then do as you're told. Get onto the bed.'

Lily did as she was told, pushing the covers out of the way and easing herself into the corner with her back to the wall. Bob stood against the edge of the bed, fiddling with his cuff links, and she felt so securely caged she began to believe her position was hopeless, though there were moments when undressing would put him at a disadvantage: when he took down his trousers or went, as he did now, to drag his half-open shirt over his head.

She lost that moment. Mr Fernon's skin absorbed light; Bob's had the soft lustre of oiled wood. His upper body was more muscular and rounded, with a quality of innocence that shocked her profoundly — a different level of dismay, that something which of itself showed no aptitude for harm should be made to serve as the means of her punishment rather than his pleasure. She flicked her eyes back to Bob's face. His expression, both eager and dismissive, sickened her. She turned her head away while he finished his undressing.

As he pulled her towards him her wrapper came open, and she had a last, foolish hope that he would see they weren't children any more, know the game had gone too far, and stop. He didn't. He put his mouth against her shoulder, the thing he'd been wanting to do all night.

'No, Bobby, don't. You mustn't.' The shame of lying naked beneath him in the sight of the moon. 'The covers. Pull up the covers.'

'It's not cold.'

'I'm cold.'

'Christ!' he said, but reached back and dragged a sheet and blanket over them. That was something. He began to stroke her face and hair, then his hand strayed to her throat again as if he liked best what he felt there.

'I have to go to the lavatory.'

'No, you don't. Draw up your knees.'

This is the least of it, she thought as he entered her, and it doesn't matter. Every night of the week women lay with their legs apart in this fashion while the men they were pleased to call their husbands grunted and sweated between them. It was what she did that was important; her senses were in her own keeping, and they could not be forced. Bob and his notions of what she might be made to think or feel were nothing.

When he'd finished he was calmer. He lay beside her and slid one arm beneath her shoulders. He wanted to talk. And how he talked! A tangled stream of memories and confidences. 'We should have married years ago,' he said. It was Jean and her jealousy that had come between them. 'I always knew you never cared for Bertie Fraser.' Then his voice changed, sounding faint and faraway. 'Bertie wouldn't have married you anyway. That wasn't what he had in mind.'

'And I wouldn't have married him. Or done anything else, for that matter. He's got no eyelashes.'

'Hasn't he?' he asked, more normally.

'If he has, they're very pale ones.'

'He's grown rather fat.'

'He has. He looks like a pet pig.'

That pleased him, but then he raised himself on one elbow and began to stroke her throat again. 'How cold you are,' he said.

'I told you I was cold.'

'That's not what I meant. I could understand it if you were a virgin.' Then he stopped, his hand still on her throat. 'Were you a virgin?'

A dangerous question. An insane question, because he'd known the answer before he came to her door.

'No,' she said carefully, 'I wasn't. But we only did it two or three times.'

As if the number of times you did anything was important. Yet it seemed the right answer; his hand came away from her throat, and his touch ceased to trouble her at all. It was only her throat that mattered. Soot and his rabbits had shown her that.

'I don't know when I first began to suspect something,' Bob said. 'It may've been that night at the theatre when you couldn't stop talking about him. Or perhaps it was later, something you said. So one evening when you told me you'd be working I telephoned the hotel. You weren't there.' He made a breathy sound which might have been laughter. 'You didn't think I'd do that, did you?'

'No,' said Lily. 'I didn't think you'd do that.'

'That's why I asked him to the ball. I wanted to see you with him, to be sure. Well, I could have saved myself the trouble, because he told me.'

'When he asked if you'd ever enjoyed my favours?'

'In a manner of speaking.'

'And what did you say?'

'What would you like me to have said? Invited him to meet

me a discreet distance from the house and then beaten him to a pulp to avenge your honour?'

'No, of course not. That would've been silly.'

'We're agreed on that, then.'

Her honour. But there'd been something there. 'So what did you say to him?'

'When?'

'When he asked you.'

'My answer was, "No, but I'd like to." And he said that sex had never interested him much with you. It was your stupidity that kept him hanging about. In that respect, he found you impenetrable.'

Mr Fernon's last shaft and his best, but if she flinched Bob gave no sign of noticing.

'Well, now you have,' she said.

'Have what?'

'Enjoyed my favours.'

Bob lay quiet, so quiet Lily wondered if he'd fallen asleep and risked a look at him. His eyes were closed, his face relaxed. She began to edge away.

He caught her forearm. 'What're you doing?'

'I've cramp in one leg.'

'Would you like me to rub it for you?'

'No. It's all right now, it's gone.'

'I don't think you're stupid,' he said suddenly, with a schoolboy's sturdy kindness. He might have been offering to help her with her sums. Then his voice became quiet and dry again. 'In fact I think you've been very clever, the way you deceived us all. Especially me.'

So that was it. For as long as Bob believed she kept herself aloof from other men he'd been secure in his possession of her. It was knowing he was wrong that had maddened him so. But he'd let go her arm.

'If you wanted money, if you wanted clothes, you should've asked me. I'd have bought those things for you. I could have brought you something from London if you'd wanted, or from Paris.'

She hadn't seen him for years before he went to London and Paris, but he'd chosen to forget that. He had what he'd always wanted now.

He said, 'We've been making love for hours.'

Making love. Lily moved a little way from him, and he didn't seem to mind. She risked a small jab. 'You could have hit Mr Fernon. He wouldn't have hit you back.'

'He'd have tried.'

'No, he wouldn't.' She thought of him looking at Bob with the same smile he'd given her when she slapped him that day. See what I made you do.

'Look, it doesn't matter,' Bob said. 'Everybody does stupid things, we all make fools of ourselves one way or another. We can't stay here — too many people know about you — but we'd be all right in the Argentine. I would've asked you sooner, but I wanted to be sure.'

Now he was wide awake and full of hope. He knew some Italian and they'd both pick up Spanish, it was easy. He was good at languages, and she was such a clever mimic she would be too. He had friends there already and they'd soon make more. 'Everyone likes me,' he said. 'I get on well with everybody.'

'I can see that,' said Lily, but it was lost on him. He was too happy.

'Even your grandmother. I used to be scared of her, remember? I always waited at the gate because I thought she didn't like me.'

'She doesn't like anybody.'

'That morning I called in and you weren't here, she asked me if I could open that window. And do you know what she told me?'

'No.'

'She said, "This used to be our son's room, and it was empty for a long time. He died when Lily was a baby."'

'Well, we knew that.'

'Yes, but I wanted to hear what else she'd say. I kept on fiddling with the window and I asked her what he'd died of. She said he started ailing and they thought he was soft. "He wouldn't do anything," she said, "anything at all, and then one morning we found him dead. It was very sudden. Do you remember old Soot?"'

'Of course I do.'

'No, that's what she asked me. Did I remember old Soot. I said I didn't, and she said, "He used to spoil that cat; a cat should earn its keep." "Oh, he will," your uncle told her. "You can make him mind the Tiger Lily when I'm dead." That's what he called you because your head looked like it'd been brushed with pollen.'

'It's hot in here. Why's it so hot?'

'You wanted the covers.' He went to throw them back.

'Leave the sheet, that'll be enough. Just the sheet. Is it hot in the Argentine?'

'I suppose it depends on where you are. We could find somewhere like here.' Bob put his arm under her shoulders again; he wanted to finish his story. 'Your grandmother said she told him not to talk nonsense, but she didn't know how bad he was. I said that I was sorry, and she said, "Well, a quick death's better than some kinds of life."' He paused. 'All the same, I don't think I could put a shotgun under my chin and blow my head apart.'

'How do you know he blew his head apart? You always said that if he stood the gun on the ground and bent over it he could've shot himself through the heart.'

'After I found his grave I asked Dan Kelly what he knew of it. He told me his father helped rake out the hay and burn it, and always used to say he never wanted another job like that as long as he lived. And how his father reckoned they got the sexes wrong in your family. Your mother was no sooner up and about than she was chopping wood and hauling coal, while her brother sat around with you against his shoulder and the face of a jilted girl on him. Nobody was surprised when she ran off again.'

How busy he'd been in pursuit of that poor ghost.

'I'm sorry we laughed at him now,' he said.

'We didn't know. It was just a game to us, and it was my mother we were laughing at.'

Bob had struck a brief spark of kindness in her; for a moment she thought about going away with him. It could never be worse than this, and might come to be better. She pictured them making their way across a crowded wharf and up a gangway, arguing as they went like their ordinary selves. At least, she thought, he wants me and no one else ever has.

Then the knowledge of just how much he'd weakened her came down on her. For that was untrue. A great many people had wanted her, one way or another. They'd wanted her for reasons of their own and often that hadn't suited her, yet how could it be otherwise?

'I shall have to go,' he said, but turned to her, and she knew he meant to do it again. 'Remember the day I had to stay in bed and you came to see me? I think that was the first time I really noticed.'

'Noticed what?'

'How pretty you were. Are. That spring I was walking past the lilacs just as the sun came out and caught them after a shower of rain. They were still quivering, and there were raindrops like prisms on every leaf and flower. When you came into my room that day you made me think of the lilacs.'

'But it was winter when I came.'

'It wasn't.'

'Yes, it was. There was snow along the drive, and I was so muffled up you said you nearly didn't know me. I had a dewdrop on my nose.'

'In that case it must've been the other way round. That spring it must have been the lilacs which reminded me of you.'

He said, 'Put your arms around me.'

Lily did, but crossed them at the wrist so that her fingers shouldn't touch him. She hoped he would finish quickly and leave, but his movements slowed and then stopped. His body slackened and grew heavy, and heavier still.

This time she didn't risk rousing him in her haste to get away but stayed motionless, taking careful breaths and listening to his, half-muffled by the pillow. When she was certain he was sound asleep she drew up one leg, and braced herself against the mattress. At first she couldn't shift him, but then their bodies came apart and he rolled off her with a sound between a sigh and a groan. Lily waited a moment more to be sure he wouldn't wake before sliding out of bed and putting on her wrapper.

She was out the verandah door at last, but there was nothing to do and nowhere to go. The drive, the gate, the scattered sheep looked as they'd always done. She went to the pump and ran water over her hands. Black Nose and White Nose were crouching in the paddock; she hadn't known they hunted so far from home. How long it seemed since she'd stood watching them from the Kellys' parlour with Mr Fernon beside her.

Lily walked round the far side of the house, not wanting to pass the window where Bob lay in possession of her room. Her grandparents' window was open, and she heard her grandfather snoring. That sound, and the fact that her world could still coincide with theirs, amazed her. She went into the lavatory and squeezed out a few drops of urine in a vague attempt to rid herself of whatever Bob had left in her. But it was thinking of her grandfather that made her go to the tall cupboard in the wash house where the guns were kept. The key was on the cupboard's roof, and she had to stand on tiptoe to feel for it.

As a child she'd been taught the guns were always loaded, as bulls were always iffy and horses always kicked, but she also understood that for them most days went by in silence. They were her grandfather's, and their lives were plain and useful like those of all his things, their spirits shaped by the necessities of work and time. Yet now, as the cupboard's door swung open on its musty breath and she saw them in the moonlight, she knew they had more cunning than she'd supposed. Their gleaming barrels struck at all her senses, and their secret, savage longings filled her heart. The shotgun came easily to her hand, and she lifted it free. It broke for her as it had for Nigel Harraway. She took down the box of cartridges and slid two into the breech, then walked back around the house to the verandah. The loose board creaked under her foot as she opened the door to her room.

Bob lay as she had left him. The shotgun's weight was on her palm. It snapped shut, and its muzzle sought the slight hollow in his cheek. Perhaps he sensed its breathless hunger, for his eyelids lifted slightly, but there was only a brief glimmer of silver beneath his lashes before they fell again. The hint of a smile lingered about his mouth.

She'd been right all those years ago. He looked gooder when he was asleep. But to wake him she would have to call his name, even touch him — things she couldn't bring herself to do. Instead she knelt and placed the shotgun beneath the bed, then returned to the verandah to wait for the dawn and her grandfather's slow tread on the path as he went to the pump for the morning's water.

Chapter 18

Michael Kelly left the ball in such a state of exaltation he didn't bother to go to bed. He was too shy to dance, but he'd gone upstairs to watch the men at billiards and see the electric lights on pulleys that hung low over the table, and the panes of glass in the ceiling to give good light by day. He'd slipped into the upstairs bathroom for a piddle in the flushing lavatory, and paused to admire the shower-bath and the rail from which winter's towels came warm and dry to the hand. It wouldn't have done to ask Bob Graham for a ride when he went off with Lily, and he hadn't felt like leaving with his parents or waiting for his uncles, so he'd strolled home alone, where he sat on the verandah and smoked the cigar somebody had given him before changing into his work clothes and going out to shift some stock.

Then he set off for the Davidsons'. They'd arranged to spend a few days in Mr Macgregor's hotel to look at houses for sale at the Bay, and had asked him to drive them to the train. He came upon Bob's Buick, half-hidden by some trees, and climbed in to sit with his hands on the steering wheel and wish he could drive that to the station instead of Mr Davidson's old wagon. He thought that since Bob was there they mightn't need him, but he went on anyway. And he said nothing that day of seeing the motorcar, nor for many years after. As things turned out, he used to say, it would have done Lily Macgregor no good and might have done her some harm.

⚜

Lily was drinking tea at the kitchen table, and hoping her grandmother would be in too great a rush to pay her much attention.

'You'd better get some clothes on before Michael Kelly gets here,' her grandmother said. And, 'Have you taken a look at yourself in the mirror this morning?'

'I haven't been in long,' said Lily. Her grandfather was already dressed and shaven and had gone outside in his suit and hat to wander among his neat rows of vegetables. There was no reason for him to go to the gun cupboard, but in case he did and saw the shotgun wasn't there she added, 'And then I thought I heard a stoat and went to see if the hens were all right. I haven't been to bed.'

'Well, you needn't think you're going to sit around here all day looking like you've been dragged through a gorse bush backwards. There's still plenty to do.'

'There is. Whether or not I'll do it is another matter.'

'Oh my! We do have a good opinion of ourselves this morning. Just as well we don't go to a ball every night of the week.'

Lily said nothing, and that annoyed her grandmother far more than a sharp retort would have done. 'One of these days, my girl, you're going to hear a few home truths from me.'

'That'll make a nice change. Why did my uncle go and shoot himself?'

But her grandmother, dressed for the Bay and with her town hat on, was ready for her. She examined the stitching in one glove. 'Who told you he shot himself?'

Her voice held a hint of amusement, as if Lily were the dupe of a mischievous gossip.

And Lily couldn't bring herself to say: my mother. She'd told Bob, she'd offered it to Ruby as a counterbalance to the sudden intimacy Ruby thrust on her, and she owed her mother nothing, but her nerve failed. 'Nobody told me. I just know, that's all.' Then the thought that she hadn't been supposed to know, would have needed to be told, even though she and Soot had sat beneath the kitchen table and smelt the burning hay, infuriated her. 'And lots of other people do as well, so don't bother to tell me anything. I'll ask around.'

'That's right, and make an even bigger fool of yourself than you've done already. You didn't think I knew about your performance at the railway station, did you? A woman said to me, "Mrs Davidson, when she started laughing at that poor man I really thought she'd gone mad."' Her grandmother paused to let that sink in. 'I don't know why Bobby Graham still has so much time for you.'

Bobby Graham, thought Lily, I could tell you a thing or two about Bobby Graham. I could grab you by the arm and drag you out onto the verandah and through my bedroom door, and there'd be your bloody Bobby Graham.

But she knew she could no more betray him in that way than she could have shot him. It was strange now to think she'd ever believed she could.

'You're nothing but an ungrateful little trollop. You showed more sense when you were at school.'

'It's a pity you didn't bother to praise me for it then.' She'd far rather shoot her grandmother.

'And you can take that look off your face. I never thought I'd live to see the day when I'd be glad to leave this place. You've made an exhibition of us all. People'll be thinking it's something in the pump water.'

And there it was, just like that. Time stopped, then started again, but this time there was no click in her head, nor any voice but her own. 'It was my uncle who went mad, wasn't it? And that's all there is to it. He was mad and he shot himself, but who cares about that now?'

'You didn't know him.'

'Of course I did.' She'd have known him better than she knew the kindly black kettle and the whispering kitchen chairs, better than she'd known Frisky and Nancy, better even than she'd known Prince.

'You wouldn't remember him.'

'I do. He had blue eyes and fair hair.' And the face of a jilted girl on him.

'You wouldn't remember what he was like. He didn't even keep himself clean. He'd spend all day sitting round without a word out of him, and then we'd hear him laughing and talking in the middle of the night when there was nobody there. And he used to say such dreadful things.'

And perhaps his pale lips had twisted in a certain way before he said them. 'What things?'

But her grandmother wouldn't or couldn't repeat them.

'Well, what sort of things?'

Her grandmother gave herself a little shake. 'Oh, just silly things. The same sort of nonsense you come out with at times. You ought to watch yourself, you know. He used to say the sheep were talking about him.'

'I daresay they were, and they wouldn't have been the only ones.'

'That's right, make a joke of it.' But in the face of her silliness her grandmother had regained the upper hand. Her expression became reminiscent, and she found her town voice again. 'He was very rude to poor Mrs Graham one day.'

Poor Mrs Graham. 'What did he say?'

'Oh, she came over with some little things of Jean's she thought might do for you. She said that seeing her latest was a boy there was no point in hanging on to Jean's clothes any longer.'

Some little things of Jean's. Never in a hundred years would her grandmother have used a phrase like that if she were being herself.

And she'd had to wear Jean Graham's castoffs. No wonder she learnt to sew as soon as she could hold a needle.

'I told him to go and bring you out so Mrs Graham could have a look at you, and he said, "Doesn't that bitch know that Lady Bountiful from the Big House has had her day?"'

From anybody else that remark would have given her grandmother nothing but pleasure. 'And what did Mrs Graham say?'

'Oh, she wasn't the least bit put out,' said her grandmother comfortably. 'She just said to him, "There's no need for that sort of language, you know." She did ask me later if I should leave you with him as much as I did, but I said the other one had gone off again and I couldn't be expected to see to everything.'

And how she must have hated admitting that to Mrs Graham, although she gave no sign of it now.

'Mrs Graham always took an interest in you. When you came back here to live she made Jean and Bobby take you to school so the other kids wouldn't tease you.'

'You should have kept something of him,' said Lily hopelessly. 'I don't believe you never had a photograph, not one. You could have spoken of him more, you could've taken me to see his grave.' And then I might have known who it was that I've been looking for all these years.

'I don't believe in living in the past,' said her grandmother. 'He was a dear little fellow when he was small, and I like to remember the good in people.'

And Lily never knew what she might have found to say to that, because her grandfather came in. 'Michael Kelly's coming down the road,' he said. And then, 'What's going on here?'

The town manner went in an instant. Her grandmother took on the aspect of a cornered child, the sort who'd be a self-righteous little bully when things were going to her liking and a whining sneak when they were not. 'Oh, I'm just having to listen to everything I should have done but haven't for her ladyship here.' Her face crumpled and turned red, as if the attempt at nonchalance had been too much for her.

'I only wanted to know about my uncle, that's all. I don't see why it's always had to be such a deep dark secret.'

'People say that sort of thing runs in families,' said her grandmother. 'It might have worried you.' Now her voice threatened tears.

'Why? He wasn't my son. Nor my father, for that matter, though I've heard it said he might have been.'

'People can be very cruel. I've always tried to protect you from that sort of talk. All my life I've done my best for you.'

'That's right,' said her grandfather. 'We did our best for you. She always tried to protect you.'

'Protect me? From what?' But Lily knew she'd gone too far. They all had. Her grandfather sidled off, muttering about Michael and the wagon. Her grandmother was gathering up her purse and umbrella. The only person she'd ever sought to protect was herself, and she was doing it now as she'd always done.

The days flecked with anger, with swats from dishcloth or razor strop, and orders to get out from underfoot, get away to bed. The jeering, the disgust, that need for distance. And now, when Lily had grown past and above all these, the show of weakness, an appeal to a kinder side her grandmother had no part in forming.

And always, underneath, the fear.

Fear that had little to do with Lily, and even less to do with her mother. For what the daughter had done and the granddaughter become were as nothing compared with the son whose life and death cast so long a shadow. He'd frightened her grandmother, and perhaps her grandfather and Mrs Graham too, but he hadn't frightened her. She must have liked him as she liked his little room, as she'd liked old Soot, as she'd liked the name he'd given her; whatever others may have thought of him he'd made perfect sense to her.

When the snowman melted, the yard dog understood his longings, for he was built around the stove rake and that's what leapt inside him when he saw the stove.

The answer was so simple; it had lain in and around her all this time, and she'd never seen it, never even thought to look for it. Bob had done better than she in that, as he did in everything.

Michael Kelly was hovering in the doorway. Her grandmother shot Lily a look intended to convey that his more than usually bewildered air was on account of her state of undress, and then they were gone.

Lily felt the house settling around her. Alone she was stronger, but there was still Bob. He might have dressed and slipped away, though that would have been difficult with her grandfather in the yard. It was more likely he was waiting for his chance to leave.

He wasn't even awake. He lay on his side now, facing the

wall. Lily took the shotgun from under the bed; it seemed diminished by day, cool and content again. She unlocked the door to the front room, opened it and banged it shut.

Bob sat bolt upright, said, 'Oh, God,' and covered his face with both hands. 'What time is it?'

'Past seven.'

'Oh, God.'

'You can get dressed and get out. No one will see you. Michael Kelly has taken my grandparents to the Bay train and it'll be a while before he comes back with the wagon.'

'Why have you got that thing?'

'Why do you think?'

'Is it loaded?'

'Of course.'

'Do you know how to use it?'

'Yes.' And to show him she drew one hammer back.

'The way you're holding it you're likely to do more damage to yourself than to me.'

But there was a great stillness in him.

He said, 'If you shoot me they'll hang you. Or lock you away for the rest of your life.'

'They might decide I'm mad. It's in the family, as I'm sure you know.'

'I think you'd have a better chance of getting yourself out of gaol than a lunatic asylum.'

'That's something you'd never know for sure.' Lily bent to pick up his shirt and underwear and tossed them onto the bed. She had no qualms about looking at him now. It would serve him right to have to dress in front of her, to feel her eyes.

'I'd find it easier to think about putting on my clothes if you uncocked that gun. Do you know how?'

'Yes.'

'Well, point it away from me first.'

Lily felt tempted not to, but did.

'You need to ease the spring. Front trigger.'

'I know. Nigel Harraway showed me.'

'Good for him.' Bob managed a smile. 'I take it you didn't enjoy it then. Last night.'

'No.'

'If you didn't want to do it, you should have said.'

'I rather thought I had.'

He reached for his shirt and turned modestly from her. 'I don't think my first wife liked it much either.'

'You must ask yourself what she and I have had in common,' said Lily, then felt suddenly ashamed of taunting him in this fashion with a loaded shotgun on her arm. It wasn't his fault she had never liked him in that way, or that his wife was dishonest enough to pretend she might — at least until a ring was on her finger.

Bob picked up his trousers, then sat on the edge of the bed and rubbed his face again. His cheeks were dark and his hair tousled, but he still looked very clean. It wasn't fair that he should look so clean. Lily wanted to mark him in some way, to soil him as he had her. She turned to lean the shotgun against the wall, and cast about for a more subtle weapon.

'What did your wife die of?'

He muttered something. A syllable pricked at her ears, the sound overheard in the discreet murmurings of Mrs Kelly and her grandmother.

'Did you say a miscarriage?'

He nodded drearily. 'The result of a fall.'

'Oh, yes,' she said. 'Did you know she was pregnant?'

'Of course.'

'Were you there when it happened?'

'What, the pregnancy?' Bob gave her one of his tolerant smiles.

'The fall.'

He shook his head. 'I had to go away for a few days. She was on her way out with a friend. The house we had then had marble steps, and she slipped and sat down heavily. She said all that was hurt was her dignity, and they went in for a cup of tea, then out again. Later she told her friend she'd been more shaken than she'd cared to admit and that when she got home she would lie down for a while. That was where she died. At home, on the bed.' His voice was flat, his face expressionless; he might have been reciting a story learnt long ago by heart. And parts of that tale could have been well rehearsed even before Bob heard it, but he'd been a lawyer as well as a husband; he mightn't have swallowed it whole.

'Where's my collar?'

'On the floor where you left it.' She picked it up and held it out to him. The domesticity of the scene. They might, for an instant, have been married. He thrust it into his pocket and bent to gather up his shoes.

'Was your wife's friend with her when she went to lie down?'

'No.'

'Didn't you have a maid?'

'She went out just after they did. It was her afternoon off.'

'I suppose you had the telephone.' Bob couldn't live without it. 'Why didn't she telephone for help as soon as she got in?'

'I don't know. She may have felt too weak, or been too shy. Or too frightened.'

Too frightened. Lily had it all now. The staged fall on the steps, a cup of tea in the house so that the maid should know, a visit to someone recommended by her friend, and a sad little story for the absent husband. Her weapon was to hand.

'Falls can be frightening, I know. Women came to the flash hotel we had in Christchurch to have them all the time. Of course they brought their doctors with them, so there was no real harm done. I had to get the room ready and clean up afterwards. As the manager's daughter my discretion was assured.'

'What are you saying?'

'Nothing, really. Your wife couldn't have done it like that, because it's very expensive and she might have had to ask you for the money. Or perhaps she just didn't know the right kind of doctor. But when she got home and knew something had gone wrong she could have telephoned Connie — I'm sure Doctor Graham would've been discreet. Though maybe not quite discreet enough for Mrs Bob Graham.'

'Connie wasn't around,' he said absently. 'She was working in Sydney by then.' He seemed to have lost something else.

'So I can see your wife's fall must have come as a surprise.'

'Shut up, will you? Just shut up.' There was a note of panic in his voice. He started hunting feverishly among the bedcovers.

'What are you looking for?'

'I've lost my watch and chain. Where did I put it?' Perhaps it was the seal that worried him, the stone like a still pool in the sunlit creek with the initials RG for Bobby Graham.

'It's over there,' she said, nodding at the dressing table. 'I'd hardly wish to keep it as a memento.'

'You might be right,' he said suddenly. 'She was young, and she was disappointed because we'd planned to go to Europe later that year and it wouldn't have been possible.'

'And now you'll never know for sure. But you went, anyway. Well, they say travelling alone's best. The company of anyone you meet along the way is bound to be an improvement on your own.'

He snatched up his coat, and a coin from the pockets rang on the floor. 'You can keep that,' he said, but it was a feeble insult aimed at her and what she'd done, not at what another might have done to her.

'I'm glad you rate your pleasure so low.'

'I never want to see you again.' He spoke as if her loss would be the greater.

'You won't have to if you go to the Argentine. As it seems you've told everyone you will.' But she knew he wouldn't now, because he'd meant to go with her. Bob wasn't good at being alone.

In the doorway he paused, and stood looking out across the paddocks as if he no longer knew where to go at all. The corners of his mouth were drooping in a way she'd never seen before.

'Where did you leave your motorcar?'

'Up the side track, by the trees. Where I used to tie the horse.' He pressed the back of his hand against his mouth.

What they had been, what they'd become. Lily felt sick with

shame. 'Somebody might have seen it there.'

'I don't think so.'

'What will you say if they ask you where you were all night?'

'I'll say I had too much to drink and slept in the Buick.'

'The first part of that's true. If you're going to tell a lie it's best for it to be as near the truth as possible.'

'I'll take your word for that.' Then he turned back, his eyes on the ground.

'Now what have you lost?'

He raised his head and smiled shyly, seeming afraid to speak.

'What is it?' For a moment she thought he was going to say that he was sorry.

He said, 'I hope you're not thinking of making a fuss about this.'

'A fuss?'

'Nobody will believe you. Half the Bay must have seen you with that shit at one time or another, and everyone here's seen you swanning round in clothes you couldn't possibly have paid for. Too many people know what you are. And your grandparents were in the house — you could have screamed, you could've struggled. There isn't a mark on you. And I'll bet you didn't say one word about it to them this morning. Believe me, you haven't a leg to stand on.'

'You must be mad to speak like that now.'

'Why don't you shoot me then?'

'I still might, but I feel sorry for you. I think I always have done.'

He shrugged, and walked away slowly along the verandah. That took courage of a kind, or maybe he also thought of death and the ease it would bring. At the top of the steps he turned to face her, perhaps to see what she intended, or he may have thought she'd hesitate to shoot him in the back. Then he slung his coat over one shoulder, thrust his other hand into his trouser pocket and went on, with an odd mix of jauntiness and despair.

Chapter 19

Michael Kelly returned with the wagon and called that he'd left the horse in the stable paddock and would be back later to see if she wanted anything done. Her grandmother had told him there was a stoat that wanted shooting.

Lily shouted her acknowledgements from the bathroom where she stood staring at the empty tub. The thought of water on her skin pained her; the rub of towels and weight of clothes would be too much to bear. And so, not being clean and dressed, she had no inclination to do anything at all, but sat on the verandah as empty as the day.

There was a bruise, just one, on her arm above the elbow. That must have been where Bob caught her, though she'd felt nothing then and it was not sore now.

The day grew brighter and she wanted to do something to dispel the numbness in her, but when she wondered what that something might be she could think only of Mr Fernon.

The times they'd been nice to each other. The first night he came to her room, so trustful she'd felt almost afraid for him; that day he'd walked smiling towards her in his white linen suit, the way they used to lie in bed talking nonsense together. Though she didn't want him to talk to her now. She wanted him still and soothing in a room filled with yellow light; she wanted him like honey, to take the taste away.

He wouldn't come. Or shouldn't come, because there was nothing to come for. She'd been spoiled. Something was gone from her, the thing Bob sneered at when he spoke of her honour, even though it went on protecting him to the very end. She was sorry, then, that she hadn't shot him on the steps when he turned to face her; that would have made her whole again.

Or perhaps not, because he'd seemed so helpless standing there. She thought again of his eyes across the ballroom, the haggard face at her door. She'd been too careless where Bob was concerned. The fault was hers for letting him drive her home; nobody could say she hadn't been warned.

And she should have locked the verandah door.

But that was a thing she'd never done; there'd been no reason to. And even if the door had been locked and she'd known Bob was there, she would have opened it. She'd never thought to fear him, and that had been her worst mistake.

He was out there somewhere in the sunlight, going about his business with the sad air he'd put on with his clothes. A wronged man, a disappointed man. A man whose life had brought him to the age of thirty and left him incapable of judging whether or not a woman wanted him, and ignorant of the pleasure he might have when she did.

He'd have washed the night away. She could see him in the shower-bath: dark-bodied, darker-haired, lavish with the Pears soap that matched the coloured tiles. He'd have shaved and dressed and eaten breakfast, pretending not to hear his sisters ribbing him about sleeping with his motorcar. Or maybe not. If they believed he and she had reached an understanding, they might have been more tactful.

Again she saw herself and Bob struggling along that busy stretch of quay, squabbling over who should be carrying which piece of luggage. A picture not without a certain charm, so long as you ignored the fact that both squabblers knew she could disagree with him only when he allowed her to.

Refusing to let her out of bed when she said she wanted to go to the lavatory. Complaining of her coldness, then asking if she was a virgin. Such arrogance, such ignorance. For what could Bob have known of virgins other than his wife, and perhaps some clever girl at the university hellbent on flouting conventions not much observed outside her own little circle? Or of tarts for that matter, since Ruby was his idea of one.

Lily went and tore the sheets from her bed, flung them into the wash house, and took fresh ones from the linen cupboard. I shall tell the Kelly boys, she thought, and then we'll see who gets beaten to a pulp to avenge my honour.

That picture also had its charms, but she knew she'd do no such thing. She accompanied them to dances and sewed buttons on their shirts, but they were no more a part of this new world than her grandparents had been.

She left the shotgun in her room; she felt a certain kinship with it now. On an impulse she took off her silk wrapper and went to thrust it in the stove, but stopped herself in time. She'd liked it until now and would do so again; it had done her no greater harm than fall open when Bob pulled her towards him, and she had never put it on because she hoped it would protect her. She'd worn it for Mr Fernon, who was out there somewhere too.

By now he and Bob might have formed a new alliance to replace the one they'd made in the Grahams' garden — whilst having a piss, no doubt. Standing there in evening dress with their cocks in their hands and their minds on an impenetrable woman. A woman who'd shown no inclination to relieve Bob of his loneliness or Mr Fernon of whatever it was that led him to betray her, and not because of anything she'd done, but for something left undone out of what he termed stupidity. He meant, of course, her ignorance of love and the cheap excuses it provided, the tawdry games that could be played in its name. Though she and Bob had proved apt pupils in the end.

Her honour, her stupidity. They'd been one and the same, and nothing very wonderful: only something to do with never giving in. Call it obstinacy, then. Not a quality ever spoken of with admiration, but it had carried her through countless petty slights and humiliations and was more than ever necessary now.

She would wash, then, and don her new summer frock and hat, and go to the Grand with an untroubled face and let Mr Fernon see how little he'd achieved.

That plan pleased her. Nevertheless she lingered at the gate, thinking of the fitness of her new summer shoes for the walk to town and of what she'd say to Mr Fernon when she found him there. And she wasn't very far along the road before she began to feel conspicuous and therefore, by the standards of the district, somewhat silly. For a moment she considered turning back to the Kellys' to see if Michael could drive her in their gig, but she hadn't done such a thing before and knew she wouldn't now.

Jack Dennehy, idle for once, was standing on the Grand's steps looking along the street. At first he seemed not to recognise her, then blinked and grinned.

'Have you seen Mr Fernon today?'

'He's just this minute gone out into the garden, Miss Macgregor.'

Mr Fernon was with a small family group, all dressed rather sportily: a middle-aged man and woman, a boy of fourteen or fifteen looking dutiful but distant as such boys do when obliged to appear in public at their parents' heels, a young woman with an awkward, lurching gait and an independent air. To her Mr Fernon seemed particularly attentive as they settled at their table by the trees.

He saw Lily, frowned, and looked away.

It was too late for that game now. She had enquired for him and he was there. As she drew nearer he rose and said, 'Miss Macgregor, what a pleasant surprise,' and introduced his companions, but she didn't heed their names.

'Won't you join us?' asked the woman, and her husband offered his chair, turning to an adjacent table to pull up another. Their daughter wanted to know where she was from; they were from San Francisco.

'Miss Macgregor is a native of these parts,' said Mr Fernon, 'and shortly to marry. Then she and her husband will travel to the Argentine.'

This for the daughter's benefit, no doubt. 'It is in connection with that I wished to speak to you,' said Lily, and smiled on his companions. 'I must ask you to excuse us for a moment.'

That left Mr Fernon with no option but to follow her a little way from the table. 'You are not honouring our agreement,' he said, taking her arm to walk beside her.

'You came to the Grahams' ball.'

'I was invited, as I assume you were, by Bob Graham.'

'But you came here, when you told me you meant to go away.'

'Perhaps you took so much of my money I had to change my plans. In any case, I like it here. Should I make an offer for your grandfather's farm?'

'I wouldn't advise it. You need to get on with your neighbours if you hope to do well as a farmer. The Kellys have no time for you, and Bob Graham's not your friend.'

'Michael Kelly was quite cordial when I spoke to him this morning. And if Bob's elder sister is to be believed, he is set on leaving. Accompanied by you.'

'You know that's not true. None of it is true now.'

'Then I'm sorry. But it was I who paid you to keep away from me, Miss Macgregor, not the other way around.'

'I never agreed to keep away from the place where I was born.'

'It's what *I* must do.'

'And if you want your money back . . .' she said carelessly, then wondered who could lend her the balance other than Bob.

'No, my dear, I do not want my money back. I paid you to stay away from me and so you shall.' He put his hand over hers where it rested on his arm. 'But do not go too hastily. People are watching.'

They were, though with no more than mild interest.

'Since when have you cared what people think?'

'Are you threatening me, Miss Macgregor?'

'Threatening you? How could I do that?'

'I am very much afraid you are about to cause a scene.'

'I don't cause scenes.'

'Oh, do you not? That isn't what I've heard. Still, I gave you the money; it's not for me to say what you must do with it. That dress is quite delightful, by the way. You might have risen from a sunlit sea. And I do think it a great pity Bob has seen fit to change his mind.'

'You needn't. It was just another of his dreams.' Then something gave in her. 'Why did you ask him . . .' she began, but had to stop. Her chin was wobbling.

Mr Fernon smiled. 'I was curious to know what place you held in his affections. You yourself were in some doubt when last we spoke of him.'

'I was shown it last night.' Her lower jaw jerked like a decrepit old man's; it seemed no part of her. She caught at it with both hands.

'And I gather the experience was not a happy one. I hope you don't expect consolation from me. I don't go about consoling people.'

They had reached the gate to the street, and Lily didn't trust herself to speak again. He said, 'I have a pleasant afternoon planned, but I may find time to call on you later. Can you manage on your own from here?'

'Why not?' Even two words were an effort.

He gestured at her face. 'You seem not quite yourself.'

She took one hand away. 'A bad tooth, that's all.' The lie came out easily; that was something.

'Then I really must rejoin my friends.' He opened the gate for her and Lily passed into the street.

So there was to be no help from that quarter. Was that what she'd expected, after all? That he would be alone, that they'd sit together at a table in the garden and that he, who'd contrived to bring this misery on her, would somehow have the power to take it off again? For what would she have spoken of, if not that? And who else was there to tell?

Perhaps some things were like the dreams Mrs Kelly said should never be told.

Long roads, watchful eyes, and one new shoe burning her heel: they were all that mattered now. The effort required to keep her back straight and her head high was exhausting; she wished somebody would come by and offer a lift, then hoped they wouldn't, because they'd be sure to ask where she'd been, got up the way she was, and wonder why her face didn't match her festive attire. Most of all she feared to see the cloud of dust that meant a motorcar.

At last she was far enough from town to sit down and take off her shoes, then quit the road and head home across the paddocks, a gaudy, stumbling scarecrow.

Lily changed into her house clothes and did the washing. She felt ready to topple over with each puff of wind as she stood at the line, but she went on with her chores. After all, she had money and nice clothes and there was nothing to keep her here; once the house was clean and orderly she could pack her things and go. And not just to one of the cities: anywhere in the world, if she wanted to. She had a brief, wonderful vision of broad streets with splendid buildings, and gardens and galleries too. Such an ambition seemed almost too large, but it steadied her. She took up the worn hall runner and the front room's carpet square, heaved them over the verandah rail, beat them, rolled them and tied them with string. Then she scrubbed the floors, comfortable on her hands and knees, unseeing and unseeable. If she didn't light the lamps as it grew dark, nobody would know she was at home. She liked that idea.

When she heard hooves on the drive she thought first of Michael Kelly and next, as the horse was hitched to the verandah rail, of Bob. This time it was her hands that shook. Only her hands, and that was odd, for she was certain that last night they hadn't touched him. She'd forgiven him, or thought she had, but her hands knew otherwise. She crept into her bedroom and picked up the shotgun; that served to make them still.

The front door opened, and he stepped into the hall. She knew that step: it was not entirely steady, but it wasn't Bob's. Pushing the shotgun under a fold in her eiderdown, she sat down on the edge of the bed and listened as he walked through the house, pausing to look in each room, then returned to the front room and crossed to hers.

'Here you are at last,' he said. He wasn't drunk, but there was an unpleasant blurriness about him. He'd been drinking brandy; she could smell it on the air.

'Have you come to gloat?'

'What have I to gloat about?' he asked, and didn't wait for her reply. 'How busy you have been.'

'My grandparents have gone to the Bay.' Her voice sounded flat and dull, scarcely hers at all.

'I know.'

'I have the house to myself till Wednesday night. There'll be nobody here but me.' But it was too late for that. 'You should have come sooner or else stayed away.'

He shrugged. 'I thought you wanted to see me.'

'Well, I don't.'

'You surprise me. This afternoon I detected a certain urgency in your manner.'

He sat beside her and, putting an arm around her shoulders, drew her towards him and began to fondle her. She leaned awkwardly against him for a moment or two, then asked, 'Why are you doing this?'

'Why not? What else have you ever required of me?'

It seemed wrong of him to touch her in this way when he knew, he must know, what Bob had done. If he had valued her at all he wouldn't want her now. She said, 'It's not as if you ever liked me.'

'I could say the same of you.'

'Oh, you can, of course you can. We never liked each other. I don't blame you for that, or for anything that passed between us.'

'That's very kind of you.'

'I was mistaken in you, that's all. You made me think — you reminded me — of someone I was attached to a long time ago. But you're just his shadow. It wouldn't have made a difference; I don't think it ever will. Though now I can see just how wrong everything has been.'

He moved away from her. 'Is there anything to drink in this house?'

'Haven't you had enough already?'

'Dutch courage, Miss Macgregor. Well, French to be precise.'

'There's only sherry for the Christmas trifle, and that's been packed.' The old instinct for usefulness made her add, 'I could run over to the Kellys' and borrow some whisky if you like.'

'That will not be necessary.'

After a little he said, 'If I have hurt you in any way, then I'm sorry.'

'It's Bob you've hurt. And if the things you do made you sorry, you wouldn't do them at all.'

'Then it's best that I go,' he said, and went to rise. That was when he put his hand on the eiderdown, and felt the shotgun there.

'Leave that alone.'

'Oh, Miss Macgregor, what strange bedfellows you have.'

'You must have known he'd do something he'd be sorry for, if not to you then to me.'

Mr Fernon broke the shotgun, smiled upon the cartridges nestled in the breech, then snapped it shut and dropped it into her outstretched hands.

'It's different today,' she said. 'Last night it thought its hour had come.'

'But not yet gone.'

There was an odd excitement in him now. He began to pace about the room touching her belongings, picking them up and putting them down: the unfinished bit of beadwork on an afternoon apron, her hairbrush and hand mirror with their painted wooden backs, the shell box she'd made to hold her hairpins. She feared for them, so cheap and small before that tireless appetite for harm.

'You'll have to go,' she said. 'I've work to do while it's still light and then I've things to think about, so I don't want you here.' His restless movements were making her giddy; she stood the shotgun on its butt and rested her cheek against its cool barrels.

'What a child you are,' he said suddenly, 'what an innocent. You should have bought yourself a doll, not those fine clothes.'

There was something peculiarly offensive in the notion of a doll, but she was glad her train set was in a drawer and safe from his eyes. 'And you should have left Bob out of it,' she said. 'Whatever went on between us had nothing to do with him.'

'Perhaps I envied him.'

'I don't believe you. I think you wanted to make him hate you, as you do with everyone.'

He swung away from her and propped himself against the wall. 'And have I succeeded in making you hate me?'

'I don't feel anything for you.' That was true for the present, yet even as she spoke she had an inkling it would change one way or the other.

'The trouble with you, Miss Macgregor, is that you do not feel at all.'

'Oh, I feel,' she said. 'I feel ashamed.'

'Ashamed?'

And it wasn't the right word, but she couldn't think of a better one. 'What Bob did shouldn't matter, none of it should matter, but it does. There's a hole in me now.'

Mr Fernon remained by the wall, his face showing nothing of what he might be thinking. In the pallid light he looked crumpled and somehow papery, his skin whiter than usual and his eyes unnaturally dark; an empty cut-out thing of studied folds and creases. Lily felt cramped and vaguely ill, as if she too were helpless before that fearful hunger. She lowered the gun and pulled one hammer back, carefully, as she had with Bob, but Mr Fernon didn't ask if she knew what she was doing.

He said, 'If you are planning a shooting party, Miss Macgregor, may I suggest that your dress is somewhat inappropriate?'

'I'm not planning anything,' she said. 'I shall have to start all over again and I want to be free of you.'

He could have turned and walked away as Bob had done; there was time enough to do so. Instead he stayed where he was and looked towards the window. 'The days are much too long here,' he said. 'It must be nearing nine o'clock, yet the birds are still so noisy.'

Chapter 20

With Pat away at high school and Cathy off to Wellington, evenings at the Kellys' were much quieter than they used to be. Dan and his brothers agreed that the shot had come from the Davidsons', and wondered who'd be shooting there. Michael spoke of the stoat, and the men waited with knowing grins for the second shot, for they had no great opinion of Lily's skill as a marksman. When it didn't come Mrs Kelly felt a chill about her neck and shoulders, and told Frank and Gerald to go over and make sure Lily was all right. Michael, who had meant to go anyway, went with them.

Lily was sitting on the verandah with her grandfather's shotgun across her knees, and the air of one who has completed a task long postponed. 'There's an awful lot of blood in there,' she said. 'And a hole in the wall where he stood. That'll have to be repaired before the place is sold.'

They'd already guessed it wasn't a matter of a stoat.

'You wait here,' said Frank to Michael, 'while we take a look inside.'

'Did you mean to kill him?' asked Michael. He was still thinking of Bob Graham, even though his uncles had identified the horse by the verandah as one from the stables in town, and he knew the Buick had gone by the time he returned with the wagon.

'One doesn't point a loaded shotgun at someone standing a

few feet away and press the trigger otherwise,' replied Lily, rather rudely Michael thought.

'You mustn't say that,' he said. 'You must say it was an accident and you don't know how it happened at all.'

'I'll have to get my things out of there,' said Lily. 'And you'll have to get a constable to come from the Bay.'

'Oh, the police,' said Michael unhappily. 'That mightn't be a good idea.' He wondered what was keeping his uncles. They read the court reports in the newspapers, and went to watch the juicy trials; they'd know what to do. Later Gerald told him they'd considered disposing of the body and freeing the horse to make its way home, but decided it wasn't the best time of year for that sort of thing, what with the days being long and the rivers low.

'She has spoilt a better face than her own,' reflected Dan when he heard their news, and then fell to puzzling over who'd said that and of whom, now the person most able to tell him was dead.

The district was excited but not much surprised to learn what Lily Macgregor had done. She'd always been a funny one, from a funny family, and God only knew who and what her real father was. It was Bob Graham they felt sorry for. And even after she'd strung him along the way she had and was known to have a considerable sum of money in her possession, money she'd got from her dead fancy man, Bob lost no time in finding her a lawyer and wanted to pay for her defence, a matter later sorted out between him and her stepfather.

The lawyer was a young fellow Bob had known at the university. He'd set up for himself at the Bay, and saw in Euphemia Davidson — otherwise known as Phemie Macgregor and seemingly most often as Lily Macgregor — his chance of fame, though the day he met her hadn't started well for him.

He was eating his breakfast in the kitchen, with the back door left open for air, when a middle-sized rat sauntered across the floor. Taking the poker from beside the stove, he followed the rat into the dining room where it disappeared under the sideboard.

He called his landlady's cat, thinking that if she drove the rat out of hiding he could kill it. The cat was keen enough for sport and thrust her head beneath the sideboard, whereupon the rat emitted a high, sobbing cry, a cry so full of terror and despair he was moved. Or deceived, for what the cat heard in that cry caused her to back away with flattened ears, snarling. The rat emerged and ran for the kitchen. He went after it, still meaning to kill it, or at least drive it from the house, but it slipped into the narrow space between kitchen bench and pantry.

The gap was just wide enough to admit his arm and the poker. He peered in to ascertain the rat's exact position and so met its eyes, round and very bright in a sweet, sharp face beneath translucent ears; he was struck by the pallor and delicacy of what he saw as its hands. It knew the time for fear or threat had passed: those bright eyes and exquisite hands contained nothing but the resolution of one about to sell its life as dearly as it could. And to beat at such perfection was beyond him. He left the back door open for the rat to quit the house in its own good time and took himself and the cat off, feeling slightly less than a man.

His encounter with Miss Davidson was more satisfying, and would be the first of many, because there was no doubt she'd shot and killed Josselin Fernon and that there'd be a case to answer. She sat before him with her eyes downcast and her hands clasped on the scarred wooden table. The police, she said in response to his query, had been very nice to her, 'though I would have liked a cell with a larger window.'

'This is not a hotel, Miss Davidson. What have you told them?'

'They said that because of the seriousness of my situation I could tell them as much or as little as I pleased, but whatever I said had better be true.' She unclasped her hands, long-fingered and fine-jointed, and pushed back her sleeve to reveal a yellowing bruise above her elbow. 'I showed them this and explained that I hadn't meant to shoot Mr Fernon, only to frighten him so he would leave me alone.' The shotgun had gone off of its own accord and she had run from the house to get help from the Kellys, but felt ill and sat down on the verandah. Then she saw the Kelly boys, 'Frank and Gerald, the pugilists, you might have heard of them,' coming across the paddocks.

He exchanged glances with his junior; it was the best they could have hoped for.

'Well, I had to tell the police something,' she added a shade defensively. 'They gave me a cup of tea.'

'Did they write anything down?'

'Oh, they wrote things down, but they never asked me to sign anything. The Kelly boys said I wasn't to if they did. They said the magistrate'll say the same.'

'In a manner of speaking, though you'll have to make a statement in due course. At this stage you need do no more than plead not guilty to murder when we appear before him.'

'But everybody knows I did it,' she said.

'My colleague here will explain the difference between murder and manslaughter later, and from now on you should not discuss your circumstances with anyone other than ourselves. Tell me, was the shotgun you used that day the one the police have?'

She nodded.

'Would you say the trigger pull is on the light side?'

'It has two triggers,' she said. 'One behind the other.'

His junior snickered. Clearly, Miss Davidson was not a woman of great penetration.

'Has anybody else used it recently?'

'Mr Harraway, who has gone to Wellington. He's a friend of Mr Fernon's.'

'A close friend?'

'Oh, yes. They were at school together. And when Mr Fernon's family wanted to send him to a lunatic asylum Mr Harraway's father persuaded them to let him come here. But I don't know much about that. You'd have to ask Mr Harraway.'

'I daresay I shall.'

'What will happen to the shotgun after the trial?' she asked.

'You would do better to think of what could happen to you if you are found guilty of murder, Miss Davidson. Or even of manslaughter, if there is no recommendation for mercy.'

'Oh, I will,' she said, 'I do,' and for the first time she raised her eyes, round and very bright, to his. He thought briefly of Bob Graham, so busy on her behalf, and of the rumours that he'd hoped to marry her, and wondered if Miss Davidson had found her erstwhile paramour something of a bind.

He said, 'When we go before the magistrate there may be a chance of bail. Your friend Mr Graham . . .'

'I want nothing from him.'

'Then all you need do is think of everything you know that will help me with your defence,' he said.

And for their next meeting Miss Davidson had ready a sad little tale of seduction and betrayal. She had met Mr Fernon almost a year ago at the Kellys', and he'd escorted her home. Then she encountered him at a house rented by the Harraways, and he pressed her to have dinner with him at the Grand Hotel. The very next evening, on her way to see Mrs Harraway, she'd called in at the Grand to return a book Mr Fernon had loaned Mr Kelly.

'And did you have dinner with Mr Fernon?'

Miss Davidson shook her head. She had some difficulty in explaining what had eventuated, but at length agreed that they'd become lovers. After that they saw a great deal of each other. 'He took a room at Mrs Morton's house, not far from my stepfather's hotel.' About six months ago they became engaged to be married, and Mr Fernon promised her a ruby ring.

'Do you still have that ring?'

'He never gave it to me. He said we had to keep our engagement secret because his family wouldn't like a barmaid in their midst, and he didn't want to lose the allowance they paid him.' It was a very generous allowance and he'd given her money for her trousseau, but all the while he continued to associate with other women, and made no secret of his desire to seduce the Kellys' daughter. And so, after several quarrels, they parted. She had gone to Christchurch to visit Mrs Harraway. 'We went shopping and I bought new clothes,' Miss Davidson added shamefacedly, 'which I said were for my trousseau.'

'You had hopes of a reconciliation?'

'From what I knew of Mr Fernon, that would have been impossible.' But he had followed her home that spring, and attended Mrs Graham's ball. She had danced with him once because it would have looked strange to refuse, and he'd reminded her he had paid for all that she had on. The next day she had gone to the Grand to ask him to leave her alone and to offer him his money back, but he'd refused to listen. That night he came to her grandparents' house. He had been drinking, and knew she was alone there; she knew what he had in mind.

'And where was the shotgun then?'

'In my room,' said Miss Davidson. 'On my bed.'

'Is that where it's usually kept?'

'No, of course not. It's kept in a cupboard in the wash house. Why are you so interested in the shotgun?'

'It is a matter of your defence, Miss Davidson. It's not usual for women to keep loaded shotguns in their bedrooms unless they have some special reason to do so. When did you take it from the cupboard?'

'Early that morning, after the ball.'

'And when did you load it?'

'After I took it from the cupboard.'

'Did you think Mr Fernon would come to the house later that day?'

'No.'

'Did you ask him to come when you saw him at the Grand Hotel?'

'Why would I do that?'

'These are questions the Crown Prosecutor may well ask if you take the stand.'

'If he's going to ask silly questions, I won't answer them.'

'You may not have to,' he said, still undecided on the matter, 'but it's his job to prove you acted with murderous intent, and mine to convince the jury otherwise. Your reason for having a loaded shotgun in your bedroom is of the greatest interest to us all.'

'You had no thoughts of killing yourself?' asked his junior hopefully. That would make for sob stuff in the final summing-up.

'When?'

'When you loaded the shotgun and took it to your room.'

'I had thoughts,' said Miss Davidson, 'of killing a stoat. After the ball there was a stoat about.'

'Did anybody else see this stoat?'

'You'll have to ask him that.'

'Ask whom, Miss Davidson?'

'Your friend Mr Graham, who drove me home from the ball. He saw me with the shotgun. And I told my grandmother about the stoat that morning.'

'How often have you used the gun?'

'Hardly ever. My grandfather showed me how when I was about ten, and sometimes I used to watch Mr Harraway shoot rabbits. I don't like killing things, but stoats seek out the dotterels' nests and I've always been very fond of those birds.'

'How do you spell Euphemia?' she asked, before she signed her completed statement with a careful hand. 'I think I know, but since that's who I am now, it's best to be sure.'

He asked his junior, 'Why would Fernon have gone to see her after he'd paid her off if she didn't ask him to?'

His junior had revised his opinion of Miss Davidson downwards. 'Perhaps the poor bastard wanted her back — there's no accounting for tastes. She's a cold fish. Did you notice she never once used his Christian name? I wouldn't put her on the stand.'

'I don't intend to. I think our Euphemia might answer the Crown a little too well.' Much better to draw out their witnesses on the habits of the dead man, and then speak last of love and of being let down, and the fear Miss Davidson must have felt when her seducer came at night to the farm. That would be the bit to test his powers, for he'd been unable to ferret out any evidence of violence on the part of the deceased apart from a tale extant among the local bogtrotters about an attempt to lame a future

Cup winner. But there'd be a bogtrotter or two on the jury, no doubt.

He said to his junior, 'Far be it from us to tell a lady how to dress for her day in court, but could you suggest she wear something to enhance her pallor? Not black, that's overly dramatic. Perhaps dark blue. And she should keep her head down, so the jury don't see too much of those eyes.'

'Miss Davidson won't need our advice,' replied his junior feelingly. 'She's as cunning as a shit-house rat.'

Which made him think again of the kitchen rat, and know it for an omen, a sign. The gentlemen of the jury would be solid, upright, unimaginative men who would not scruple to kill a cornered rat, but they'd be kinder to a woman, especially one as fragile and simple-seeming as Euphemia Davidson — farm girl, barmaid, nobody's child — who'd seen her dreams of love and a life free from drudgery made flesh in the person of a soulless bounder.

And he was right. The testimonies of a number of respectable people supported Miss Davidson's story, and while some witnesses could not be manoeuvred into speaking ill of Josselin Fernon, nor did her lawyer think it always wise to try, the jurors heard nothing that was good of him.

Euphemia Davidson was found guilty of manslaughter with a strong recommendation for mercy, and sentenced to three years' hard labour.

She wasn't grateful.

'Three years is not long,' her lawyer said. He'd scarcely dared hope for fewer than five.

'I don't care about that.' Miss Davidson didn't look at him, but sat staring at the wall. He rose to go. Suddenly she burst out, 'That man had no business showing my drawings to the jury.'

'I thought it an error of judgement on his part too.'

'Well, I want them back. And you didn't have to say all those things about Mr Fernon.'

'Were they untrue?'

'No,' she said, after a brief, unhappy silence. 'Not really. But he showed me no less kindness than I showed him and as that man said, it wasn't Mr Fernon who was on trial.'

She ought to have thought like that before she pulled the trigger. 'Then what else could I have said?'

'I don't know. I was too afraid of being locked away, so I didn't stop to think how it would sound. And I knew what you wanted.'

'As you knew what Mr Fernon wanted?'

'Oh, yes,' she said.

After a little she added, 'But I never wanted people to feel sorry for me, and you made me out to be so helpless, you made me sound so needy. And they won't be feeling sorry for me now, they'll all be laughing at me for a fool. And I let you do it. I just gave in, you see.'

He didn't see. 'People generally reserve their derision for those who seek to disprove their most cherished beliefs about humankind, Miss Davidson. They rarely mock those who confirm them.' He felt rather proud of that, off the cuff as it was.

Miss Davidson seemed not to have heard him. 'And now I've given in,' she said, 'there's nothing left of me.'

'You have considerable talent,' he said, in an attempt to sound improving. 'And a long life ahead of you. You must think what you'll do with it once you're out of gaol.' All the same he was glad to see the last of her, and never knew what she made of herself.

Upon her release she was said to have left the country and taken a new name; at one time she'd spoken of going to Australia. 'And that's the right place for you,' said her grandmother, to which the amiable Miss Davidson replied, 'I shot the wrong person. I should have shot you.' She is also reported to have sent Bob Graham a message to the same effect when he tried to see her before he went off with the Mounted Rifles. But these are stories put about by Michael Kelly, who lived to grow talkative and then tedious before dying at the age of ninety-six, and even he, who liked to know things, never knew what became of her.

J. Dennehy, R. J. Graham, N. H. Harraway, F. Kelly, G. Kelly, P. Kelly have their memorials in every town and city, in weeping walls of greenstone, in church windows and school halls; J. Fernon's grave in the local cemetery is marked by a small stone erected by A Friend, and The Scatterling has a plaque in the paddock where he was born. Doctor Graham's name appears in chronicles of notable New Zealand women, and that of Miss Ruby Ellis in memoirs of the popular stage; even the unexamined lives of Mesdames Graham, Davidson and Kelly can nowadays be relied upon to yield a thesis or two.

But of the elaborate invention that was Lily Macgregor, nothing remains at all.